"You know why I came," Jordan said, his voice quiet and solemn. "Your father said he told you about the arrangement we made."

I suppose it was the word 'arrangement' that made me clench my teeth together. I lifted my chin and stared into his eyes. I opened my mouth to speak but he smiled and lifted his hand.

"I know what you're going to say, Shelley. But please, just hear me out. I want a wife. And it seemed practical to marry someone I can talk to easily, someone I respect and genuinely like. A friend," he said, looking into my eyes. "I asked myself who my best friend was. The answer was you, Shelley."

I was flattered and hurt at the same moment. Not once had he mentioned love. "We aren't the same, Jordan. We aren't children anymore to scamper through the forest and hunt for seashells at daybreak."

"I know that," he said, frowning at me. He reached toward me and took my hand, pulling me up from the driftwood. "But it's a beginning, isn't it?"

I pulled away. "What about love, Jordan?" I felt so breathless that my voice came out as a mere whisper, and I could hardly believe I had asked him such a thing.

He pulled me into his arms. His kiss, so warm, so persistent, took me completely by surprise. I felt myself weakening and I moved willingly into his embrace as I reveled in that kiss. The kiss deepened and I told myself that the hunger in him was because he had been alone so long. But when he finally pulled away, I knew with a quiet sense of triumph that I was not the only one who was shaken . . .

CLARA WIMBERLY
THE BRIDE OF SEA CREST HALL

ZEBRA BOOKS
KENSINGTON PUBLISHING CORP.

ZEBRA BOOKS are published by

Kensington Publishing Corp.
475 Park Avenue South
New York, NY 10016

Zebra and the Z logo Reg. U.S. Pat & TM Off.

First Printing: December, 1993

Printed in the United States of America

Chapter 1

Jordan Waverly was the first man who ever kissed me. I was thirteen and he a very mature and totally devastating young man of fifteen. He was the first man I ever loved and the first man who broke my heart.

As children we had roamed our island home like gypsy vagabonds. Jordan, myself, and Mary Louise, my best friend and my fiercest enemy. We were together constantly and were happiest that way, even though we were from two entirely different worlds.

I was from the north end of the island, the only child of Joshua and Lucinda Sheldon Demorest. Before settling on St. Catherine's Island, father had been a sea captain, one of the most skillful ones, I was often told, ever to navigate between the hazardous shoals on the seaward side of the island and the river that lay inland. He met my mother when she and her brother came to play their music at the island's hotel one summer—he the piano, she the violin.

After my mother's sudden death from a quick, rare fever when I was small, my father would often sit on the front porch with me on his lap. And there in the velvety darkness of night, with the sound of the ocean crashing against the shore in the distance, he would speak to me of my mother and her beauty.

"The most beautiful woman I ever met," he would say, his dark eyes gazing into the distance beyond the sea. "She had the face of an angel and when she played the violin, the entire room would become still and enraptured. Your mother was the only woman who could have made me give up the sea forever. After I met her, I was never content to sail away from this island again."

I would smile and snuggle against my father, satisfied then to listen to the quiet rumble of his voice and the whisper of the wind in the sago palms that surrounded our modest home. I would often fall asleep there, secure in his arms, dreaming of my mother in a beautiful lace dress, playing her violin for the only man she had ever loved.

In this tropical paradise, reared with such stories, was it any wonder I grew up to become such a romantic?

We were not a wealthy family. Most islanders from the north end were farmers and traders. A few, like my father, were retired sea captains who felt at home on the small island off the coast of Georgia. There, I suppose, they felt that the ocean they loved could still be an integral part of their lives.

But Jordan and Mary Louise's lives were markedly different from mine. They were from the south end, and because of an odd lack of communications between the two ends of the island, they might as well have been from a different country. They came from the wealthy gentry of the south, whose ancestors were plantation owners and politicians who, even after the War Between the States, still held power and influence and still retained most of their landholdings. It was told that Jordan's great-grandfather was a Revolutionary War hero and that because of that, the Waverly family mansion was never seized by the Union troops during or after the war.

Mary Louise's father was not as wealthy as Jordan's. He was the owner of the island's only hotel—the Camden. But as my papa often said, Mr. Camden knew how to use people to his advantage. America's wealthiest families came to the island in the summer, and everyone knew that Mary Louise's father was not above using his position to obtain favors that often included political and monetary gain.

Mary Louise was his princess, a beauty even as a child. Even while the two of us roamed the beaches in search of turtle eggs, my long bare legs would be caked with salt and sand, while Mary Louise remained dry and pristine. She was an odd girl, given to flights of fancy and daydreams about princes and pirates. But she always knew what she wanted and there never seemed to be a doubt in her mind that she could have whatever she set her heart on.

Sometimes I loved her. And sometimes I hated her, for Mary Louise had set her sights on something rare and breathtaking, something that I wanted for my own. She swore that when we grew up, she would marry Jordan Waverly.

"I'll wear a beautiful gown of white," she'd say, her voice breathless, looking starry-eyed and giddy. "All our relatives will ride the *Emmeline* across the sound from the mainland. There will be roses strewn before me as I walk the long path through the garden. All the best newspapers on the mainland will write about me and my wedding." Mary Louise had decided that she and Jordan would be married at his home, in the beautiful formal English gardens of Sea Crest Hall. "Children will gather phlox and fashion an arch for us to walk through."

She hugged her arms around her slender body and turned to me, her blue eyes sparkling with excitement. "You will be my bridesmaid, Shelley—my only attendant. You will wear a flowing gown of pink moire antique satin with a disposition background."

We'd had that conversation many times. But I remember the last time, before I went away to college in Savannah, when Mary Louise and Jordan's wedding seemed finally more a certainty than a dream. We were strolling quietly along the beach near the Camden Hotel—at eighteen I no longer raced with my dress above my knees. I can remember making a sound of disgust and seeing Mary's gaze dart quickly to my face.

"What is it?" she asked. "Don't you want to be my bridesmaid?"

"Of course I do," I said. "But you know very well how I hate pink. Don't you know that women with auburn hair should never wear pink?" I knew my voice and my manner were more stern, more harsh than I intended them to be. But I didn't care. I was so sick of hearing about Mary Louise's dreams, Mary Louise's wedding, Mary Louise's dress. And I admitted, only to myself, that I was really sick at heart, because I knew that finally, I would have to put my dreams about Jordan Waverly aside forever.

"Oh, pish," she said, waving her dainty hand toward the ocean. "Who cares what one should or should not do? Pink is my favorite color and it's what I want you to wear. So it's settled."

And so it was—as was anything when Mary Louise Camden made up her mind about what she wanted. There was simply no room for anyone else's wishes or opinions.

I remember that day so well. The tang of salt in the breeze, the touch of a spring chill in the air. Sandpipers danced away from the advancing sea and gulls soared above the white-capped waves. I looked away toward the barrier islands as I usually did when walking, fascinated by the daily change in the shifting of sand. I loved St. Catherine's, from its saltwater marshes and flat white beaches to the dark, moss-draped maritime forest that separated the two. And that day I knew I was saying goodbye, for a while at least, not only to my island home, but to Mary Louise and Jordan.

I didn't want to argue with her, for in the end, as much as I resented and envied her, I loved her.

I glanced beneath my lashes toward her, noting the way the ocean breeze teased her hair away from the confines of her straw bonnet and the way the sunlight glittered in the fine blonde curls and warmed the rosy skin of her cheeks. Her blue eyes twinkled and the corner of her mouth dimpled into a smile of self satisfaction. Her figure, though slender, had grown lush and womanly, while I still looked like nothing more than a long-legged, coltish girl.

Could I blame Jordan for noticing her instead of me? For loving her?

We parted on good terms, when I left the island that week. It was hard to say goodbye to her, she reminding me for the hundredth time about my dress and I only nodding with amused agreement to anything she wanted. No one could resist Mary Louise for long, not even me.

I didn't see Jordan before I left. I couldn't bear it. And even though I received several letters from him in Savannah, I did not return the courtesy. I wouldn't see him again until I returned in late summer for the wedding.

My father would not attend the affair. He resented the powerful Waverly family as much then as he ever had and he said he did not belong at such an occasion. As a child, I'd often had to sneak away to be with my companions, but as we grew older, I realized more and more that my father had other interests and other concerns. He became lost in his land and his investments, in his gambling pleasures, until there seemed to be little time for a young girl's growing up, so I was not really surprised that he refused to attend the wedding.

That weekend, Mary Louise insisted that I stay at Sea Crest Hall, the Waverly mansion on the south end of St. Catherine's island. She had already moved her things to the house and there seemed no good reason why I should not spend the weekend there as well.

It was a beautiful day and the large castle-like house was over-run with wedding guests. The sound of laughter rang through the spacious flower-filled sitting rooms. Outside on the wide sunny lawn, one could hear the ocean in the distance, and nearer the house, the sound of wood against wood as players in a croquet match shouted good-naturedly to one another. Horseback riders and carriages came and went along the sandy driveway to the house.

It was a perfect weekend, and the scene was set for a

perfect wedding. Even though Mary Louise was nervous and strangely irritable, I thought I'd never seen her looking happier or more beautiful.

And Jordan. Oh, Jordan Waverly was so handsome that I could hardly bear to look at him. I would catch his dark-eyed gaze on me sometimes at dinner, and I saw the question in his look. We had once been so close and now I found myself avoiding him whenever possible and made certain that I was never alone with him.

But the night before the wedding, when all the guests gathered in the great ballroom of Sea Crest Hall, I could no longer avoid him. He came unexpectedly to pull me into his arms and whirl me around the room beneath the sparkling lights of the exquisite gold and crystal chandeliers. I caught the familiar spicy, sun-warmed fragrance he wore and for a moment I had to close my eyes against the longing that rushed through me.

"What's wrong, Shelley?" he asked, his voice deep and impatient, his lips very close as he whispered against my hair. "I have the feeling you've been avoiding me ever since you arrived. And you didn't answer any of the letters I sent to Savannah."

"I'm sorry," I said, gazing at the material of his dark suit that fit so superbly across his shoulders.

"Are you?" he asked.

For a moment he hesitated in the dance and I stumbled against him. I could sense him staring down at me and still I could not force myself to look up into his eyes. With a muttered curse of impatience that I knew so well, he took my arm and pulled me through the opened doorway and out onto a sheltered balcony.

Outside there was only the light from the ballroom

11

and from the Chinese lanterns that lined the garden. But I could see him well enough to note the determined set of his shoulders.

"Look at me," he demanded, his voice a harsh whisper.

I took a deep breath and forced myself to look up into his eyes. That was almost my undoing.

"I want you to tell me what's wrong, Shelley. Are you angry with me? Is it something to do with the wedding?"

"No," I lied. "No, of course not."

"Then what?" His voice was soft, a deep plea that caused my knees to tremble. And when his fingers closed around my wrists, I found myself longing to throw myself into his arms and tell him how I felt, how I'd always felt about him.

That sun-washed day when we were hardly more than children came rushing back to me. Jordan and I had wrestled over a sea conch and had fallen together into the ocean. He had pulled me against him and kissed me, a teasing kiss, the mischievous exploration of a boy's curiosity.

The effect of that first kiss, though innocent, had grown and blossomed in me over the years, while he was falling in love with my best friend.

We were children then, but now he was a man. And I knew, standing there so close to him, that I had to be careful.

"God, Shelley, you mean so much to me and Mary Louise. And yet, the past year, you've become so distant. We were best friends. Have you forgotten?"

"No," I whispered, feeling my heart pounding. "I haven't forgotten." The look in his eyes, the anxiety

12

across his handsome face swept all my selfish concerns away.

I couldn't bear to see him hurt, even now. And for a moment, I remembered his laughter, the light-hearted banter of our childhood. Jordan had always been the devilish one, the one to make us laugh. And as I stood staring at him on the night before his wedding, I wanted to see him smile again and hear his laughter. I wanted to take that memory with me back to Savannah. And perhaps one day I would find a man who would love me the way I loved Jordan.

"I want you to be happy," I said, gazing into his eyes. "That's all I've ever wanted for you, Jordan—your happiness. I'm sorry if I seem distracted. It's just that I've grown homesick in Savannah and being here makes me regret having to go back."

"Are you sure that's all it is?" he asked, bending his head so that he could see my face more clearly.

"Of course that's all," I said, forcing a smile to my lips.

He bent his dark head to kiss me, a light whisper of a kiss that took my breath away. And yet, glancing up into his eyes, I knew he meant it only as a sweet gesture of friendship.

"I miss you," he said, stepping away from me. "I wish you were still living here on St. Catherine's. At least—"

"Well," we heard from the doorway. "I wondered where you two were." Mary Louise swept out toward us, and her presence in a pale, sequined dress seemed to suddenly light the darkness. "My husband-to-be and my best friend," she said, stepping to put an arm around each of us.

"I am so happy tonight," she sighed, gazing out toward the colored lanterns.

When she turned to Jordan, her look was uncharacteristically serious and for a moment as she stared up into his eyes, I felt a twinge of foreboding wash over me.

"Promise me we will always be this happy, Jordan," she said, staring hard at him. "Promise me it will be this way forever."

Chapter 2

That night I did not sleep well. I attributed it to the fact that I was in a strange bed, in a palatial house that, although elegant and beautifully furnished, could also be daunting to someone unaccustomed to it.

I was still awake when I heard the first scream. It seemed almost to be in the same room with me and echoed with an eerie intensity down the long hallway.

I sat up in bed, not moving, waiting to see if I had only dozed off into a nightmarish sleep. Then I heard it again—a woman's scream, shrill and frightening, and filled with such anguish that it caused me to throw back the covers and leap to the floor.

By the time I pulled on a dressing robe and went to the door, I could hear the sound of other doors being opened. Guests peeked out into the hallway and several men stood looking about.

"What is it?" someone asked.

"Did you hear it?" asked another.

Together, in an odd assortment of nightclothes, we all trooped down the long, drafty corridor to the top of the curving stairs that led to the first floor. I suppose we felt secure in numbers, for none of us hesitated until we had come downstairs into the wide entryway. There we found the front door standing wide open. There was a stiff breeze from the ocean that night and already the tangy scent of salt air filled the house. Leaves and twigs lay on the tiled floor and wet, sandy footprints left a trail from the doorway toward the back of the house.

I saw Jordan then, coming from the study. He wore a hunter green robe and as he approached his anxious guests, he ran his fingers impatiently through his tousled black hair.

"I'm sorry," he said, attempting a smile. His gaze moved over my face, hesitating for a moment as if he wanted to speak directly to me. Instead he turned and closed the front door before coming back to face the group. "I'm afraid one of our guests, General Roberts, was taken ill earlier this evening. We've had a doctor with him, but moments ago the General passed away. His wife was understandably distraught."

"Then it was Mrs. Roberts we heard?" one of the women asked, her eyes round with fright.

"Yes," Jordan replied. "It was."

The woman turned to her husband, and although she attempted to whisper, all of us heard her words very distinctly in the quiet hallway.

"It was the *Sea Witch*," she whispered, her voice filled with fear. "Last night just before dusk, someone saw the Sea Witch off the coast."

"Nonsense," Jordan said. "I've already told Mary Louise that what she saw could not have been the *Sea Witch*. The stories about a ghost ship are nothing more than that—childhood stories, fantasies passed on from one generation to another."

When I looked at him, I thought I had never seen his eyes so cold and dismissive. As children we had both reveled in the stories about the ghostly *Sea Witch*. We had watched for hours for the blood red sails and the flag with its skull and crossbones, though none of us had ever seen it. Had he really changed so much since then?

"But Jordan," the woman insisted. "There must be some truth to the stories—about how its appearance is a portent of death. How else do you explain what's happened?"

"Please," he said, his eyes closing wearily. "All of you—go back to bed. General Roberts's death was something that could have happened to him anywhere. I assure you it had absolutely nothing to do with the *Sea Witch*. My bride-to-be has a vivid imagination and I'm sorry if her story disturbed any of you."

Finally, with muttered remarks, the guests turned to go back upstairs. But I stayed, staring hard at Jordan and noting a certain wariness in his eyes.

"Jordan?" I asked. "I had no idea it was Mary Louise who saw the ship. I heard the rumors, but—"

"Shelley." A frown creased his forehead and he shook his head as he looked down at me. "Not you too."

"Where is she?" I asked. "Knowing Mary Louise, she could hardly have slept through such a scene. Mrs. Roberts's screaming could be heard all over the house."

"She is sleeping," he said. Then turned from me, as if to dismiss me completely.

I followed him back into the study and closed the door behind us. My eyes went immediately to his favorite chair and I did not miss the coffee that sat on a table nearby, nor the hint of cigar smoke that still lingered in the air. Obviously, he had not even been to bed.

"Jordan," I said, trailing behind him. "I won't be dismissed like one of your servants. I know you too well. Now, you must tell me what's wrong. Is it Mary? Is she ill? Why do you look so troubled?"

"For God's sake," he muttered, slumping down into the chair and taking a deep breath. "You are as inquisitive as ever, aren't you?" But for all his gruffness, he could not hide the smile that tugged at the corner of his lips as he looked up at me. "Don't you know that educated, well-bred young ladies are not so inquisitive?"

I laughed then, and for the first time in a long while I felt close to him again. I felt the inhibitions that loving him had brought fall away, and in their place was the deep friendship that had always lain beneath.

I sank down onto the floor beside his chair, resting my shoulder against his knee.

"I am not well-bred, nor a lady—not yet anyway, according to my teachers. So, you might as well dispense with such talk. It won't put me off anyway, you know."

He smiled then, and for a moment his smile was wistful and sweet. He reached to touch my hair, and I saw the troubled look cloud his eyes again.

"It's Mary," he said, his voice almost a whisper. "She was almost in hysterics last night after her walk on the beach. I don't know what possessed her to go out again tonight. I swear, Shelley, I almost believed myself that she saw the ship."

"Perhaps she did see a ship. Maybe one passed off the coast as she walked. You know how imaginative she can be."

"No captain in his right mind would sail so close to the south end of the island, especially in a darkening sea."

"Perhaps he was off course," I said. "The wind has been very balmy the past few days."

His fingers moved over his lips as he turned his eyes toward the darkened windows that looked out toward the ocean.

"I found her near midnight, wandering along the beach. She was barefoot and her gown was wet from the spray. I've never seen her like that before, Shelley," he said, turning his gaze back toward me. "Never."

"So it was you who left the footprints in the entry-way?"

"Yes," he said, frowning as he remembered. "She was in such a state that I carried her in and put her to bed. Mother gave her a sedative and I suppose that's why she didn't awaken when Mrs. Roberts screamed."

"But, Jordan," I said, staring at him and trying hard to understand what he was saying. "Why on earth would she need a sedative? What was wrong with her?"

"I don't know. After she saw the ship last night, she seemed frightened to death. I couldn't calm her—no one could. But I had no idea she would go out in the middle of the night tonight trying to find the *Sea Witch* again."

"It's only anxiety," I said. "You know how high-strung Mary Louise can be." I wanted to comfort him and to reassure him, but for the life of me, I couldn't understand why an energetic, powerful man like Jordan would want a wife who was frightened of everything. "She's just a little apprehensive, that's all."

"I know that," he said. He stood up quickly and stalked across the room to the windows. "Do you think I don't know what's wrong with her? Tomorrow is her wedding day."

19

"Jordan," I whispered, feeling a wave of understanding sweep over me. "What are you saying?" I went to stand behind him and even though my fingers curled together with their need to touch him, I did not. "Mary Louise loves you. All she ever wanted was to be your wife."

"God," he muttered, raking his hand through his dark hair in that impatient gesture I knew so well. Even as a boy he had done it. "I don't know what's happening to us. She can hardly bear for me to touch her, Shelley." His eyes bored into me and there was such pain behind that look that it almost took my breath away. "Anything beyond a playful kiss . . ." He shrugged and gazed again out the window. "I tell myself it's only natural. She's young. And within a few short hours, she will be a new bride, away on a honeymoon cruise. I suppose that's all it is."

I had to bite my lips to push away the unbidden thoughts that those words conjured up in my mind. What woman wouldn't be ecstatically happy at the prospect of marrying this man? Mary Louise was no more naive than I. Yet the very thought of sailing away with Jordan Waverly was almost more than my trembling heart could bear.

"She's marrying *you*, Jordan," I said. "Not some stranger or someone she barely knows." I could feel my cheeks burning, but not from embarrassment. I was angry that Mary Louise could be behaving this way, that she could cause Jordan this anguish.

And I was envious.

He turned to me then and placed his hands on my arms. He smiled down at me, his look wistful and sweet.

"You were always the strong one, Shelley . . . the

practical one. And no matter how badly I behaved, you were always my defender."

He pulled me into his arms then and it was all I could do to keep from whispering, "I love you."

"Always," I said instead. "I will always be your defender, Jordan. When the three of us are old and surrounded by grandchildren, I will still believe in you."

The tender look in his eyes was only gratitude. I knew that, and I told myself, there that night in his study, that it would have to be enough.

"Go to bed, Shelley," he whispered. "I don't want to be the cause of tiredness in those beautiful brown eyes tomorrow."

I didn't sleep the rest of the night. Instead I walked the floor, feeling sad and lost. Feeling angry that Mary Louise could not even be grateful now that she had everything she had ever wanted.

I was still awake at dawn when two men in a wagon pulled up to the house and carried a long pine box inside. And I watched until they came back again, and saw their shoulders bent, their muscles strain with the burden of what lay inside.

I shivered, thinking about the tragic death of a man in this house on the night before Mary's wedding.

My eyes moved automatically toward the sea, as if I too might catch a glimpse of the ghost ship *Sea Witch*. As if the death of General Roberts had indeed been foretold by Mary Louise's vision of the death ship.

I couldn't seem to stop shivering. There in the cool morning hours I watched the light of dawn touch the top of the trees and turn the hanging Spanish moss to strands of gold. It took all the strength I possessed to admit that I would never marry the man I loved, and that I would never live in a house like Sea Crest.

By noon, as we gathered in the magnificent gardens for the wedding, no one could ever guess what lay in my heart. The pink moire satin dress that Mary Louise had chosen for me was lovely, and with my heavy auburn hair swept atop my head and partially covered with a lace mantilla, I'm sure no one noticed that the shade did not suit my coloring. I smiled and performed the duties of bridesmaid as skillfully as if I had been trained for the stage. It was indeed an act, for all the while my heart was breaking.

Later the guests gathered at the dock on the inland side of the island to see the newlyweds off. Mary Louise came to me and there were tears in her eyes when she said goodbye.

"I'm so afraid," she whispered in my ear as she hugged me close.

I pulled her aside, away from the shouts and laughter of the others.

"Not of Jordan?" I asked. "Surely you must know how much he loves you. He would never hurt you, or offend you, Mary Louise. You must know him well enough by now to know that much at least."

"I know that Jordan is wonderful and kind. It's just . . . oh, how can I explain such a feeling?"

"What, Mary?" I insisted. "You know you can tell me anything."

"I suppose it's just that I never thought about the actual physical aspect of marriage. I thought only about the handsome husband who would adore me and shower me with gifts, and the magnificent house like Sea Crest that I would reign over. I want to be respected,

Shelley, as a woman of prestige and wealth. If my father has taught me anything it is that one needs the power of such things. And I always expected to have a husband who would live his life for me and who would do anything to make me happy."

"You have all that now, Mary. And more."

"Oh, Shelley—you're so practical and I know you're probably right. It's just that Jordan is a . . . a powerful man." She almost gasped when she said the words and her eyes darted toward her new husband who stood even now watching us. "So . . . so physical." She said the word as if it were distasteful to her. "And I find the idea of what will happen tonight disagreeable, to say the least."

I was stunned by her words.

"Mary Louise," Jordan called. "We should go. The captain is anxious to leave."

I waved to them and watched as the children threw rose petals into the frothing water of the ship's wake. I could not explain the feeling of disquiet that swept over me as I watched the two people I loved most sailing away.

It was to be the last time I would see Mary Louise alive.

Chapter 3

I spent a few hours later that day with father, but he was so distracted that I soon grew restless. I could hardly wait for the *Emmeline* to carry me back across the sound to the mainland.

I returned to Savannah and to my studies with a new determination. I had always been an outgoing person and now I forced myself to make even more friends than before. There were many social engagements and my studies to keep me occupied, and soon I convinced myself that I was happier than I'd ever been.

I received letters from Mary Louise. She and Jordan were in the Caribbean, then South America. If her letters were less than enthusiastic, I told myself it was because she had a fear of water and had never really liked to sail.

I kept the letters in a box beneath my bed. After they returned home to Sea Crest, the box grew more full still with Mary's letters and a few from Jordan. But always when I wrote, it was to both of them.

Months passed and I was not surprised to learn that Mary Louise was expecting a child the next summer. I never told anyone, not even my best friends at school, how the news tore at my heart. Those dreams I had of marrying Jordan had to be put aside for good now—the ones that no one on earth knew about except me. Still, despite my vows, sometimes I dreamed of having Jordan's children—Jordan, myself and our black-haired, black-eyed children, so like their father, as carefree as the seabirds that ran along the shore. Then my heart would ache and I would grow impatient with myself and my self-indulgent thoughts, and I would plunge myself even deeper into my studies and social life.

I was almost relieved when the weather that winter was too bad for travel. Mary Louise urged me to come home and sometimes I wanted to very badly. Then I would imagine seeing the two of them together, their faces glowing with happiness and love, and I simply could not do it.

Even today I find it hard to forgive myself for that. If I had gone home the way she begged me to do, at least I would have seen Mary Louise alive one last time.

In the early spring I received the news.

There had been an accident. No one knew how it happened or why Mary was out in a small boat alone, especially in her condition. By the time anyone missed her, it was too late; a few hours later, Jordan found her lifeless body floating in the inlet near Pelican Banks.

I could hardly believe it. Not only that Mary Louise was gone, but that she had drowned. Even though she was afraid of the water it had not kept her from becoming an excellent swimmer, and I found it difficult to comprehend that she could not have swum the short distance to shore, pregnant or not.

She was buried in the Waverly family cemetery, not

far from Sea Crest Hall. I stood beneath the huge moss-draped oak trees and watched the faces of the people gathered there. Even my father came to the funeral that day.

Jordan was surrounded by his family—his mother and father. Even his brother Benjamin was there, although most of us had not seen him in years. Mary Louise's parents were devastated. I think that all of us that day were in shock.

As much as I wanted to comfort Jordan, I barely saw him. When we did speak, he was distant, even angry. It was as if he didn't want to talk to me—as if my being there reminded him of those youthful carefree times when the three of us had been together.

That week was the first time my father mentioned our growing financial difficulties to me.

"I'm not sure how much longer you will be able to continue your schooling, daughter," he said to me.

"Not continue?" I asked, surprised. "But, why?"

"There's not much money, I'm afraid. 1893 was not a good year for the country and I'm afraid it was not good for me, either. There were a few poor investments, and—"

"But I thought mother set aside money for my schooling years ago, when I was still a baby."

He turned from me then, but not before I could see the distress on his face. He looked old to me that day, and very troubled.

"Yes," he said, his voice a mere whisper. "She did. But I'm afraid I've had to use some of it for my own expenses."

I bit my lips to keep from arguing with him. My father had never been a good provider, but I loved him and I respected him. I told myself that I should count myself lucky to have received whatever formal schooling I had.

When I went back to Savannah, I quietly took a job tutoring some of the other girls, hoping it would help me continue my education as long as possible. I wasn't sure how my father did it, but together we managed to pay the tuition for another year.

By the first anniversary of Mary Louise's death, I had decided to stay in Savannah. There were many opportunities there for a young woman with an education. Besides, the thought of going back to St. Catherine's was still too painful for me. But as fate always seems to intervene when we have settled our minds about something, so it was with me that spring.

The letter from my father was short and to the point:

Daughter. You must come home at once. There has been an unfortunate turn of events in which I desperately need your help.

All the way home my mind was turning and twisting as I wondered what was wrong. Was Father ill? Dying even? Guilt tore at my heart as I recalled all the times I could have gone home to visit and did not. Now all I could do was hope and pray it was not too late.

Imagine my surprise when my father greeted me at the dock, looking fit and healthy.

"Father," I said, trying to catch my breath. "What is it? What's wrong? Your letter sounded ominous. I was afraid—"

He took my arm and pulled me toward the waiting carriage. "Let's go home," he said tersely, looking about at those waiting to board the *Emmeline*. "It's a long story and needs the privacy of our own house for the telling."

It was a beautiful day and the sun was very hot. Against my will I felt a sweet sense of homecoming wash over me. The familiar scents of the island, the sight of a raccoon scurrying across the road and the sound of the ever present wind, welcomed me and made me sigh with pleasure. We were soon into the dark canopy of the maritime forest, where the roar of the ocean was muted and the cry of the sea birds sounded far, far away.

Once home, Father seemed as anxious to talk as I was. We had hardly settled my trunks in the bedroom when he pulled me out onto the porch, his favorite spot for talking.

"You know how much this land means to me," he said, his eyes glazed oddly as he looked toward the sea.

"Yes, Father, I do."

"I would not have taken such desperate measures if the land were not involved. I want you to know that." The look he turned my way made me catch my breath. There was indeed desperation there and something else as well—a pleading sense of regret and shame.

"Father, what are you talking about? Have you sold the land? This house?"

"No, no," he said, taking my hand and looking into my eyes. "But I'm pleased that you are concerned about that. You would not want me to lose our home, would you lass? This land?"

"No," I said, frowning at him. "No, of course not. But if—"

"That is exactly what would have happened if I had not made these arrangements."

My heart skipped wildly in my chest. He was looking at me so oddly, and I think in that moment I knew that the arrangements he spoke of had everything to do with me and his summons for me to come home.

"What arrangements, Father? Tell me exactly what you're talking about."

He sighed and looked away from me for a moment. When he spoke, he did not lift his eyes to meet mine.

"Last year's economy, my own poor investments—that wasn't all of it, I'm afraid. There were some gambling debts too. Debts I would never have been able to pay without selling the house."

I waited, unable to speak for the fear that choked at my throat.

"I have made arrangements for your marriage, Shelley," he said, squeezing my fingers tightly. "The gentleman wants a wife and he wants a son. He has very graciously agreed that in exchange for your hand in marriage, he will pay all my debts, which are considerable, even to restore this old house to the way it was when your mother . . ." His voice trailed away wearily.

I pulled my hands from his grasp and jumped up from the chair. As I turned to face him, I was breathing as heavily as if I'd just run a long distance.

"No," I gasped. "I won't do it, Father! Debts or not. This is barbaric! People don't arrange marriages anymore—not like this. What you're talking about is the buying and selling of another human being—your own daughter! How could you expect me to marry a man I don't even know? Just forget this idea, Father. Tell the man no. I'll find employment in Savannah. If we have to, we can—"

"Shelley," he said. The sad break in his voice stopped me cold and as I stared at him I saw tears in his eyes. "This is all I have," he whispered. "This land, and the sea. I'm an old man and you have your whole life ahead of you. You'll have wealth and security—"

"No, Father," I said. I placed my hands over my ears and walked to the edge of the porch, staring out to sea as I felt the shame and humiliation wash over me. "I can do without wealth. I won't marry a man I don't love."

"Look around you, child," he pleaded. "Look at the oleander there near your mother's grave. See how it's grown? Every year the scent of it invades the house and it's almost as if she's here with me again. Would you ask me to leave her here—to give up her burial place to the bushes and wild animals?"

"Father, please," I said, feeling tears sting my eyes.

"You love this island, Shelley. I can see it in your eyes when you're home. You'll be able to have it all—your beloved island, wealth and position . . ."

I turned then to stare at him. "The island? You mean the man lives here? On St. Catherine's? But who . . . ?"

But he was lost in his own reverie and he continued to talk as he stared out to sea.

". . . and Sea Crest, daughter," he said, his eyes brightening. "Just imagine that. My little girl will be the mistress of Sea Crest Hall."

I gasped aloud then as I stood very still, staring into his face.

"Sea Crest? Father, what are you talking about? Who is the man you've arranged for me to marry?"

He smiled then and I thought for a moment there was a hint of insanity in his eyes.

"I did forget to mention his name, didn't I? How could I forget? It's Jordan, my dear. Your old friend, Jordan Waverly."

Chapter 4

I doubt that my father even saw me leave that day. He was staring out to sea, rocking back and forth in his chair.

"Consider it well," he said, although he didn't turn to look at me.

I backed away from the porch and from him, unable to breath, unable to speak even after hearing the name of the man who had offered to pay for my hand in marriage.

I turned and ran then, and my legs carried me as easily as when I was a girl. Across the narrow expanse of yard, past the barrier palms and out to the open beach. I have no idea how far I ran. Until the wind had ripped away all the pins from my hair. Until I began to feel a heavy wetness at the flounced hem of my day gown. Until my heart pounded heavily and I could barely breath. But nothing could banish the words from my mind.

Your old friend, Jordan Waverly . . . Jordan Waverly.

Why had he done this?

Years ago I would have been reeling with delight. But

31

now, after his having chosen Mary Louise first, after his having made this arrangement with my father in such a cold, calculated manner, I thought nothing could ever be the same. I knew it even though my heart tried at first to convince me otherwise.

Couldn't he at least have come to me? Asked me to marry him? Deep inside I knew I might have considered it even knowing he did not love me. But not like this. Not this distant offering of money for a wife, as if I were someone he'd never met.

"No," I whispered fiercely to the wide expanse of ocean. I took off my shoes and felt the cold sand beneath my stockinged feet. "I won't do it. I will see the land sold first," I swore, even as guilt tore at my heart.

I must have walked for hours. At first I stayed on the beach, letting the foaming water lap at my feet. When the sun warmed and turned the spring afternoon to a seeming summer, I retreated to the shade and shelter of the sago palms and live oaks.

The diversity of St. Catherine's was what I loved most. When the tide was out, the island's marshes looked like a broad plain of tall grasses. Here and there were bright, glittering streams that wended their way to tidal creeks. Wading birds stretched long legs through the grass and fiddler crabs scurried across the mud flats.

On the highest plane of the island was the forest. A quiet, sun-filtered area of live oaks, draped with Spanish moss that gave a touch of the exotic to the area. Then, emerging from the darkness of the forest to the white, sun-drenched beach, the light was so bright, so blinding, that one might momentarily lose one's sight.

Father was right. I did love it here. More than any place I'd ever been.

I walked deeper into the forest and stopped, turning slowly around to allow my gaze to take in everything. It was quiet here with the sunlight diffused through over-arching trees and vines. I could hear the sound of small animals in the underbrush and the gentle splash of water through the nearby salt marshes.

I knew it was my heart rather than my head that whispered to me there in the still forest. It told me that if I married Jordan I would never have to leave this place again. That at last I could realize the dream of seeing my children scampering happily along this very beach, searching for turtle eggs, chasing mischievous raccoons through the trees.

Black haired children, with black eyes. Like their father's.

I gasped then and closed my eyes against the rush of emotion that those thoughts carried.

Loving Jordan. Seeing him every day. Living with him in the intimacy of marriage with all that those words meant.

"Oh . . . heavens," I whispered aloud.

I was aware of the quietness. There I could hear the rush of air from my lungs and feel the tripping of my heart. I think until that moment I had convinced myself that those feelings for Jordan were gone forever. As long as I was away from the island with all its unique beauty and all its memories, I could make myself believe it.

I loved him; I had never stopped loving him. And I wanted him—beyond the girlish simplicity of youth, beyond the irrational dreams of children. I knew that what I felt that day was what a woman feels for a man.

I returned to the beach. This time as I walked in the waning sunlight, my steps were slower, more studied. I felt a sense of awe at the emotions I'd experienced in the quiet forest.

Father was not at home when I returned and I was thankful for that. The last thing I wanted was another discussion of the proposed marriage. I needed time to think and to decide what I wanted and what I was willing to sacrifice for it. At this point, I was beginning to think any sacrifice I might make would only be one of pride. For no one knew except me all I would really be gaining if I married Jordan. All I had to decide now was if I could marry him knowing he did not love me as he had loved Mary Louise.

Next morning was bright and sunny. I awoke to the sound of birds singing in the trees outside. As I lay in bed I also became aware of voices—the deep rumble of men's voices from somewhere near the front of the house.

They were standing outside on the porch, my father and Jordan. They seemed to be engaged in a serious conversation and I sensed that they did not realize or remember that anyone else was around. I peeked through the windows quickly, before running back to my bedroom.

It had taken only one glimpse of Jordan's handsome figure in tan riding pants and white shirt to send my head into a spin. Even as I quickly dressed, my fingers trembled at the long row of tiny buttons on my dress and my face felt unnaturally flushed and warm.

How could I face him? What was I to say?

I tied my unruly hair back with a ribbon as best I could. Then I glanced into a mirror, studying my face and eyes. My cheeks were as rosy as if I'd been out in the island sun and I could not deny there was a new sparkle to my eyes.

I bit my lips and took a long, steadying breath. Then, with a lift of my chin, I walked through the house and out to the front porch.

Jordan had changed since I'd seen him last. He looked leaner, although his shoulders and arms were as muscular as always. It was his face, I suppose, that had changed the most. There was a tiredness etched across his features, a weary cynicism in the black eyes that I once knew so well.

When he saw me, he smiled, though only slightly, in a sweet, wistful way. I didn't understand that look. He was so different from the young boy of my happiest summers. Jordan loved nothing better than chasing us across the sand until we fell with exhaustion, laughing. And he was the one who always laughed hardest.

This was not the Jordan I remembered. He was older, mature beyond his years it seemed. But even though the laughter was gone from his eyes, they were still the same sparkling eyes I remembered, and his face was still the one I had loved all my life.

I felt my heart skip a beat. I had been in his presence for only a moment and already I felt my resolve slipping away.

"Shelley," he said, stepping forward. "You look beautiful."

I looked up into his eyes, wondering if he was as anxious to be alone as I was. Almost immediately, he answered my unspoken question.

"Would you like to walk to the beach? There are a great many things I'd like to talk to you about."

"Of course," I replied.

I felt his hand touch my arm and I moved quickly out of his reach and off the porch. From the corner of my eye, I saw my father's hopeful nod of approval. He could see the change in me when Jordan was near, I was sure of that, and he was no doubt feeling quite secure that his wishes would be carried out.

Jordan did not speak until we had walked past the live oaks and barrier palms and out to the open beach. Sandpipers danced along the sand, following the motion of the waves. An osprey flew above the water, screaming as he searched for an unsuspecting mullet.

"Shelley," Jordan said, taking my arm and pulling me to a halt. He turned me to face him and his eyes were troubled and searching. "Why do I have the feeling you're running away from me?"

I didn't know what to say. Conversation with him had always come so easily, but now I felt suddenly shy and awkward.

"I don't . . . I didn't mean to give you that impression. It's just that this is . . . awkward, to say the least."

His eyes changed as he touched my face, his fingers caressing softly down my cheek. For a moment, I saw that flash of amusement in his smile, that mischievous grin of a little boy.

"So formal," he murmured, intending to tease me. "Have you finally grown into a lady then, little tomboy?"

I relented a bit then, letting his teasing chase the icy reserve I felt away, if only for a moment.

"Your mother once said I'd never be a lady," I reminded him, unable to resist smiling.

He laughed and for a moment, he seemed like the old

Jordan. His eyes twinkled and his lips parted to reveal white, even teeth.

"I remember. I had caught a butterfly and told you I'd take it in to my father for his collection. You came at me like a little swamp cat as I recall, declaring I could not do such a cruel thing to something so beautiful and so helpless. And when mother found us, we were rolling about on the ground like two wild bear cubs."

I laughed too, remembering. "No wonder she said I'd never be a lady."

We continued walking and he glanced at me from the corner of his eye.

"She'll be pleasantly surprised when she sees you. You look as sweet and demure as any young lady I've ever seen."

I blushed then beneath his steady gaze and looked out to sea. I was finding that now, with the question of marriage between us, there was something different, something exciting and forbidden in every word, every look.

"Appearances can be deceiving, as they say."

"How well I know that," he said.

He grew quiet—distracted even—and I was certain he must be thinking of Mary Louise. Had her reluctance made him doubt her? There were so many things I longed to ask about her and about her death, about their life together, but I couldn't. I simply could not, with this strange new uneasiness between us.

He motioned me away from the water and up the sloping beach to a large piece of driftwood that had washed in with the tide.

I sat on the sun-bleached log and Jordan propped his booted foot nearby, leaning forward over his bent knee.

"You know why I came," he said, his voice quiet and solemn. "Your father said he told you about the arrangement we made."

I suppose it was the word 'arrangement' that made me clench my teeth together. That, and the fact that he admitted freely that the deed was already done. I lifted my chin and stared into his eyes. I opened my mouth to speak but he smiled and lifted his hand.

"I know what you're going to say, Shelley. But please, just hear me out before you give me your answer."

I sighed, but kept my silence as he asked. I settled myself back on the log, staring stubbornly into his face as I waited for him to begin.

"I know that look," he said, grinning. But when I said nothing he grew serious again. "The money isn't the important part, Shelley. Knowing your scrupulous honesty, I have to tell you that first. I would have helped your father anyway."

I'm sure my eyes gave me away as I wondered if my father had been the one to approach Jordan.

"I want a wife. And it seemed practical, after Mary Louise, to marry someone I can talk to easily, someone I respect and genuinely like. A friend," he said, looking into my eyes.

"Without the complications of love," I said, still seething.

He ignored me and continued. "Once I sat down and thought about the qualities I wanted in a wife, it seemed too obvious to ignore. I asked myself who my best friend was. I asked who understood me better than anyone, who I always came to when I wanted to talk . . . the first person I wanted to show a new shell to, or explore the forest with. The answer was you, Shelley."

I was flattered and hurt at the same moment. Of course I wanted to be his friend, to be the one he respected and admired. But not once had he mentioned love. It was what I wanted from him so badly, what I longed to hear more than anything.

"We aren't the same, Jordan. We aren't children any more to scamper through the forest and hunt for seashells at daybreak."

"I know that," he said, frowning at me. He reached toward me and took my hand, pulling me up from the driftwood. "But it's a beginning, isn't it? What could be better than friendship?"

I thought he was going to kiss me and I pulled away. He knew me so well. Had he guessed how I felt about him? Did he intend to pacify me with a kiss, to give me some encouragement?

"What about love, Jordan?" I felt so breathless that my voice came out as a mere whisper, and I could hardly believe I had asked him such a thing.

He pulled me into his arms, holding me tight when I struggled to free myself.

"There will be love, Shelley. I want a son. I want us to have a child together."

I closed my eyes against the onslaught of emotion those words brought. And when I felt his lips on mine I did not pull away.

His kiss, so warm, so persistent, took me completely by surprise. I felt myself weakening and I moved willingly into his embrace as I reveled in that kiss. The kiss deepened and I told myself that the hunger in him was because he had been alone so long. But when he finally pulled away, I knew with a quiet sense of triumph that I was not the only one who was shaken.

"You surprise me," he whispered, his voice husky. "That kiss was a long way from the first one we shared . . . remember?"

"Yes, I remember."

I stared into his eyes, feeling myself under his spell as I'd always been. And he knew it. When his lashes lowered, then lifted again, I saw the quiet possessiveness in his eyes. He pulled me against him again, holding me hard against his chest as if he might make me relent.

"Marry me, Shelley. There will be love, I promise you that."

"I . . . I have to think." How could I possibly make a reasonable decision when he held me that way, when he looked into my eyes the way I'd always dreamed he would. And when his lips were so close, how could I decide if what I saw and felt was real?

"Why?" he asked, brushing his mouth against mine again.

I managed to drag myself away from him that time, but I was certain he could see me trembling as I stood away from him.

"Because," I said, trying to catch my breath. "I . . . I can't think straight when you . . . when you kiss me that way."

He smiled, but he made no effort to come closer.

"That's a start." His eyebrows lifted as he gazed at me. "When?"

"When what?"

He laughed aloud then and shook his head.

"Oh, Shelley, you are still so refreshingly guileless. You always could make me laugh. It seems like a hundred years since I've laughed." He stepped toward me so quickly that I was taken by surprise. His lips captured mine again in a sweet searching kiss that left me trembling and breathless. "When will you tell me your decision?" he whispered against my mouth.

"I . . . I don't know. The weekend—Saturday."

"Thursday," he demanded in a half teasing, half serious manner.

"That's tomorrow, Jordan," I protested. "I can't possibly."

"Friday then," he said, smiling the way he'd always done when he knew he'd won. "Wear your prettiest dress. I'll drive here and pick you up. We'll have dinner at Sea Crest."

"Jordan Waverly," I began, shaking my head at him. "You are an exasperating, overbearing man."

"And you like me that way," he teased.

I could not deny how he affected me—how his smile could brighten the darkest day for me, or how his strong, hard kisses had left me trembling for more.

Perhaps he knew me better than I was willing to admit.

Chapter 5

Father wanted to know everything. His eyes had the oddest look and I could not explain how disturbing his excitement was to me.

"I haven't given him my answer yet," I said.

"That's clever," he said, nodding. "It will make him want you all the more."

"But that's not . . ." I stared at him, unable to believe his behavior. Had he grown so desperate, so greedy that he was eager to sell me to the highest bidder? It seemed like a game of some kind to him. But I told myself I should count my blessings that the man he had chosen was Jordan and not a stranger, or some lecherous old man who would disgust me.

"He's coming here Friday, to take me to dinner at Sea Crest," I said, trying not to reveal my frustration with him. "Like Jordan, you will have my answer then, Father." I turned and went into the house, for I found I could no longer bear to see the bright glitter in his eyes when we spoke about the subject.

Those next two days were torturous for me. No matter how hard I tried to remain calm, to make a reasonable decision, I found that I was just as confused as ever. By the time Jordan arrived on Friday afternoon, I was no closer to knowing what to do than before.

He looked so handsome that he took my breath away. The day was very warm and he had discarded his jacket, leaving it draped across the carriage seat. His shirt was sparkling white, and it emphasized his dark hair and skin.

I had worn my very best gown, debating all the while about whether it would be too formal or not. It was a pale, creamy, lightweight brocade, with chiffon flounced inserts in front, caught up with ribbons from the knees to the hem. Now, seeing Jordan so elegantly attired, I was glad I had chosen the dress.

His dark eyes moved over me, and I hoped it was admiration I saw in them, but he said nothing. Instead he took my hand and led me to the carriage, then he walked around to the other side.

As he made a quiet noise, urging the horse on, he leaned toward me, although his eyes never left the narrow, sandy roadway.

"You've grown into a beautiful woman, Shelley."

"You don't have to say that," I said, without thinking.

He turned to me, his eyes wary and brooding. "Why would I say it if I didn't mean it?"

I looked away and shrugged, feigning indifference. "I don't know," I murmured.

I could feel his eyes on me, studying me. But I did not turn to meet his gaze. Instead I began to chatter about the scenery. It was a long drive to Sea Crest and I found that I was growing more and more reluctant to discuss anything personal with Jordan. That was something I could not explain, not even to myself.

We moved inland, into the densely twisted forest. We passed the place where an old settlement had once been, now marked only by ghostly tabby chimneys that stood silently beneath the trees. Past the old settlement, the island narrowed. We passed the road leading to the dock, the only way to the mainland, and then we were on Waverly property.

Was there any other place so lovely as this? My eyes drank in the beautifully kept vistas and carefully pruned hedges and trees. Exotic wildflowers and tall stately palms rustled softly as we passed.

I realized that I was holding my breath in anticipation of seeing the house and its surrounding gardens again. I must have made a sound when it appeared before us, for Jordan turned to me and smiled. Then he stopped the carriage.

"It is beautiful, isn't it?"

"Yes," I said, awed as always when I saw the house.

It sat on a small rise overlooking the marshes. It seemed impossible for such a mansion to exist on the quiet simple island of St. Catherine's. Its stuccoed walls gleamed in the waning sunlight and the dark green gabled rooftops rose upward and upward toward the sky. It was a huge house with many sections and levels, its tall cream-colored chimneys rising well away from the top of the third story. A square balconied addition with windows all around made a fourth floor at the very peak of the house. It looked somewhat like the top of a lighthouse and I wondered if perhaps that was its intent when the house was built.

"It will be ours one day, Shelley," he said quietly, still gazing at the house. "And our children's."

When he turned to look at me I wondered if he knew

that my desires lay not in the owning of such a house, but in being near him.

"Will you make me wait until the evening is over?" he asked, his voice light and teasing.

"I don't know what to say."

"Say you'll marry me. Say that you will come here to brighten this house. Say that you will be the mother of my children." His last words were spoken in an emotional, husky whisper.

"Jordan," I began.

He pulled me into his arms and kissed me, his mouth hard and demanding as if he had lost patience with me.

"Say yes, Shelley," he demanded, his breath soft against my lips. "You know it's what you want."

I couldn't deny it, any more than I could deny him. It was *all* I wanted, and God help me, I was willing to sacrifice my pride, willing to marry him even without his declaration of love. For now, after all these years, after all my forsaken dreams, it had taken only his kisses and a few softly whispered words to make me change my mind.

"Yes," I whispered, finally giving in to all the emotion I felt. It *was* what I wanted, what I'd dreamed of.

When he finally pulled away, he laughed, a quiet sound of jubilation, but for some reason, the sound of it made small chills race along my spine.

We drove through the arching, wrought iron entrance and up the drive to a wide, tiled area in front of the house. There were two young men waiting to take the carriage. Jordan helped me out and held my hand as we made our way up a short flight of steps, then another longer one that led to the front porch.

Inside, the house was cool and quiet. The entryway

45

with its black and white Spanish tile was so wide and spacious that it looked as though it could serve as a ballroom. Another servant took the wrap that I had brought for the drive home and, with a bow to Jordan, he turned and disappeared toward the back of the house.

I had been here many times as a young girl, but Jordan, Mary Louise, and I would usually enter at the back of the house, more often than not stopping in the kitchen where the cooks teased and laughed and fed us cookies and lemonade. And of course, I had been here the weekend of the wedding.

I turned to look at Jordan now, thinking of that weekend, that strange, disturbing weekend when I knew I'd lost him forever. The weekend when Mary Louise had seen the ghost ship.

"Are you nervous?" he asked, frowning when he saw my look.

"Yes," I admitted, nodding. "Your mother always frightened me to death and I hardly know your father."

"He's a good man," he said. And I wondered why his words sounded defensive, as if someone had questioned Mr. Waverly's goodness before. What he hadn't said was whether or not I'd like his father and I began to wonder if that was a deliberate omission.

The dining room was as elaborate and beautiful as the rest of the house, with lovely old pieces mingled with fashionable oriental ones. There was a beautiful French watercolor over the long ornate sideboard.

The others were already there when we arrived. I wished that Jordan had not removed his hand from mine before we went in, for I felt my legs trembling inexplicably and I needed someone to hold on to.

They all turned. There were more people in the room

than I'd expected. As they looked at me in their cool, aristocratic way, I felt an urge to turn and run from the house.

Jordan touched my elbow, moving me toward a tall, graceful woman in a black silk dress.

"Mother," he said. "You remember Shelley."

"Yes," she said, her look cool and assessing. Her gray hair was immaculately swept up, emphasizing her pale eyes and long patrician nose. "Welcome to Sea Crest, Shelley."

Jordan looked very much like his father, a man still attractive despite his advancing years. His hair was a gleaming silver and I wondered if this was the way Jordan would look when he was older.

The man stepped forward and before I knew what was happening he had wrapped me in his arms. His lips against my cheek were warm and moist, and I caught the strong scent of liquor on his breath.

"You have yourself a beauty, son," he said, his words slurred. He stepped away and holding my arms, let his gaze deliberately rake up and down my figure.

I was blushing when he finally released me.

"Yes indeed. A fine, strong-looking beauty."

For a moment I was stunned. I felt as if I were a racehorse at an auction. I saw the disapproval on his wife's face and when I glanced at Jordan, I saw a look in his eyes, one of embarrassment and sadness. He took my arm and directed me toward a man I recognized.

"Shelley," Benjamin said with a smile and a slight bow. "I'm Jordan's big brother. You haven't forgotten me, have you?"

"No," I said, smiling with relief. I felt such gratitude

at finally meeting someone who seemed open and friendly. "I haven't forgotten you, Benjamin."

"This is my wife, Ella," he said.

Ella was a small woman, petite and rounded. And although she was too pert ever to be described as a classic beauty, I thought that her large gray eyes and beautiful ivory skin gave her an attractive appeal that mere beauty could not. She looked not much older than I was, evidently much younger than Benjamin, who I reasoned was in his mid thirties. He had been a grown man when we were children and away at college most of the time.

I was pleased when Ella and I were seated together at dinner, although neither of us said much during the evening. I was too afraid of making a mistake, so I preferred listening. Luckily Jordan and Benjamin did most of the talking, discussing property and business ventures.

"I think we should invest in the new shipline," Benjamin was saying. "The turn of the century is going to usher in a new prosperity, you mark my words. Americans will have more leisure time than ever and more money to spend. I think we should consider cruises to every major port in the world."

"I agree," Jordan said. "Who knows, Shelley and I might be among the first passengers ... for a honeymoon cruise."

I'm sure I blushed and there were murmurs of congratulations. For some reason I glanced at Mrs. Waverly. She sat very still, her eyes riveted on me, her face expressionless. For a moment I thought I saw resentment in her eyes, dislike even, and I glanced away quickly.

Ella touched my hand beneath the table. She'd seen Mrs. Waverly's disapproval too.

"It will be wonderful having you here," she said beneath her breath. "This past year has been so quiet and lonely."

I wondered then if she and Mary Louise had been close friends.

The men began talking again about other things.

"You mustn't mind Jordan's mother," Ella whispered. "I don't think she realizes how possessive she is of her sons. But she has treated me very kindly since Ben and I married."

"Do you have children?" I asked. There was no reason for me to whisper and I was aware that everyone could hear my question.

Suddenly the room grew very quiet. I glanced at Jordan and saw him take a long deep breath, saw him look toward his brother. Their eyes barely met and in that moment I felt the awkwardness between them, a resentment of some kind.

"Ah, there's the rub, my dear," Mr. Waverly said.

His jaw was slack and as he lifted his wine glass into the air toward me, the red liquid sloshed over onto the white damask tablecloth, where it spread slowly like a pool of blood.

"The first born grandson shall inherit," he shouted.

"Father, that's enough," Jordan said quietly. But his look was hard and disapproving.

"You hate it, don't you?" his father continued. "You hate ultimatums—always did. You were a willful boy, Jordan . . . willful and too independent for your own good." His father turned bleary, red eyes toward me as he continued to splash wine from his glass over the table. "I must warn you, my lovely Shelley, that the man you are marrying is in-intractable," he said with a loud hiccup. "But he loves this land and this house and he will do anything to keep it."

Jordan stood then, looking toward the dining room doorway where a uniformed servant stood.

"Edgar!" he barked. "Please take my father up to his bed."

The servant came immediately and pulled the old man up from his chair, propelling him unsteadily toward the doorway.

"Mary Louise was a weak and useless creature," the old man shouted. "He should have chosen you from the beginning." The wine glass fell from his hand and shattered against the tiled floor in the hallway. I could hear Mrs. Waverly's quiet murmur of dismay behind me, but I could not take my eyes from the drunken old man as he struggled against the servant. "Ella has not been able to produce a son—hell, she can't even produce a daughter! It's up to you now, Shelley. Give Jordan a son before Benjamin and your reward will be Sea Crest."

We could hear his laughter from the hallway, the laughter of a madman. His words rang in my ears as I turned to stare questioningly into Jordan's black eyes. They were cold and lifeless, and completely defensive as he deliberately turned and picked up his wine glass.

Those black eyes, so passionate before, dismissed me now as if I were someone he hardly knew.

Chapter 6

The evening was ruined. Mrs. Waverly seemed to make an effort to compose herself. She walked past me, her head held high with the regal appearance of a queen. Her eyes barely brushed over me.

"Good evening, Shelley," she said.

Benjamin took his wife's arm and although his glance my way was a bit more sympathetic, he walked past me without speaking, taking Ella with him.

"Jordan?" I turned to face him when they all had gone, expecting to hear him explain.

"I'm sorry," he said. "This is something you'll have to get used to, I'm afraid. Father has ruined dinner parties before and I'm sure you will have to endure it again in the future."

"It's not the drinking," I said, staring at him. "Or a ruined dinner party." He knew what was troubling me and I could not understand how he could dismiss his father's shocking words so casually.

"Let me get your wrap," he said, ignoring me and turning to leave the room.

I watched with dismay as he walked out of the room.

I noted the tenseness in his shoulders and the way he held his head with such pride and arrogance. Was it only pride that made him reluctant to discuss his father's drunken words? Or could it really be that what his father had said was true?

I was completely alone in the huge dining room. I turned and let my eyes take in the house and its lovely furnishings, the elegantly appointed table with its unfinished meal laid out on exquisite china. I realized that for all its beauty, it was a cold room—cold and impersonal, like a museum. I shivered then and ran to the doorway to wait for Jordan.

Jordan came back and placed the wrap around my shoulders. But even though I gazed up at him, waiting for him to explain his odd behavior, to say something, he did not.

With his hand at my waist, he moved me through the house and out to the front where the carriage sat waiting. Jordan glanced up at the sky.

"There's a ring around the moon. The old sailors say it's a sign of rain."

This time he drove toward the beach instead of through the forest. Here, in the moonlight, the white sand stretched like a gleaming ribbon as far as we could see. Waves crashed against the shore and shimmered like fireflies.

"Jordan . . . stop," I said finally. I couldn't bear another moment of his silence, or of the unanswered questions that burned within me.

He did as I asked and when he turned to me, his hands were warm and gentle on mine. But this time I couldn't let him distract me.

"How could you do this?" I asked. "How could you use me as a pawn between you and your brother?"

"Shelley, you musn't let my father's drunken rantings upset you. I promise that when you move to Sea Crest, he will not be a nuisance."

"That's not what I mean, and you know it. Is it true?" I persisted. "Are you marrying me so that we might have a child before Ella and Benjamin? Are you using me to help you gain Sea Crest?"

"Shelley . . ." His hand cupped my face and as he bent to kiss me, I saw the glitter of moonlight in his eyes. For a moment, he looked sightless and his dark hair cast a furtive shadow across his features. I gasped, but when his lips touched mine, they were warm and familiar and I told myself that my imagination was only playing tricks.

"Don't think your kisses will quiet me this time, Jordan," I said. But even as I spoke, I could feel my insides trembling with emotion.

"No?" he asked, a strain of laughter in his voice.

I wanted to shake him. My hands went to the lapels of his jacket and I grasped them with growing frustration.

"Answer me," I whispered. "I can't marry you . . . I won't, if it is to be under false pretenses."

Jordan grew very still. He pulled away from me, leaning back against the seat and staring hard into my face.

"I told you I wanted a child. I'd hardly call that false pretenses."

"Then it's true. What your father said is true."

"My father does not run my life. I decided long ago I wanted to remarry because I wanted children. I want a son." He sounded so cold, so completely uncaring of my feelings, and he still had not denied his father's words.

I stared at him there in the moonlight for long moments. Then I jumped down from the carriage and ran. I didn't think about where I was going, or that we were miles from my own home on the other end of St. Catherine's. All I knew was that his words brought an aching grief to my heart and I could not bear to hear any more. I wanted so badly for him to love me and he seemed to think nothing of letting me know he did not.

"Shelley!" I heard him shout. I heard muttered curses and then the sound of footsteps running in the sand behind me.

I screamed when I felt his hands grasping at my billowing skirts. "No!" I shouted. "Leave me alone. Just go away! Leave me alone!"

"Shelley," he growled. "Stop this. Damm it. Listen to me."

My foot caught in the sand and we both fell, sprawling together as I tried to get away from him.

He pulled me around so that I was on my back, then he grasped my wrists and held them over my head so that I could not fight him. His leg imprisoned both of mine and for a moment we lay staring into one another's eyes, our breathing ragged and labored.

"Shelley, I want to marry you. Is it so shocking that I also want a child . . . a son to carry on my name?" His voice was soft and cajoling as his lips touched my cheek, then the corner of my lips.

I couldn't suppress the shudder that coursed through me. When he felt it, he released my wrists and placed my arms around his neck. Slowly, deliberately, his hands moved downward, caressing and warm. I could feel his

54

gaze in the darkness, looking into my eyes, as his hands moved to touch my breasts.

I closed my eyes, trying to breathe, trying to protest. "Jordan, don't."

"When will you ever stop denying what's between us, Shelley?" His fingers slid to the small covered buttons and his thumb flipped them open with quick ease as if he'd done it many times before. "Can't you see that what we're feeling is much more appropriate to a marriage than love?"

"No," I murmured. But my voice was weak and I groaned as his head bent and he placed quick, hot kisses against my naked skin.

"You want this," he growled. "Admit it. Admit you want me, Shelley. That you want me to make love to you right here, right now." His breathing was harsh, his hands hard and demanding.

I wanted to deny it; I knew I should. But I couldn't. His hands, his lips were taking away all my conscious thoughts. I could only feel and need and want.

"Say it," he whispered, his mouth against my neck. "Say you want me no matter what the cost, no matter what the reason." His teeth nipped at my skin, causing delicious, uncontrollable shivers to race through me.

I gritted my teeth, knowing I should resist. But his voice, his touch was slowly driving me mad.

"Yes," I whispered finally, my words barely discernible against the sound of the wind and the sea.

"Say it. I want to hear you say the words to me, Shelley." His voice was a quiet growl and his hands held me, shook me.

I was trembling then, physically shaking with my need for him.

"I want you. I do . . . want you."

His arms tightened possessively until I could hardly breathe.

"No matter what the cost," he demanded.

"No matter . . . what . . . the cost."

His mouth was not gentle. It was a kiss of triumph, of possession, and I could feel his teeth as they ground against my lips.

His breathing was unsteady as he pulled away and stared down into my half-closed eyes.

"And you'll marry me."

"Jordan . . ." I began, trying one last time to regain some composure, to push away the burning need that made me feel insanely out of control.

"Answer me," he rasped. "Say you'll marry me."

"Yes," I replied, unable to resist him any longer. I couldn't fight him and my own traitorous body. I felt a wave of shame wash over me as I admitted that I was marrying Jordan for this. Not for guilt because of my father, not even for wealth and possession of Sea Crest Hall as Mary Louise had.

It was because I wanted him, because I wanted to spend every night like this, in his arms.

"Yes," I repeated.

Chapter 7

When Jordan walked me back to the carriage, he held me so tightly that I had the feeling he could hardly bear to let me go. I knew that it had taken all his strength to pull away from me that night on the beach and to wait for our wedding night. I even imagined for a while that he might love me.

How could one have those feelings—those sweet, overwhelming feelings—and not be in love? Surely this excitement that burned so brightly between us was at least a precursor to love. I wanted to believe that more than I had ever wanted to believe anything.

I even thought there was a new sweetness between us that night when he told me goodbye. His nearness, his attention, seemed to make his father's words insignificant, and it was much later that evening, as I lay awake in bed, before I even thought of his rantings again.

In the next few days, Jordan showered me with gifts and attention. He brought stacks of magazines and catalogs that contained pictures of bridal gowns.

"You must have the most beautiful dress that money can buy," he declared. He seemed to know exactly what

I should wear and if his interest in such things seemed odd, I chose to pretend otherwise. I told myself it was because he cared and because he wanted to make me happy.

"But Jordan," I said, "I prefer something simple. I'm hardly used to being dressed to the height of fashion. It doesn't really matter to me."

"It should," he said. "You will be a Waverly now," he continued, ignoring me, ". . . and you must look the part." He kissed me then, and as always, his kisses made my protests seem foolish and insignificant.

Finally we settled on a frothy dress of billowing silk chiffon, cut low in front and covered with a beautiful, ruffled collar of Battenburg lace that fell to the tops of my breasts.

We were at Sea Crest that day, and when Jordan was called into the study to discuss business with Benjamin, I slipped away for a look at the house and grounds.

I ventured past the edge of the lawn to the dark overhanging trees of the cemetery. I sought out Mary Louise's grave and saw that another smaller tombstone had been added. It read only "Baby Waverly" and the date of death was the same as that on Mary Louise's larger, more elaborate stone.

"Oh, Mary," I said, staring down at her grave. "How did this happen?" It seemed impossible to me that she was really gone, that I'd never see her again, or hear her funny, high-pitched voice. Sometimes I thought I could still hear her childish laughter echoing through the halls of the rambling house by the sea. Or see the image of her strolling along the long, white beach.

I had been in the house all day, planning the last details of the wedding. Or I should say, listening to Mrs.

Waverly make the plans she thought were appropriate. It was only a few short days now until the wedding and I found myself almost delirious with excitement. I was content to let Mrs. Waverly take care of the details. Whatever she wanted was fine with me.

But for all the beauty of the mansion and its immaculate grounds, I felt suffocated in that environment. It was a beautiful day and I decided a walk along the beach was just what I needed.

A warm breeze played against my skin and soon I was feeling more like myself than I had since the idea of marriage to Jordan had been presented to me.

As I walked I saw a man, from a distance at first. I put my hand up to shade my eyes from the bright sunlight and watched him walk toward me. I didn't recognize him. In fact, I was certain I'd never seen him before.

But he knew me. As soon as we were within six feet of one another, he stopped and smiled at me, a smile of recognition.

"You must be the new bride of Sea Crest," he said.

"Why . . . yes, I am. But how—?"

He was dressed in light-colored trousers rolled up above the ankles and a white shirt, open at the neck to reveal sun-darkened skin. He was barefoot. I thought he must be near Jordan's age and would have been handsome if not for the ruggedness of his features.

He had a rough, swarthy appearance, not unappealing, but certainly not classically handsome either. His eyes were as brilliant and blue as the sky that glistened above the ocean.

"Andrew Benson," he said, extending his hand toward me. "I have a little shack on the other side of the island."

"Oh," I muttered. I couldn't help noticing, when I placed my hand in his, how rough and hard his palms were. I thought he must be a fisherman.

"I've heard a great deal about you," he said.

"About me?" I couldn't hide my surprise. I was certain I had never seen this man in my life, nor heard anyone mention his name for that matter.

"From Mary Louise," he said, his blue eyes shifting out toward the ocean.

"You . . . you knew Mary?"

"Why, yes," he said. His voice was quieter now, his eyes speculative as he turned his attention back to me. "Does that surprise you?"

"Well, no," I said, hardly knowing how to answer him. Suddenly he seemed defensive and wary, as if I had insulted him somehow. "It's just that Mary Louise never mentioned you to me. And I thought I knew everyone on St. Catherine's."

"But you've been away at school for a while, in Savannah, I believe."

"Yes," I said, surprised. "I have." I must have stared at him oddly because he laughed then and his manner seemed to soften a bit.

"I never asked Mary Louise specifically about you, or anyone else on the island for that matter." His smile held a slightly apologetic look, as if he had intruded somehow. "But I suppose she was so anxious for me to know all about you that she just chattered on without thinking you might object. Actually, she told me some rather personal things."

"Really?"

It wasn't so hard for me to imagine Mary Louise telling a stranger such things. But now as he stood looking at me with those odd blue eyes, I felt a shiver race down my spine. I thought I'd never had any man look at me in quite that way. Then, almost as quickly as the look appeared in his eyes, it was gone.

"Just things about your childhood on the island," he said. "About how she had always loved Jordan Waverly and wanted to be the first bride married at Sea Crest Hall."

I began walking, hoping the man would take the hint and conclude our conversation. I didn't like the direction his words were leading, nor the way his eyes darted about as if to make sure no one saw us together. It was the first time in my life I had ever felt a tingle of fear at being alone on our deserted beaches.

"She was anxious to make Sea Crest her home," I said.

"And you?" he asked, falling into step beside me.

"That was not my first priority in agreeing to marry Jordan," I said, glancing away from his questioning eyes.

"Ah," he said, flashing brilliant white teeth. "A love match, then."

"Mr. Benson," I protested. "Really, I—"

"I'm sorry." He stopped just at the edge of the ocean. For a moment there was only the sound of the waves to break the silence, and the crying of gulls as they soared and wheeled above us. "I suppose that sounded very presumptuous of me, speaking to you of such a personal matter."

"Yes, it did."

"I apologize. It's just that I feel I know you so well. I've forgotten that you don't know me at all."

"Have you been here long?" I asked, wondering how well Mary knew him.

"This is my second summer. I met Jordan and Mary Louise when they came home from their honeymoon cruise. She was a delight." Still, his words seemed non-committal and I felt I knew no more about him than I had before.

"And you make your living . . . fishing?"

He laughed then and I thought that his smile fairly transformed his rugged features.

"Hardly," he said, still laughing. "Or I would probably starve to death. No, I'm an artist."

"Oh."

"Surprised?" he asked, grinning at me. "I'm putting together a book of paintings about birds in their native habitat. And I was told that St. Catherine's would be the perfect place to start. I'm afraid I've fallen so completely under the island's spell that I don't want to leave."

It was my turn to smile now, even though I was sure it must seem a self-conscious one.

"I am surprised," I admitted. "Actually, you look more like a fisherman."

"Thank you," he said. "That's rather a compliment, considering a year ago I'd hardly spent any time outside the city. I've learned a great deal living on the island. I hardly knew fish from fowl when I first came." He glanced at his rough hands and I thought it odd that as an artist he didn't seem to mind the calluses and rough textures.

"I'm surprised I haven't met you before. I mean, I

have been at Sea Crest quite often lately. I know Mrs. Waverly is very interested in art and—"

The sound of his laughter caught up in the sound of the wind and the sea.

"Now who's curious? Actually, I was there quite often at first."

"At first?"

"After Mary Louise's wedding." His eyes looked so strange, as if he meant to convey some hidden message to me somehow. "But your groom-to-be soon put a stop to my visits."

"Jordan?" I felt a jolt rush through me. "But . . ."

"He thought his new bride and I were spending too much time together," he explained.

"I find that hard to believe," I said. "Jordan isn't like that. He's . . . he's . . ."

"At a loss for words?" he asked mockingly. "My dear Miss Demorest . . . are you so sure after all this time away, after what happened to Mary Louise, that you really know him so well?"

I turned on him then, angered by his insinuations and by his audacity. I'd hardly even met him and already he was taking far too much advantage of our acquaintance.

"Of course I know Jordan. I've known him since we were children. He might be moody and intense, but he's . . . he's—"

"A jealous man? Temperamental—given to uncontrollable rages?"

"Of course not," I said, staring at him.

"Odd. We don't seem to be describing the same man. Have you never noticed his need to possess, then, Miss Demorest? Even Mary Louise could see that and I dare say she was far less astute than you."

I was seething. And yet I could not think of one thing to say which would counter his opinion. What exactly had Mary Louise told him about Jordan? Knowing her flights of imagination, how much of it was true?

"Again, I must apologize," he said, his voice becoming contrite. "When I saw you walking along the beach I only wanted to meet you. I certainly had no intention of upsetting you."

"What exactly was your intention then, Mr. Benson?"

"I wanted to meet you, if for no other reason than I'd heard so much about you. Now that I have, I find myself quite anxious to paint you one day."

"That's impossible," I said. How could he ask such a thing after the accusations he'd made against Jordan?

"Yes," he murmured, his eyes showing regret and sadness. "Under the circumstances, it probably is. But perhaps one day you will stop by my cabin. I would love to show you the paintings I did of Mary Louise."

"I don't think so," I answered abruptly.

But to myself I had to admit just how curious I was. What exactly had Mary Louise been to him? And more than that, how had she felt about this rugged, mysterious artist? If she had found Jordan too physical, what must she have thought of this earthy, masculine man?

I turned to go and was surprised to feel his fingers clutch my arm from behind.

"Wait. Miss Demorest . . . please. Mary Louise loved you. And out of respect for her, I feel there is one other thing I must say."

"What?" I asked, jerking my arm away from his rough, broad hands.

"She was afraid here. I'm not sure anyone ever knew except me exactly how afraid she was. If she could speak from the grave, she would plead with you to be careful. And not to make the same mistakes she did."

"You're mad," I whispered, backing away from him. "What on earth are you talking about?"

"I'm speaking of Jordan Waverly, Miss Demorest. I think you know very well what I'm talking about. He has a way of controlling everyone around him. He manipulated Mary Louise and he will you too, if you aren't very careful. He's a dangerous man and I'd hate to see you end up the same way the first bride of Sea Crest did."

"How dare you suggest that Jordan had anything to do with Mary Louise's death," I gasped. "You really are insane. Her death was an accident. Everyone knows that."

"Do they?" he shouted above the rising wind. "Are you so certain you know what he's capable of?"

I turned and ran and I could hear his voice behind me, louder and more urgent.

"I'm a stranger here, Shelley. Not bound by any loyalties to the Waverly family. Remember that, if you ever need someone to talk to. Remember it!"

Chapter 8

Andrew Benson's dire warning would not leave me. I debated even telling Jordan that I had met the man. But Jordan always knew me best and as we were walking one day, he asked what was troubling me.

"Is it the wedding?" he asked. "Are you having second thoughts? Regrets?"

I should not have said anything. But before I could think I had simply blurted out the words. "I met Andrew Benson the other day, Jordan. And I must confess that what he said worried me."

I saw the coldness wash over his face immediately. His dark eyes held no glint of light, and his lips, usually curved and sensuous, tightened into a disapproving line. "Stay away from him," he growled. "I'd prefer that you not even speak to the man."

"But Jordan . . ." I began. "What on earth has he done? He seems a very nice, respectable—"

Jordan stopped and turned to me. His fingers clamped upon my arms, digging painfully into my skin so that I frowned up at him. For a moment I felt as if I did not know him at all.

"You're—you're hurting me," I gasped, pulling away.

I saw the change in his eyes then, saw the pain and regret almost instantly. He stepped back, allowing only his hands to touch my cheek very gently. "I'm sorry. Forgive me. It's just that . . ." He hesitated for a moment, then turned away, staring out to sea before walking slowly away from me.

I fell into step beside him, not thinking that, as always, all he seemed to have to do was show a little tenderness, a little affection, and I was all too willing to forgive him anything.

"What?" I insisted. "Tell me what makes you so angry."

"I don't want you to be hurt," he said, still not looking at me. "I don't want anything to happen to you, too."

I stopped, hardly able to believe what I was hearing.

"To me too? Like Mary Louise, you mean?" How strange that his warning was so similar to Andrew Benson's. "Are you saying that Mr. Benson had something to do with what happened to Mary?"

"No," he said quickly. "No, I'm not saying that at all. I'm satisfied that her death was an accident." He smiled then, that sweet, sensual smile that warmed me to my toes. "It's a beautiful afternoon. Our wedding is in two days. Let's not spoil it with talk of such unpleasant things."

Only later when I was in bed did I realize that Jordan had used his smile and his kisses that day to make me forget. Just as he always did.

An uneasy feeling remained with me. I wasn't sure if it was caused by Andrew Benson's words, or Jordan's refusal to discuss him. I was so curious about Mary Louise and I found myself desperate to know what kind of life she and Jordan had had together. Were they happy? Pleased about the child they were expecting? Did they kiss and touch as young lovers do—the way Jordan and I did? Or had Mary remained afraid as she'd been that day on the dock before they left on their honeymoon? I wondered if that same fear made her turn to another man for companionship.

I found myself asking quiet, seemingly innocent questions of the servants. I even asked Ella, and her answer took me completely by surprise.

"What woman wouldn't be happy, married to a man like Jordan Waverly? If Benjamin treated me nearly as well as Jordan treated Mary Louise, I'd be an extremely contented woman." It wasn't her words so much that surprised me, but the tone of her voice. Ella was always gentle and soft spoken. But that day I detected an edge of bitterness, a resentment even as she spoke.

"Mary Louise was a fool," she said, turning a stormy, gray gaze toward me. "I know she was your friend, Shelley. But Mary Louise was a selfish, self-centered fool. Jordan gave her everything. He was kind and gentle, patient when the rest of us thought he should just strangle her and have done with her whining." She smiled wistfully then as if to soften her words. "He gave her a child." She was quiet for a moment, seeming to focus all her attention on the sewing she held in her lap. "I could hardly believe she was stupid enough to give it all up for—" She stopped and immediately stood up. She seemed flustered and embarrassed.

"Oh, my. I've said too much. Please forgive me, Shelley. I hope you won't mention any of this to my husband, or to Jordan."

"No," I said. "Of course I won't. But what were you going to say? You think Mary Louise gave up Jordan's love . . . for what?"

She only stared at me, her dark eyes troubled.

"Forget what I said. All that matters now is that you're marrying Jordan. And you love him—I can see that."

"Yes," I whispered. "I do love him. I think I've always loved Jordan."

"Good," she said with a nod. "That's very good. You mustn't let anything or anyone change that."

After she had gone, I sat staring out the windows of the parlor. I put aside the dried flowers and ribbons that I had been weaving into a bridal headpiece. Had Ella intended to say that Mary gave up Jordan's love for someone . . . another person, instead of some thing?

"No," I whispered to myself. That could never be true. Mary Louise might have been foolish and self-centered, but she would never do such a thing to Jordan,—never.

But I couldn't shake the feeling that something was terribly wrong. That something dark and secretive had occurred at Sea Crest. Something that no one wanted to talk about. I could find no one who would tell me about Mary Louise, not even the servants. When I asked, I would see their eyes dart away, or to meet those of another servant, as if I had mentioned a forbidden subject. And sometimes as they hurried from the room, I saw their glances turn my way again, as if they couldn't wait to be out of my presence.

There was a tenseness in Jordan too, an almost calculated politeness that he erected between us, as if to keep me at arm's length. And yet beneath that was still the intensity, the breathtaking allure that drew us together, that insisted on our touching whenever we were near. It was a new, completely captivating feeling for me and I found myself giving in to it more and more as our wedding day approached. I think at that point, I would have said anything, done anything that Jordan asked.

Mrs. Waverly suggested that we have the wedding in the gardens. But I wanted nothing of my wedding day to be like Mary Louise's, so I insisted on having it inside. The ballroom seemed like a perfect setting, with its huge chandeliers of Austrian crystal and the elaborate gilded mirrors that lined the walls. I left the placement of flowers to Mrs. Waverly and her staff and I was delighted the day before the wedding to see huge baskets of fresh flowers, palms, and sweet grass placed between the gold mirrors. Chairs had been placed on either side of the room, leaving a space between for an aisle. For a moment that day, I convinced myself that everything about the ceremony was going to be perfect.

I had not counted on the rain.

It began that evening, at first as a light sprinkle that glistened on the trees and hovered in a mist out over the ocean. My trunks were being moved into the house and they were covered with drops of water. As Mrs. Waverly gave orders for them to be dried and carried upstairs, we heard the first heavy rumble of thunder.

"Oh, dear," Mrs. Waverly said. "I had so hoped it would not rain, not tonight when all the guests will be arriving for the pre-wedding dinner."

"I'd hoped not, too," I said.

Mrs. Waverly was not a demonstrative woman. But that day, she reached to touch my cheek and her smile seemed genuine.

"Don't worry about it, my dear," she said. "The rain tonight will only wash away all the dust. And it means that tomorrow's skies will be beautifully blue and clear."

"I hope so," I replied, trying to sound optimistic. I was feeling grateful that I had asked Jordan not to plan an ocean cruise for our honeymoon. And even if the weather delayed our crossing to the mainland for a few days, what difference did it make?

Later, after I had dressed for dinner, I stood in the upstairs bedroom, staring out to sea. It had grown dark and gloomy early that day and I could barely see the glimmer of the water through the misty rain. When I first saw the image, I frowned and shook my head. I rubbed my fingers across my eyes, thinking that the busy day had left me more tired than I thought.

But when I looked again, it was still there—just off-shore, hovering in the mist. I thought I actually saw the outline of billowing sails, glinting red against the dark skies.

"My God," I whispered, clutching at the neck of my dress.

"Shelley?" I heard from the doorway.

I turned to see Jordan standing there, staring at me.

"What's wrong?" he asked. "I though I heard you cry out."

"Jordan! It's the *Sea Witch*. It's there, just like it was the night Mary Louise . . . oh, God, Jordan, look. Look."

But when I turned back to the window it was gone. Whatever I'd seen or imagined was no longer there. There was just the rain and the ocean and the darkening gray skies beyond.

Jordan took my hands and turned me to face him.

"Sweetheart," he said. "What is this foolishness? Your hands are freezing. Are you sick? Are you feeling feverish?"

"I'm not sick," I said. "And I'm not crazy. I know that I saw something."

His eyes darkened for a moment. "Of course you're not crazy. What's this all about? Has someone said something to frighten you? To make you remember Mary Louise's sighting of the *Sea Witch?*"

Suddenly his look turned distrustful and his black eyes narrowed. "Where have you been all day? Did you see Benson again after I asked you not to?"

"No." I studied his face and saw the suspicion there. "Jordan, what is this bitterness between you and Mr. Benson? Can't you tell me? We're to be married tomorrow, and—"

"I've told you," he said. "The man is not what he pretends to be. He was not a good influence on Mary Louise, that's all, and I suppose I'll always resent him for that." His look softened and he took me in his arms. "Now, let's have done with all this talk." He stepped away and his eyes raked slowly down my face, to the expanse of ecru lace at the throat of my dress. I knew the new dark green silk fit the slender shape of my body very well. It was the only dress I'd ever had that made me feel confident about the way I looked. I didn't feel boyish in the lovely gown, and now as Jordan looked at me, his eyes warm and mysterious, I thought I might never feel that way again.

"You're beautiful," he whispered. "I want to take you down to dinner and show our guests what an exquisite bride I shall have tomorrow. Come along, sweetheart. You'll feel much better after you've eaten."

For a moment, as he escorted me through the beautiful house with its glowing chandeliers and vases of fragrant flowers, I felt secure. I felt safe and the look in his eye made me feel more desired than I'd ever have thought possible. For a little while I forgot the *Sea Witch* and the meaning behind its appearance. I was beginning to wonder if it was anything more than my imagination, fueled by nerves and anxiety. For those few precious moments, I was happier than I'd ever been. There could be love for me after all. A life with the man that I loved.

I saw the look on Mrs. Waverly's face when we stepped into the dining room. It was practically empty except for the Waverly family and a few neighbors who lived on St. Catherine's. All the rest of the chairs were empty.

"What—what's happened?" I asked, feeling a suffocating sensation clutching at my chest. "Where are the guests?"

"Oh, Jordan," Mrs. Waverly said, going to him and putting her hands on his arm. "The most horrible thing has happened. The ferry was on its way across in the storm. Many of the guests were aboard and the rest waited on the dock. The captain should have waited for the storm to pass . . ." She turned then, fluttering her hands toward the table as if that would help her explain.

"Mother," Jordan said, frowning at her. "What in God's name are you trying to say? What's happened?"

"It sank," she gasped. Her eyes, brimming with tears, darted about as if she were confused. "The ferry, Jordan—we've just learned that it went down . . . with all our friends . . . my sister and her husband. Oh, dear Lord . . ."

She fainted then, sank to the floor, her elegant, chocolate-colored, taffeta dress spreading gracefully around her. I heard Ella's gasp and felt Jordan's hand slip from mine as he went to his mother. The room seemed filled with noise and light, but for a moment I felt only a numb coldness.

Then I gazed across the room and saw Jordan's father. He had not even bothered to get up from the table, but sat sipping his wine as if nothing had happened. When his eyes met mine there was jubilation in them, almost as if he were pleased. That look actually brought a quiet whimper from deep inside me. For a moment I wasn't even sure where the sound came from.

Then he smiled. Still staring into my horrified eyes, he lifted his glass toward me.

"Welcome to Sea Crest Hall," I heard his raspy voice say. Then he laughed. "Welcome, welcome, welcome."

Chapter 9

Miraculously, there were no deaths in the ferry accident, only a few injuries among the frightened people. The passengers were close enough to shore to be brought safely back to the docks, even in the nasty weather. A few of the guests even managed to make it to Sea Crest that night. Mostly those who had been waiting on the dock, hearty seafarers who were not frightened to death by what they had witnessed.

But the accident changed the entire atmosphere of the house. Mrs. Waverly took to her bed, not even able to act as hostess for the guests who did come. Some of the servants were terrified, and there was talk of the *Sea Witch* and comparisons to the night Mary Louise saw the ghost ship.

I didn't dare mention what I'd seen for fear that they'd all desert the house and the wedding.

Jordan and Benjamin were among those trying to minimize what had happened. They and some of the others even managed to make a festive evening out of the remainder of the night.

When Jordan walked me to my room very late that

night, he took me in his arms and whispered against my hair.

"I'm sorry all this has happened. I hadn't wanted anything to spoil the wedding for you . . . for us."

"It hasn't," I said, although I'm certain my voice reflected my lack of confidence.

"Are you sure?" he asked, looking into my eyes.

"I'll admit I was frightened," I said. "But now that the guests are here safe and sound, I feel much better."

"Good. Then I suppose the next time I see you, you will be walking into the ballroom on the arm of your father."

"Yes," I whispered. I still found it impossible to believe. I would actually marry Jordan Waverly tomorrow. "I only hope the weather doesn't delay his trip from the north end of the island."

"Don't worry." He smiled at me as if he had enough confidence for the both of us. "We'll get him here somehow. I hope he won't be too uncomfortable, being in this house with my father."

"Surely he can manage it for one day," I said, attempting to be as optimistic as he was.

"Tomorrow then," he said.

I suppose that conversation set me to thinking about my father and why he and John Waverly were such bitter enemies. No one had ever explained that to me. I suppose as a child I never asked. But after being around Mr. Waverly and seeing his behavior, I was sure that his attitude and his drinking must be part of it. But as I went to my room that night I wondered. Had Jordan's father always been this way? Might not he have been different as a young man? For a moment, the thought came to me that if Mr. Waverly had changed so drastically since his youth, couldn't Jordan also change? Hadn't he changed already since we were children . . . since Mary Louise died?

"No," I whispered. "Stop this. Nothing is going to spoil this wedding, or this marriage. Now, just stop it."

The next morning two of the maids arrived to help me prepare for the wedding. I sat in my dressing gown, sipping a cup of hot, soothing tea while one of them arranged my hair. Then, just before eleven, they helped me into my fashionable, lace-trimmed wedding gown.

When I turned to look into the mirror, I was pleasantly surprised. My auburn hair was swept upward and the flowered wreath I'd made was placed like a small crown on my head. Pale wispy ribbons in spring colors mingled with the same frothy chiffon as my dress was made of to make a veil.

"You look as lovely as any bride I've ever seen, miss," one of the girls said shyly. Both of the girls were smiling broadly as I turned about and stared into the long cheval mirror.

"It's the dress," I said, still bemused.

The girls giggled and one of them handed me a bouquet of spring flowers. "It's you, miss," she said. "If I was as nice and slender as you I'd be a happy young woman, I would. Dresses don't hang right on a round woman, me old grandma used ta say."

The rest of the morning passed in a blur. The beautiful ballroom, the guests gathered there in their splendid clothes . . . Jordan looking so tall and handsome. I simply became numb. I hardly remember what was said during the wedding ceremony. All I remember is Jordan and the look in his eyes as we were pronounced man and wife.

"I can't wait to get you away from here," he whispered as we embraced.

I'm sure my cheeks must have been flushed. I glanced toward my father, and met his smile of approval. And if there was also a glint of relief on his weathered face, I felt too happy to acknowledge it. I had been too distracted even to ask how he was, or if he'd had problems getting to Sea Crest in the bad weather.

As it was, the weather would delay our honeymoon. I was disappointed that we would have to spend the night here at Sea Crest Hall, but I knew it couldn't be helped.

After a long, sumptuous luncheon in the formal dining room, we came back to the ballroom. The chairs had been moved to the edge of the room and musicians sat on a raised platform at the far end of the ballroom. The sound of violins filled the air. Even the dark gloom of the day added to the beautiful atmosphere—made it brighter inside, even cozy, if one could call the gigantic ballroom cozy.

For a while that afternoon as Jordan and I danced and laughed and enjoyed our guests, I forgot about the weather. I even managed to forget my first vision of the *Sea Witch*. And I forgot Mary Louise.

Later I saw my father motion to me from across the dance floor. Jordan was dancing with his mother, who had managed, after last night's near tragedy, to compose herself for the wedding. In fact, she seemed to have gotten over last night's incident quite well. I signalled to Jordan that I would see my father out, then I went across the room to catch my father's arm and walk with him through the house.

We stood at the front door.

"Don't bother coming out, lass," Father said. "You'll get your beautiful gown wet."

The wind was blowing rain across the porch and it looked as if the storm might last through the evening, possibly even the entire night.

He took me by the hand and looked into my eyes.

"You are happy, aren't you? This is what you wanted? It's taken a heavy burden from my old shoulders, child. But I'd like you to be happy too."

"I would like it to have been Jordan's idea, Father," I said.

I saw his frown, and for a moment there was a troubled look of guilt in his weary eyes.

"But yes," I added. "Marrying Jordan is what I've always wanted."

"Good," he said with an audible sigh. "I trust Jordan," he said. "I trust him to take care of you and . . . keep you safe."

He seemed to be staring at me as if he might never see me again. I touched his face and smiled.

"Of course he will, Papa."

"But if anything happens—if John Waverly, or any of his family tries to interfere in your life, you've only to come to me. You know that, don't you lass?"

His words puzzled me. But then a great deal of what he'd done the past year or two puzzled me.

"Yes, Papa. I know I can always come home."

"Good . . . good. Well, give me a kiss, girl. I'll be seein' you from time to time. You and Jordan will come and visit, now, won't you?"

I assured him we would and waved goodbye as he climbed into his battered, old, black carriage. For the first time, I realized that I would be a wealthy woman, that I would no longer have to worry about money for school and clothes, or household expenses. I could even buy my father a new carriage.

I was smiling when I walked back to find Jordan.

His mother was still with him and she took my arm, pulling me around so that she stood between me and her son.

"I know what I'm about to ask isn't traditional, children. But the weather has caused changes in all our plans. I thought perhaps, since you won't be leaving until tomorrow for your trip, you might like to change clothes, then we'll have a lovely dinner with our guests."

Jordan smiled at me and there was a look in his eyes that took my breath away. His look was indulgent and patient and for a moment I thought I saw a hint of his old humor returning.

"Whatever Shelley wants," he said, his gaze never leaving my face.

"That sounds very nice, Mrs. Waverly."

"Good, then it's settled. Jordan, why don't you take your bride up to your new suite of rooms to change. I'll announce dinner to the others."

I was trembling with anticipation before we ever reached our rooms. As soon as we were away from the others, Jordan reached for me, pulling me into a darkened alcove and kissing me until I was breathless.

"God, how I wish we could forget dinner," he whispered. "Forget the guests, forget everything except us."

"Do you?" I could hardly believe he felt that way. It seemed impossible that he could feel the same way I did. But I told myself quickly that if Jordan did not yet love me, that I could settle very well for this that was between us. Very well indeed.

"Of course I do," he said, smiling that teasing smile of his. "Am I being too forward? Does it frighten you having such an ardent, impatient husband?"

His kisses, his hands, left me trembling.

"No . . . never."

He groaned slightly and pulled me back into the hallway.

"Don't encourage me," he teased. "Or I shall embarrass mother by not showing up for her dinner party."

What we were experiencing was so new, so fragile that I couldn't tell him what I was really thinking. If I could have, I might have told him I wanted to forget his mother and the party as well. At the moment I didn't care about anything except Jordan and the way he made me feel.

He insisted that we change clothes in separate rooms. It was the first time I'd seen our new suite and I found it quite beautiful. There were two large bedrooms, separated by a smaller sitting room. My clothes had been placed in one room and Jordan's in the other. I felt too shy to ask if it would remain that way. I supposed I would just have to wait and find out.

"I don't want to be tempted," he said, giving me a gentle nudge toward my room.

"I need someone to help with these buttons," I said. There were scores of buttons down the back of my dress, but both of us knew very well that all I had to do was call one of the maids.

Jordan shook his head at me and his look was warm and sweet. Slowly he turned me around. I could not suppress the shiver that ran down my spine when I felt his warm fingers moving from button to button down my back. I felt his lips against my bare skin at the back of my neck, then moving lower to the edge of my lace trimmed camisole. I closed my eyes and leaned back against him, breathing a heavy sigh of pleasure.

"You like that?" he murmured against my skin.

"Yes," I whispered. "Oh, yes."

He laughed softly and turned me around to face him.

"Oh, Shelley, how I love your honesty," he murmured. He removed the flowered wreath from my head and brushed strands of hair away from my face. "You are so warm, so open and straightforward. Promise me you will always stay just the way you are today."

His words made me think of Mary Louise and her poignant wish before her wedding that she could always be so happy.

She had such a short time for happiness.

"I can't imagine I'll ever change," I said, pushing those unpleasant thoughts away. "Except to grow more happy as the years pass."

For a moment, a line appeared between his eyes. His hand stopped, then he bent to place a soft kiss on my lips.

"I hope so," he said. "God, how I hope that is true."

Chapter 10

If the wedding had not been everything I'd hoped for, due to the terrible weather and the accident, then the dinner made up for it somewhat. Everyone seemed to have gotten past the fright of the ferry's sinking, and I suppose that our having survived such an ordeal put everyone in a thankful, even festive mood.

But for me, it was not the gaiety of the evening. It was Jordan. The dark glow of his eyes upon me, the touch of his hand on mine beneath the table, the way he leaned toward me when he spoke. I was in a daze, in a heartstopping, overwhelming daze of love and desire. I found I had quite forgiven him and Father for arranging a marriage behind my back. In fact I was feeling grateful, and finding that all the longings, all the unrequited love I'd felt for Jordan for years had come back in one overwhelming crash, like a giant wave sweeping over the shore. I could hardly wait for us to be alone.

Finally, the moment came. It had been a long day for the household and after the delicious dinner, everyone seemed happily subdued and content. With best wishes to the bride and groom, everyone slowly drifted away to their rooms. By the time Jordan and I reached our suite, the house was quiet. So quiet that even inside the large structure, we could hear the wind buffeting against the eaves and slashing at the windows. Thunder made a long, low rumble that shook the house and set the glass prisms of the hallway sconces into a melodious jingle.

We stopped for a moment in the dimly lit hallway outside our door.

"I'm happy that you're my wife," Jordan whispered as he opened the door.

As I stepped into the room the scene that met my eyes wiped away my smile and caused me to catch my breath in horror. I seemed to hear Jordan's words echoing around and around inside my head . . . 'happy you're my wife . . . happy you're my wife.' The terror of what I saw, what we both saw, was like a nightmare. I felt as if I had just stepped out of heaven into a hellish netherworld.

On the settee in the sitting room lay a figure dressed in white like a bride. The white airy material that fell in soft drapes to the floor was covered in blood. Streaks of brilliant red blood. The hair beneath the bridal veil was blonde and I knew immediately who it was.

"Mary Louise!"

The scream I heard rang through the room. It echoed down the hallway and when it stopped I felt the room growing dark and shadowy. As I felt consciousness leave my body I knew that the screams I had heard were my own.

I don't know how many minutes passed before I woke. I remember waking up, lying on a bed. There were several people in the room and as I lay there I realized that the two people nearest the bed were Mrs.

Waverly and Ella, who was holding my cold hand in hers.

"Shelley," she said, her eyes large with fright. "Are you all right? Can you hear me?"

I found my throat too dry to speak. I nodded and reached toward a crystal water glass at my bedside.

Ella was very kind. She lifted my head and helped steady the glass of water as I drank.

"Jordan," I managed to whisper. "Where's Jordan?"

"He's downstairs with some of the men," Mrs. Waverly said, stepping to the bed. "I suppose you know you gave him quite a scare."

"I . . . ?"

"Fainting that way when you saw the mannequin."

For a moment her words didn't sink in. I frowned and shook my head against the pillow.

"A mannequin? But you mean—"

"I'm sure you must have been frightened to death," she said, her voice soft and condescending. "I must admit, it did look much like a real person in the dim lights. But you don't have to worry now, dear. We've had it taken away. Jordan's downstairs at this very moment trying to find out who would play such a tasteless trick. But you know how some of the young people behave at weddings. They simply have no finesse in these matters."

I stared up at her, hardly able to believe my ears.

"Trick?" I managed to say. "You think finding a dead body in our room, dressed in a wedding dress, is only a trick?"

Her laugh was forced and I saw an odd exchange of glances between her and Ella.

"But it wasn't real," she said with a shrug of her

85

shoulders. "It was tasteless, I'll admit. And I apologize, Shelley, that something like this has happened in my own home. I promise that when Jordan gets to the heart of the matter, we shall dismiss anyone involved in such a thing."

I heard murmurs from the back of the room and I realized that the other people I'd seen were the two maids who had helped me dress for the wedding. Their faces reflected their resentment at Mrs. Waverly's insinuation.

Mrs. Waverly glanced at them over her shoulder, giving them only a haughty look.

"We'll go now, dear, and let you rest. Jordan will be back shortly. You won't be afraid, will you?"

"I'll stay with her, mum," one of the maids said, stepping forward.

"That won't be necessary, Jilly," Mrs. Waverly said.

"It's all right. I'd be happy for her to stay," I said.

Ella bent and brushed my hair away from my face.

"You'll be all right," she said. "We'll talk as soon as you're feeling better."

After the others left, the girl that Mrs. Waverly had called Jilly stepped to the side of the bed. She was a very pretty girl and I recognized her as the one who'd made the comment about being round. But in her black dress and white starched apron, I thought her soft, curvaceous body was quite perfect. She stood staring down at me, and as I glanced up at her face, I recognized a flash of resentment in her blue eyes.

"Jilly," she said, mimicking Mrs. Waverly. Her pretty mouth twisted into a pouting grimace.

I had no idea what she meant. "Would you like to sit down?" I asked.

The girl sighed and pulled the chair closer to the bed.

"I'm sorry, miss. I don't mean to be so disagreeable. But that woman knows how to get my goat, that's for sure. She knows very well that my name is Jillian and she insists on calling me Jilly, as if I was a house cat or worse yet, one of her lap dogs."

"Oh," I said. I couldn't resist smiling at her. "Then I'll be sure and call you Jillian," I said.

Jillian rolled her eyes and finally she smiled.

"Sorry," she muttered.

"It's all right," I assured her. "Really. I understand. I feel like a stranger here myself sometimes."

"You have to be careful, Miss," she said, suddenly growing serious again. "That's why I asked to stay—to warn you. What happened tonight, it wasn't just some harmless trick like Mrs. Waverly claims."

I sat up in bed, feeling the room spin for a moment. I swung my legs over the side of the bed and leaned closer.

"What do you know about it, Jillian?"

"I know that something similar happened to Miss Mary when she came home from her honeymoon."

Her words chilled me. I could feel the hair standing up on the back of my neck.

"Then why is Jordan downstairs trying to find out who did it? If he knows that the same thing—"

"He knows," she said, her voice growing quiet.

I took a deep breath. Something, some quiet thought in the back of my mind, warned me that I didn't want to hear anything else. I didn't want to hear what she was about to tell me.

"Jillian . . ." I said, lifting my hand to still her words.

"You have to listen, miss," she said, leaning toward me. "There's something evil in this house. The servants know it, even if no one else will admit it. All the things that's happened here, they can't all be accidents."

"What things?"

"The first Mrs. Waverly ... your husband's grandmother. Surely you've heard about her?"

"No," I said. Suddenly I was beginning to feel as if I were trapped in a nightmare. Somewhere odd, among strangers, somewhere I'd never been before.

"Killed herself, she did."

"But ... but I've known Jordan all my life. I don't remember his ever mentioning—"

"Oh, they don't talk about it. It was a disgrace to the family, her killin' herself and all."

I shrugged, trying desperately to ward off the dark slither of apprehension that crept over me.

"A suicide is—is unfortunate, but—"

"Don't you think it's odd that Miss Mary Louise committed suicide the same way?"

"Suicide? Mary Louise? But it was an accident. She was in the dinghy and—"

"That's what the Waverlys said—it was an accident. But they know she killed herself. They just don't want the rest of the island to know." She frowned and shook her head at me. "If you don't believe me, you can ask that artist that lives over on the Sound. He talked to her that day. He knows."

"Andrew Benson? He knew that Mary meant to kill herself? My God, if he did, why didn't he try to stop her? Why didn't someone try to stop her? No," I said, leaping from the bed. I began to pace back and forth, glancing at the girl from time to time. "Mary Louise would never do such a thing. She loved Jordan. She was going to have a baby, for heaven's sake. She would never do anything to jeopardize the life of her child."

"She would if she thought it was going to be like the rest of the Waverlys."

Her voice was quiet but the impact of her words was like an exploding shell in my brain. Was John Waverly really insane as I had suspected? Was it hereditary? Did that mean that the changes I'd witnessed in Jordan were significant?

I went to the bed and sat down. I grasped Jillian's sleeves in my fist.

"Tell me everything you know, Jillian. Jordan was not involved in this conspiracy of silence. He would never be. He loved Mary Louise and he wanted a child more than anything. I came to the funeral and I saw him. He was devastated."

"He didn't cry," she said, her voice quietly accusing. "He never cried."

"That doesn't mean anything. He's a strong man who would never show his emotions in front of other people. Perhaps he grieved in his own way when he was alone."

"Huh," she grunted. "He didn't mind showin' his anger in front of everybody else. You don't know how he treated her, miss. How he ridiculed everything she did, everything she said." Her eyebrows lifted as she spoke. "And it didn't take much time for him to hunt another bride."

I must have gasped at her words.

"Lord," she muttered. "I'm sorry. I almost forgot for a minute who I was talkin' to."

"It's been more than a year since her death."

"Oh, but there was talk of a new marriage right away," she said, her eyes bright. "Jordan Waverly knew exactly what he was doin' when he threatened to foreclose on your Father's debts."

"Threatened to foreclose? Jordan . . . ?"

"Gor," she whispered. "You didn't know. Well, me and my big mouth." Her look was sheepish and apologetic. "It's true—leastwise it's what everyone on the island says. Your Papa owed Jordan Waverly a great deal of money—more than he could ever pay in his lifetime."

I couldn't believe it. Couldn't believe that Jordan had actually planned such a thing. Didn't he know that he could have married me anyway? Didn't he know that I'd always adored him and would have married him without his having to go to such elaborate, deceitful lengths?

"I'm not sayin' that anything will happen to you," she continued. "All I'm sayin' is that you should be careful. I believe that someone in this house drove Miss Mary Louise to do what she done. And he might try to do the same to you."

I think she slipped when she said the word 'he'. But I knew immediately who she meant. She thought Jordan, the man I loved, had tormented Mary Louise, driven her insane, and that in her fragile state of mind, she had taken the only way out that she could see. Suicide.

"No," I whispered. "No, it can't be true. This can't be happening."

I don't know what I was thinking at that moment. All I knew was that I had to get away, out of the stifling confines of the beautiful cold house. I had to think and I knew that I'd never be able to reason everything out if I let Jordan touch me . . . kiss me. I couldn't let him try to convince me nothing was wrong, for I knew it was. Terribly, terribly wrong.

Chapter 11

I didn't even bother to take a wrap and I didn't think about the storm or the pouring rain. I just ran from the room, not thinking where I would go. I heard Jillian's voice behind me.

"Wait . . . Miss . . . Mrs. Waverly, please wait."

I stood in the hall for only a moment before deciding to go down the back stairs and out through one of the rear entries. I didn't want to see anyone. Most of all, I didn't want to see Jordan.

I ran outside, mindless of the lightning. My steps faltered for a moment when the crash of thunder seemed to shake the earth. But I continued on, running past the gardens and around toward the front of the house. My skirts grew heavy from the rain and my shoes were immediately soaked through. As I ran I managed to find my way by the intermittent flash of the storm's light.

Jillian must have gone to Jordan right away, for by the time I reached the edge of the lawn I heard him calling from behind me.

I knew that once I was past the tree line and out onto the beach he would not be able to determine in the darkness which way I had gone. I ran harder, my mind so confused that I did not realize the consequences of what I was doing or what Jordan must think. I only knew that something was terribly wrong and I had to be alone, to think. If the wrongness was in Jordan, I didn't want to know—not now, not tonight.

As I came from beneath the trees, I felt the soft rasp of sand beneath my feet and I knew I was on the beach. Here the sound of the ocean overrode the storm, together combined into a deafening roar.

In the next flash of lightning, I saw a glimmer in the distance and I remembered the small pier and fishing shack that everyone on this end of the island used. I bent low, staying just at the edge of the trees and I ran as fast as I could toward the glimmer of light. As I grew nearer, I could see the dark outline of the building.

I was weak and panting for breath by the time I reached the shack. I pulled myself up the long line of wooden steps and as I went I could feel the wind and the stormy ocean shaking the tall poles that served as the structure's foundation. I told myself that such storms were common, like many that buffeted the island from spring until fall. The shack had withstood storms worse than this one.

Once I was inside with the door closed, it was amazing how much of the howling storm was locked away outside. From time to time the structure would shudder from the gusty wind, but the thunder and lightning seemed to be moving out to sea.

I quickly found a box of matches and lit one of the lamps. The small warm glow of light made me feel immensely better even though I was still shivering from the wet and cold. I held the lamp up and looked around the inside of the cabin. It had been years since I'd been there.

There was a small bed in one corner, bookshelves containing supplies and a few books. Two battered chairs and a square wooden table stood in the middle of the room. On the table, its scope facing seaward, was an old, weathered telescope. This place had served as a resting place, shade from the hot sun, and as a shelter from sudden summer storms for as long as I could remember.

I looked now out toward the rolling sea. Wide windows and a door overlooked the long pier that stretched out into the ocean past the breakers. I watched the lightning flickering in the black clouds for a while before I turned back to the small room. I barely had time to think about what I would do when the door suddenly burst open.

Jordan stood for a moment in the doorway. The lightning behind him threw the lines of his face into a dark, menacing shadow. He stalked quickly across the short distance between us. His black eyes looked shadowed in the dim light and I could see rivulets of rain dripping from his hair onto his face. Without a word, he clasped my arms and shook me, pulling me toward him until I was within inches of his face.

"You little fool! What in God's name do you think you're doing? You could have been swept out to sea . . . and I'd never have found you . . . never have known . . ."

His teeth were clenched, his eyes filled with some wild fury that I'd never seen before. And for the first time in my life I felt afraid of him.

"Jordan . . . don't." A shudder ran down my spine

and I tried to pull away from him. "Please . . ." I whispered. His fingers held me tight, biting into my skin until I felt the sting of tears in my eyes.

An odd look flashed across his face and he frowned. "Shelley?" he whispered. His hands released me and moved upward to touch my face. "What are you afraid of? My God—not of me?"

"Should I be?" I said, finally managing to free myself from his hands. I backed away from him, moving toward the door that led to the pier.

"I'm surprised you could even ask such a question."

"Why didn't you tell me that you threatened to foreclose on my father? Why didn't you tell me that you were the one who suggested this marriage," I demanded, near hysteria.

"Where did you hear such a thing?"

His eyes flashed again, anger apparent in their black depths as he moved toward me.

"Don't, Jordan," I said, warning him away with my hand. "Don't come any closer."

"You're my wife," he said, his voice deep and ominously quiet. "And I have every right to do as I please where you're concerned."

"No." I ran for the door. Where I intended to go I have no idea. I only knew that I was afraid and confused.

His arms went around me from behind and he dragged me against him. We struggled as I struck out at him. I was crying desperately and the feel of his body against mine bewildered me even more. He pinioned my arms between us, holding my wrists and shaking me again. I could feel the rumble of his voice in his chest, hear the quiet growl of exasperation as he struggled with me.

"Stop this, Shelley. God, what's happened to cause you to act this way? Listen to me. Just be still for a minute and listen to me."

I went still for a moment and he grunted, pulling me against him, his arms tentatively releasing mine, before moving gently around my waist. For a moment I felt trapped and panic stricken. I tried to pull away again.

"Stop it," he said. His voice was quieter, calming somehow. "I would never hurt you. Don't you know that?"

I held myself very stiff and unyielding. But the warmth of his body, the feel of his strong arms around me was taking its toll. I wanted to trust him, wanted to believe what he was saying . . . but I had never been so confused in my life.

"Look at me," he demanded, turning me and placing his fingers under my chin.

I looked up at him there in the dimly lighted shack. The storm still raged around us, but suddenly in the cozy warmth of the cabin it was so quiet I could hear my own heart beating, its rhythm odd and irregular.

His eyes were shadowed, unreadable, as he stared down at me. I swallowed hard and I could feel my breathing growing more steady as he held me tightly against him. He wiped the tears from my face, his hands as gentle as I could ever ask.

"I know what happened tonight frightened you, and I'm sorry. I should have been there when you woke. But I was so damned angry."

"It . . . it's not that," I said.

"Then what?" He pulled me around toward the light

and I could see his eyes. They were so tender, so different than they'd seemed when he came storming into the shack a few moments earlier.

I didn't know what to tell him. I knew that if I told him everything I'd heard it would only be a matter of time before he and his mother figured out that Jillian was the one who'd told me.

"There have been rumors . . . things I'd heard before tonight," I said, lying. "But I ignored them. I—"

"What things?" he asked, his voice hard and demanding. "What rumors?"

"About . . . about Mary Louise."

I saw the clench of his jaw and his eyes bored into me for a moment before he turned away and walked to the windows. His hands rested on his hips and I could see the tension in the set of his shoulders.

"She committed suicide, didn't she? Why didn't you tell me, Jordan? Why have you never told me that?"

"God, Shelley." His voice was a soft curse as he whirled around to face me. "God! Do you know how long it's taken for me to be able to hear that word . . . even to say it out loud? How can you even begin to know how I felt? After I ignored her pleas, after I dismissed her threats. It was my fault," he said, practically shouting. His eyes were wild, filled with some long hidden guilt and fury. "Mine!" He turned again, lashing out at the table and sending a cup flying across the room to land with a loud crash against the wall. "I should have listened. And I should have believed her. I lost a child because of my own stubborn resentments."

"You lost a wife as well," I reminded him, wondering at his choice of words.

His eyes met mine then and there was a hint of sadness and apology. "Of course. I didn't mean to sound as if I were dismissing what happened to Mary Louise. But she was an adult, Shelley. Capable of making rational decisions, capable of saving herself if—"

"If she'd been stronger," I said.

"You know it was true." He turned away again in an impatient, restless gesture and I could hear his long slow intake of air. "She was never like us, Shelley. You know that. Mary Louise was different, and I took that difference as a sign of weakness. At first, I found her dependence flattering. But after a while, it became a cloying, destructive thing between us. The more I tried to pull away, the more I tried to instill a little life and independence in her, the harder she clung to me and the more irrational and insecure she became . . ." His next words were muffled and so low that I could hardly hear them.

"I was a bastard. And I've never regretted anything more in my life."

I felt a tingle in my chest, felt the warmth of love that I'd always felt for him, returning with a single jolt. There was an explanation for every single thing Jillian had told me. There had to be.

I stepped to him and put my arms around his waist. The chill of our wet clothes touched my skin and I shivered. Thunder crashed outside, rattling the windows and the floor.

Jordan turned and pulled me into his arms with a quiet groan. I could feel an impatience in him, almost a desperation as his mouth took mine in a hungry, demanding kiss.

I couldn't escape. I no longer wanted to escape. I responded to him. Responded without conscious thought, my actions seemingly fueled only by emotion, my body acting on its own.

If this was insanity, then I would let it claim me completely.

My hands moved upward to his chest and I could feel the sinewy muscles beneath his wet shirt.

"Are you afraid of me?" he murmured, moving his mouth only inches from mine.

"No," I whispered.

It was my wedding night. Despite the strange happenings, despite all my misgivings, I knew that I wanted it to be complete. I wanted to belong to Jordan. Had to. This had been my destiny since the moment I agreed to marry him. As his mouth devoured mine and his fingers pushed away the wet material of my dress, I was overwhelmed with the urgency of that need.

He pulled away for a moment, tossing his wet jacket over one of the chairs and unbuttoning his shirt. I stood, staring at him in the lamplight, memorizing every line, every muscled curve of his chest, gazing into those black, passion-filled eyes.

I could hardly breathe.

"It will be different for us, Shelley," he whispered. "I promise you, everything will be different."

He stood away from me, not touching me and yet his eyes made me feel loved, caressed. The desire I saw in his eyes thrilled me, made me forget everything except that moment.

In that instant I felt an almost spiritual connection with him, such as I'd never experienced with another human being. It was exciting and frightening, like nothing I'd ever known. I must have moaned as I stepped into his arms.

"Shh," he whispered against my hair. "There will never be any secrets between us, Shelley. Promise me."

"I promise," I said. At that moment I would have promised him anything.

"I want you," he groaned, pushing my dress away further until it fell onto the floor. His eyes were hot as they raked down my trembling body. "God, I've never wanted anyone as much as I want you at this moment."

His kiss held all the passion and hunger I could ever have dreamed of.

"I love you," I whispered against his mouth. "Love you . . . love you."

He picked me up in his arms, and swung me around toward the bed as he continued kissing me.

"Tell me you have no doubts about this, Shelley," he whispered. "About me."

"No . . . no doubts," I said, desperate to feel his warm strong body against mine. Desperate for some fulfillment that I couldn't even know existed. I pushed everything from my mind except that. Pushed away every doubt, every question until there was room for nothing except Jordan and the way he made me feel.

"Tell me this is what you want," he said, his deep voice demanding. "I want you to be sure. We can wait if—"

"It is," I said, reaching almost desperately for his lips again. "Oh, yes, Jordan. It is what I want."

How could I not have said yes? How could I ever regret having him finally for my own? It was what I'd wanted all my life.

Chapter 12

I find it difficult, even now, to describe the emotional intensity of that night. The power of the storm that raged around us, the almost forbidden allure of being alone in the primitive shack. There was a force, a wild, abandoned passion that both of us felt. Giving in to it was exciting and sweet.

Afterward, we lay in each other's arm, breathless and content. I can still see the look on Jordan's face as he stared down at me in the dim lamplight. It seemed one of awe and surprise.

"I can hardly believe this," he murmured. "I feel as if I've been carrying a rare gem in my pocket for years without knowing it."

I laughed and hid my face against his neck. "You mean me?" I whispered. I looked into his eyes. "Then you're not . . . you're not disappointed."

"God, no," he said, his voice growing husky and warm. His eyes twinkled mischievously as he brushed a kiss across my lips. "Such a question. I suppose I'll have to spend a great deal of time convincing you of that."

"Yes," I said, smiling again. "A great deal."

By morning the weather had cleared and Jordan and I walked hand in hand along the beach, littered by broken palms and long strands of spanish moss. We must have looked quite bedraggled with our damp clothes and disheveled hair.

I almost laughed aloud when we met Mrs. Waverly just inside the door at Sea Crest. I should have felt some remorse, I suppose, some embarrassment, but the puzzled look of horror on her face just struck me as funny.

"What on earth . . . ? Jordan . . . Shelley, where have you been? Your clothes—you're both soaking wet."

"Never mind, Mother," Jordan said, bending to kiss her cheek. He tugged at my hand, pulling me past her as she stood sputtering and gazing after us.

"If you'll excuse us, we have a ferry to catch," he called over his shoulder.

Those days of our honeymoon were among the most wonderful of my life. We spent long, leisurely, sun-filled days traveling along the coast, just the two of us, visiting small quaint villages and staying in out-of-the-way inns.

After dinner we would often go to our room early. It was as if neither of us could wait for evening and the privacy of our quarters. I'm sure the innkeepers and the other guests could see it written on our faces. There were smiles and nods of approval. It was spring and everyone, it seemed, was in love with love and with lovers.

When we arrived back on St. Catherine's, I could not imagine anything could ever change what was between us. I had completely dismissed the warnings that Jillian and Andrew Benson had given me. In doing so, I underestimated what some called the evil forces that lived within Sea Crest Hall.

Things between us began to change almost as soon as

we returned to the mansion. I told myself that his work, and seeing to the running of the estate, would keep us from being together as we'd been on our honeymoon. It was only natural, I told myself. But as days and weeks passed, I began to see a disturbing new pattern to our lives.

Jordan seemed to keep himself apart from me during the day, almost deliberately, I thought. His demeanor toward me was cool and detached. But when the long shadows of evening fell across the island, when the house grew quiet and we retired to our suite, he was once again my ardent lover, the man that I adored and could never seem to resist.

The first time I approached him about my concerns, he seemed surprised and as deftly as always, he convinced me I was wrong. But I could feel him distancing himself from me, though I couldn't understand why.

Ella and I had become very close, although I felt she was too much under the thumb of her husband and mother-in-law. The poor girl could not seem to do anything to suit either of them. Many of our conversations focused on her fears and disappointments.

"If only we'd had a child," she would say. "Maybe everything would be different between Benjamin and me, if we'd had a child."

I found that sometimes even Ella's company was not enough for me. I would grow restless, eager to be alone with my own thoughts and my own fears. And although I had never expressed any of those fears to Ella, I thought she was beginning to see that all was not well between Jordan and me.

It was one of those days, one of those sweltering hot summer afternoons, and I simply had to escape. I walked down to the beach, and as I often did when I was in a melancholy mood, I found my steps taking me to the pier and the fishing shack where Jordan and I first made love. It seemed to comfort me somehow, even reassure me that things could be that way between us again, that bonding of the spirit that we experienced the night of our wedding.

I saw a man walking toward me that day and I knew who he was. I also knew I should turn back and away from Andrew Benson. My seeing him could cause nothing but further problems between my husband and me, and I did not want that.

But I was lonely, and I was growing more and more desperate to understand what was wrong at the Waverly mansion. I had a feeling that Andrew Benson knew some of the answers and that idea intrigued me.

"Good afternoon," he said, coming to stand near me. For a moment his tall form shut out the lowering sun and cast a shadow across me.

"Hello," I answered.

"Out for a walk?" he asked.

"Yes. I find I can stay confined in the house only for so long. Sometimes I find myself longing to toss away my shoes and race across the sand the way I did as a child."

He laughed softly and turned to walk beside me.

"You should do it," he said. "I've found, since coming to the island, that exercise is a wonderful way to relieve the stresses of the mind and body."

We walked for a way, neither of us saying anything.

"Is everything all right?" he asked.

I glanced at him quickly, studying his profile for a moment.

"Of course. Why wouldn't it be?"

"I didn't mean to imply that it wasn't."

I stopped, forcing him to stop and to turn and look at me.

"Mr. Benson . . ."

"Andrew . . . please."

"Andrew, I was wondering . . ."

"What?" he asked, his odd blue eyes boring into mine.

"About Mary Louise—those things you told me about her."

"Why?" he asked, stepping toward me in a protective manner. "Has something happened? Is everything all right at the estate?"

"I'm fine," I said, frowning up at him. "It's just that I've heard things . . . rumors about my friend. Someone even told me that she'd threatened to kill herself . . . and that you knew about it."

He turned away from me and took my arm, motioning me along with him. He glanced about us, down the beach and back toward the line of barrier palms that partially hid Sea Crest Hall from view.

"We shouldn't be speaking of this here. Walk with me across the island. I want to show you something."

We walked down the beach, well past the boundaries of the beautifully manicured Sea Crest estate, then across Pelican banks at the end of the island. From here we proceeded inland. The further we went, the more apprehensive I became.

I knew I shouldn't be walking with Andrew Benson anywhere. In my heart I knew how upset Jordan would be if he found out. And I was not at all sure I could trust the mysterious artist.

But I kept walking, mostly out of curiosity I suppose. I had to learn what was wrong at Sea Crest Hall and I had a disturbing feeling that the key might lie in unearthing the secret of Mary Louise's suicide. This man whom I followed seemed to know her better than anyone, even Jordan.

As the water of St. Catherine's Sound and the river inlet appeared, I began looking around, wondering where Andrew Benson lived. There was not much of a beach on this side of the island. It was mostly scrub palm and marshy grassland.

"Here we are," he said.

I saw the house then, sitting well into the trees on a level above the marsh. Spanish moss draped from the gnarled tree limbs above the same gray-colored cabin. It could not have been more concealed if it had been done so by design.

"I . . . I probably shouldn't go in," I stammered, suddenly unsure.

His smile was understanding, but he stood for a moment looking at me oddly. Then he motioned toward a bench on the front porch.

"Why don't you sit here? I'll be right back," he said.

He went inside the small house and I took a moment to catch my breath. It was lovely here, and it was not a part of the island I was really familiar with. I felt myself growing relaxed as I watched the tops of the grasses swaying in the nearby marsh. It was hard to distinguish where land ended and water began. The beauty here was quieter, more serene than that near the pounding ocean's surf. Here small animals and songbirds could feel protected by the grass and trees and the shallow water.

When Andrew returned, he held two glasses in his hands. There was a book tucked beneath his arm.

"It's hot today," he said. "I thought you might like some lemonade."

"Thank you." I watched him, amazed at the diversity of the man. He still had the look of a rugged outdoorsman to me, yet there was no doubt of his skills as a host and conversationalist. Somehow it seemed an odd combination, here at the ramshackle cabin in the marsh.

As he sat down opposite me, he handed me the book he'd brought with him.

"What is this?"

I set my glass down and took the book in my hands and I was struck at once by the small, feminine look of the embossed leather cover. It didn't look like something Andrew Benson would own.

"It belonged to Mary Louise," he said, his voice cautious and almost warning. "It was a journal she kept."

I was speechless as I stared open-mouthed at him.

"She asked to keep it here, for safekeeping. She gave it to me just before she died."

"Have you read it?"

"Oh, yes."

"Does it give any insight as to why she did what she did?"

"It certainly reflects her unhappiness," he said, his blue eyes searching as he drank from his glass of lemonade. "You might be interested in what she had to say, especially about her marriage . . . and Jordan."

"I . . . I'm not sure I should," I said, staring at the book in my lap.

"Afraid of what you might find?"

"No," I snapped. "No, of course not."

"Then why not read it?"

"I will," I said, slipping the book into the wide pocket of my skirt. "But if you don't mind I'll take it home with me and read it in the privacy of my room."

He shrugged his shoulders as if he didn't care. But in his eyes I thought I saw a look of optimism.

"What do you think of my place?" he asked. I sensed that he wanted to put me at ease by changing the subject.

"It's beautiful. This was one part of the island where we rarely ventured as children. Mary Louise was always afraid of the marshes . . . afraid of the muddy sand. We saw a small deer floundering in the mud flats near here one day, long, long ago. We couldn't get to it and finally, still struggling, it just disappeared. Mary Louise never forgot it," I said, my voice a whisper as I remembered.

"Perhaps you didn't either."

"No," I said, mesmerized by my memories of that muggy day and those times. "I guess I never did."

"One has to be careful here, it's true," he said. "One misstep could be treacherous, even life-threatening."

I shivered then. I don't know why or what it was about the scene or his deep, soothing voice. But when I turned to look at him there was something in his eyes, some quiet hidden warning that made me come slowly to my feet.

"I really should go," I said, handing my glass back to him.

His rough calloused fingers touched mine and I jerked away, letting the glass fall with a tinkling shatter.

"Oh, I'm sorry," I whispered.

I saw his frown, saw him shake his head as if to say

it didn't matter. But suddenly I was afraid. I even had the feeling that somewhere in the marsh someone watched us, making note of our conversation and the touch of our hands. What on earth would Jordan say if he knew I had come here?

"I have to go," I said, fairly leaping from the porch. I turned back, my eyes barely meeting his. "I'll bring the journal back as soon as I've finished."

Then I ran. I could feel the book in my pocket, slapping against my thigh. I could feel the cool dampness of the sand tugging at my shoes.

But I didn't look back. I just ran.

Chapter 13

Once I reached the beach, I was able to breathe a sigh of relief and slow my steps somewhat. I glanced back toward the marsh and the line of trees to my left. If there had been anyone there, I was certain they were gone now.

I walked toward the shack, thinking to go inside for a few moments and read Mary Louise's journal without any interruption. But as I approached, I heard a noise, and I hesitated.

There were footprints in the sand leading to the steps of the house. A man's footprints, with wide, sunken steps, and smaller ones—I wasn't sure if they were those of a woman or a child. I heard laughter and my question was answered. I was certain it was a woman's voice. It was soon answered by the deep rumbling laughter of a man, a sound so familiar that for a moment my heart stood still.

Why was Jordan here, and who was the woman inside whose laugh seemed so intimate and teasing? I moved up the steps, my shoes making no noise above the roar of the ocean. I was mid-way up the stairs and

I could not see inside the house. I hesitated, uncertain what to do. What if the man I'd heard wasn't Jordan? I couldn't just go barging in on one of the island's young couples.

I heard the woman's voice then, plain and clear, rising above the sounds of the wind and sea.

"Oh, love," she cried. "You are the most magnificent lover I've ever known."

Quickly I turned and fled down the steps and across the beach. My heart was pounding furiously and the nape of my neck was wet with perspiration. The sun was low, almost to the edge of the ocean's horizon when I turned and shaded my eyes to look back at the cabin.

It couldn't have been Jordan, I told myself. I simply was mistaken. Those words went round and round in my mind. I knew him so well. He would never do such a thing.

Would he?

If he had ever said he loved me, I might have been able to convince myself that what my mind was saying was true. Perhaps it was because the shack had such significant meaning to me that I saw it in such light. But suddenly it seemed all too clear that Jordan would use it for such purposes if he were inclined to. He was a passionate man. I knew that all too well. And he'd never said he loved me.

When I reached the house, I stopped the first servant I came upon.

"Do you know where Mr. Waverly is?"

"Which Mr. Waverly, ma'am?" he asked, his face perfectly expressionless.

"My husband," I said, still breathless from the run. "Jordan . . ."

"I couldn't say ma'am. Haven't seen him all afternoon."

"But . . ." Even as I stammered, the man turned and walked away.

I know I should have calmed myself before bursting into the parlor. As it was I must have looked like a madwoman with sand still clinging to my skirts and my hair disheveled from the wind.

Mrs. Waverly turned to stare at me. Her mouth flew open and her hand was suspended in midair as she started to take a sip of tea from a delicate china cup. Ella was there, her eyes huge and round.

"For heaven's sake, Shelley," Mrs. Waverly said, frowning at me. Her eyes moved quickly from my wildly disarrayed hair to the tips of my wet, sandy shoes. "What on earth is wrong? You look as if you've seen a ghost."

"Where's Jordan? Have either of you seen Jordan?"

"Shelley . . ." Ella said. She put down her sewing and walked to me, taking my hands in hers. "What's this all about? Is anything wrong?"

"No," I said, attempting to calm myself. The last thing I wanted was for them to decide that I was a clinging wife, or worse yet, that I was demented. "No, nothing. I'm sorry," I said, rubbing my hands down my wrinkled skirts. "I must look a mess. I was walking on the beach and I . . . I hadn't seen Jordan this afternoon and I wondered where he was . . . what he was doing."

"Well, I'm sure I don't know," Mrs. Waverly said. Her eyes were cold as she sipped her tea. "Waverly men have always led separate and independent lives. I suppose that's something we all must adjust to. I suggest that you might want to freshen up a bit before you find him."

"Yes," I said, stepping backward to leave the room. "Yes, I will. If . . . if you see him, would you tell him I'm upstairs? That I'm looking for him?"

She nodded and I saw her glance toward Ella with an impatient little smile. Ella looked down and away from me, as if something had embarrassed her. It was almost as if they knew something that I did not.

It was not like me to behave in such a way, or to be suspicious of everyone's words and looks. But my obsession with Jordan was making me do things, *feel* things I'd never felt before.

I ran up to my room. Quickly I took Mary Louise's journal from my pocket and hid it in the bottom of a drawer. Then I asked one of the maids to draw a bath for me in the large bathroom across the hall.

I bathed and changed into evening clothes. By the time I returned to my suite, the door leading from the sitting room to Jordan's room was closed. I could smell the heady fragrance of his shaving soap and hear his muffled footsteps as he walked about the room.

I went to the door and lifted my hand to knock. But I could not. My heart was pounding and I had no idea what I was to say. I could hardly accuse him of doing something when I'd seen nothing. I turned and walked back to the settee of the sitting room and for a moment I remembered the mannequin, stained with blood, that had been there on my wedding night. That mystery had never been resolved. Everyone had dismissed it as unimportant—a silly wedding prank.

I stood up and paced the room, my hands smoothing the skirts of my Irish green muslin dress. My fingers caught at the long streamers of satin ribbons that fluttered about the bodice as I walked. When the door opened behind me, I turned, my heart in my throat as I watched Jordan step from his room into the sitting room.

He stopped, his eyes raking over me with cool detachment. And when he looked up to meet my eyes, I thought I'd never seen such disdain in all my life.

"Jordan," I said, almost gasping for breath at his look. "Where have you been? I've been looking for you."

"Have you?" he asked. His eyes bored into mine for long moments as his fingers tugged at the wrist of his shirtsleeves. "What did you want, Shelley? Finding life at Sea Crest boring already?"

I frowned at him, puzzled by the accusatory tone of his words, but he had turned away as if he could not meet my eyes.

"Jordan . . ."

He shrugged his broad shoulders and went to a small mahogany cabinet that sat in the corner. His manner was cold and dismissive; he seemed so very different than he had been in the beginning. What was I to say to him? What does one say to a man who has obviously found someone else? And why shouldn't he, I chided myself silently. He had asked me to marry him and to have his children. But at no time had he ever said he would remain faithful to a woman he obviously did not love.

I turned then and ran from the room. I could hardly bear to watch his brown fingers as he poured wine from a crystal decanter. The same sensitive hands I loved, the same hands that only this afternoon had given pleasure to another woman. My heart twisted with agony as I envisioned slender white hands clinging to those broad shoulders, lips reaching for the same lips that had kissed mine so passionately. It was more than I could bear. It was simply more than I could bear.

By the time I came downstairs, I had managed to calm myself. As I walked down the hallway toward the dining room, I could see servants moving in and out the doorway, where the family was already gathered.

Outside the door I took a long deep breath, squared my shoulders and walked in. As heads turned my way, there seemed to be no recognition in their faces of what I was feeling. I was encouraged that I had managed to fool them well enough. I smiled and joined the others.

Ella came immediately to my side.

"You look wonderful in green," she whispered. "Where's Jordan? I thought I saw him come in not long after you did."

"He's . . . he's getting dressed. He should be along any moment." I said.

Her dark eyes studied me.

"Jordan cares about you, Shelley. I don't think you know how much."

"Oh," I said wryly, turning to face her. "Is it so obvious that I'm worried about my husband?"

Her smile was gentle and sweet. "It's obvious you're worried about something. And every time I mention his name, I see a little spark in your eyes."

"I hardly know him any more," I said, my voice catching in my throat. I wanted so badly to talk to someone and share my feelings.

"He has a lot on his mind. Perhaps you remember him as a boy . . . an irresponsible young man full of fun and mischief. He's no longer a boy, you know. He's a man, with a man's worries and responsibilities." Her words were gentle, full of encouragement, and I couldn't help smiling at my diminutive sister-in-law.

"Thank you, Ella," I whispered. "Sometimes I think you're the only one in this house who understands."

Her eyes moved toward her husband and I thought I saw sadness in her look. "Oh, I understand," she said. "I understand all too well."

When Jordan walked into the room, I felt my heart flutter. He was so tall and handsome, and he carried himself with a combination of pride and ease. He met my eyes almost immediately and, if my heart was in my own eyes, I couldn't help it. My resistance to him was very low and after today, I knew it was something I'd have to work on. I remembered his words all too well about Mary Louise's clinging nature. I vowed that I would not make the same mistakes that she had.

Chapter 14

I could not tell you what I ate that evening, nor what the conversation was about. Mr. Waverly was there, drinking as usual, making wild, oddly garbled remarks and waving his glass until finally he had to be escorted from the room.

But I was hardly aware of any of it. I only remember the touch of Jordan's black eyes on me, the cool way he sipped his wine. He was as distracted as I was and I couldn't understand why. What if it really had been him there at the shack and he had heard me? Had he seen me running away perhaps?

It was disconcerting and the look in his eyes confused me. There seemed to be desire mingled with the anger and I found I didn't understand him at all.

"You're awfully quiet tonight, brother," Benjamin said. His gaze darted from Jordan to me. He was smiling and he seemed in especially good spirits.

"Am I? I was just thinking about some business on the mainland."

"Oh, that's right, the bank you spoke of. When are you going over?"

"Tomorrow," Jordan said, his look swinging over me, then away. He stood up then, not looking at me again. "And since I'll be taking the early ferry, I think I'll retire for the evening."

"You mentioned the other day that you might take Shelley," Benjamin said. "Make a day of it."

I bit my lip, holding my breath as I waited for Jordan's answer. How I would love to relive our honeymoon, if only for one day.

"Oh, I think Shelley is much too impatient to spend a long boring day waiting for her husband to emerge from a stuffy business meeting."

I didn't say a word, but I was filled with a mixture of disappointment and relief. I didn't know what was wrong with our marriage and I wasn't sure it was something I wanted to face.

I sat perfectly still, uncertain if he meant for me to accompany him upstairs or not. When his hand reached toward me, I didn't look up, but merely placed my fingers in his warm grasp and rose from the table.

As soon as we were outside the room and away from the others, Jordan released me. He walked slightly ahead of me, enough so that I could study the set of his shoulders and the disapproving line of his jaw.

When we reached our small parlor, I turned as if to go to my own room. I felt Jordan's fingers biting into the flesh of my arms as he turned me back to face him.

"Tired?" he asked, a disapproving sneer on his handsome face.

"I . . . no, I'm not, but I thought—"

His actions stunned me. He pulled me roughly into his arms. His mouth raked across mine, his kiss almost punishing in its intensity. I was breathless when he lifted his head and gazed down into my eyes.

"You are mine, Shelley," he growled, his voice husky. "Mine forever."

I wanted to cry, for I knew I was lost. All the vows I made concerning Jordan just vanished when he kissed me, when he looked at me with such fierce intensity.

When I didn't reply, he stepped to the door, and turned the lock, even though one hand never released me. When his mouth claimed mine again, I felt a lifetime of hunger for this man, surging through me. And even though his lips were hard and demanding, I clung to him, returning kiss for kiss, reveling in the feel of his hands. I sensed a rage in him and it frightened me. Yet I could not pull away. I could not deny him anything and I wondered if I ever could.

"Undress," he said, his voice deep and raspy.

"Here . . . now . . . ?"

"Here," he growled, ripping off his jacket and tossing it aside.

He excited me. His demands, his hungry kisses, the way his eyes raked over me with such intensity. It made me forget everything.

He watched as I unbuttoned my dress and stepped out of it. I heard his soft murmur as his eyes moved down over my body. His fingers reached out slowly, caressing my shoulder, moving across my collarbone and down to my breasts. I gasped and closed my eyes, swaying toward him against my will. His sweet provocative assault seemed to go on for hours, until I was trembling, until I wanted to beg him to take me into his arms.

"Jordan . . ." I whispered finally, my hand reaching toward him.

He gathered me into his arms then, the strength of him making my breath catch in my throat.

"I shouldn't have forced you into this marriage," he said, pulling away and staring down at me. It sounded very much like an apology. There was such pain in his eyes, such doubt.

I put my hand against his mouth, closing off his words the way I wished I could stop his doubts.

"Don't," I whispered. "If you regret having married me, Jordan, don't say it. Not now . . . not now."

My words seemed to fuel his passion even more. With a quiet growl, he gathered me up in his arms and walked to my bedroom door. He kicked at the door and slammed it shut behind us.

I clung to him, unwilling to let him go, wanting only to savor his kisses, his touch. I didn't want to think about anything—not about this afternoon, not about the mysteries of Sea Crest, and certainly not about the wisdom of what I was doing.

Neither of us were able to withstand the onslaught of emotion that swept over us as we fell onto the bed. There was still some kind of fury in him, some rage that I couldn't understand. Yet slowly, surely, the fury subsided and all that was left was the sweet intensity of his lovemaking.

"You belong to me," he whispered. "I was blind not to see that years ago." He words were possessive, like a demand and I could feel it in the touch of his hands, in the hunger of his kisses.

I felt speechless with all the emotions he aroused. It had never been like this . . . not this wild, furious fragmentation, as if I might shatter into a million tiny pieces of ecstacy. I felt his hands tangling in my hair, his mouth ravaging mine and I clung to him, crying out his name over and over again.

Later as we lay in each other's arms, touching and caressing, our movements were slower, less hungry. Nothing was said. Nothing to explain his odd behavior, or the rage that had consumed him and made him come to me in this powerful and almost frightening way.

I snuggled against him, wishing I could find the words to ask what was wrong. But in my heart I suppose I thought that the beauty of what we experienced together would change everything.

I was so naive.

I woke later in the night. The bed beside me was empty and cold. I sat up, touching my swollen lips and feeling a tingle rush through me at the memory of Jordan's touch. When he came to my room at night, he usually stayed. But for some reason, this night, he went back to the privacy of his own bedroom. I felt a chill then, down my arms to the end of my fingers, and I wondered how he could leave me after what we had shared.

Suddenly I felt more alone than I'd ever felt in my life. I got out of bed and threw a wrap around my shoulders. I turned up the lamps and walked to the window to gaze out over the trees.

The evening with Jordan had been breathtaking. But as I paced the floor and thought about it, for some reason the words that came to me were those of Andrew Benson.

". . . his need to possess . . ." I heard, echoing through my mind. He seemed so sure that Jordan's intensity was due to his need to possess.

I realized that my fingers were clenched so tightly

that my nails dug into my flesh. I remembered the words Jordan had said last night. There had been no declarations of love, only whispered words of passion and need. He had merely claimed me, made me his in a wild hungry proclamation of possession.

"You belong to me," he'd said, growling the words.

"Oh, Jordan," I whispered, remembering. I shook my head, wishing his words meant more, yet knowing they didn't. "I love you so much . . . so much."

I wanted to go to him then. Wanted to pound on his door, throw myself across his bed and demand that he explain everything. Had it been this way between him and Mary Louise? Did they experience this burning passion that seemed to consume everything? Knowing her as I did, I could not believe they had.

And what about this afternoon? Had it really been Jordan in the fishing shack? Was he the one who made the mystery woman swoon with pleasure and declare him her most magnificent lover? After last night I could not imagine those words could be spoken about any other man. But who was she? One of the maids? Someone from the mainland, spirited over here for a day of forbidden passion? All the thoughts swirled and spun in my head until I felt dizzy and sickened.

I went to the dresser where I'd hidden Mary Louise's journal. With trembling fingers, I pulled it free and walked to a chair that sat beside a green-shaded reading lamp.

The journal began just before Mary Louise's wedding. At first her words soothed and comforted me, made me remember those carefree days of our youth when the most important things had been the sun and water and our pleasure for the day.

She spoke of me often in those first pages. How she missed me, how she longed to share certain things with me. But as I read on, her writing changed. And the change definitely occurred after she moved to Sea Crest Hall. She seemed troubled, concerned about the wedding and about Jordan.

I don't think I realized exactly what marriage meant until now. Belonging completely to someone seems strange and a little frightening. The entire household seems obsessed with our having a child. It's all anyone talks about. I had hoped to wait and I hoped that Jordan would understand. But whenever I broach the subject to him, he only seems amused. He dismisses my wishes as if I am a child.

It hurt terribly reading about such intimacies between Mary Louise and the man I loved. It seemed I had almost forgotten that she was ever married to him. Since coming to Sea Crest, since my obsession with Jordan, I sometimes found it hard to believe that he had ever shared his life with anyone except me.

But I read on, not wanting to miss one single word, lest it had some meaning that Andrew Benson intended for me to find. My eyes grew tired and gritty and my head began to ache.

Mary Louise told about her fears and then her happiness when she discovered she was to have a child. And about how Mr. and Mrs. Waverly seemed to treat her more kindly.

I can hardly tolerate the long evenings and the family dinners. Jordan's father, although sometimes intelligent and clear-thinking, is more often drunk. He rambles about the past, and about things that I don't understand. Those are the nights I hate the most, when he is drunk. It frightens me. This house frightens me and Jordan seems to have no idea what I'm talking about.

Several pages later, just when I intended to put the journal away and go back to bed, I spotted the name "Andrew Benson" in the middle of a page. Quickly I read on.

Mary Louise told about meeting him, about how he had come to dinner at Mrs. Waverly's request.

At last, someone I can talk to. Someone who understands the isolation of the island and the limited capacity for change here. Mr. Benson is charming and ruggedly handsome—the most delightful man I've met in quite an age. He invited all of us to come to the marsh where he is staying and he insists on painting me. He said my coloring is absolutely perfect. What a wonderful evening!

I flipped through the following pages and found them filled with references to Andrew Benson. But I found I was so tired and sleepy I could not concentrate on another word. Finally I crawled back into bed and, with Mary Louise's words running through my mind, I slept.

Chapter 15

My sleep was restless, filled with odd, disoriented dreams that frightened me and made me thrash about upon the bed. I would waken, feeling as if a hand gripped my heart and threatened to stop its beating. Then, exhausted, I would fall asleep again, only to return to the same dreams and the same fears.

I saw Jordan's face and once I even thought I heard him speaking to me.

"What have you done to me?" he whispered. His voice actually had that husky, emotional quality that I loved. "You're a wild, siren from the sea . . . determined to bewitch me."

"Jordan?" I whispered.

But when I woke, there was no one there.

The birds were singing outside and even though it was barely dawn and I had slept little, I dragged myself from bed.

Jordan was already gone and I felt a wringing sense of regret that I would not see him today. I wanted to look into his black eyes, I wanted to see the same emotions I'd seen last night, hear his softly whispered words of passion and fire. I was so preoccupied with thoughts of him. He was all I could think about. I wanted to repeat our lovemaking over and over again.

There it was, the plain and simple truth, I told myself. I was totally, completely obsessed with him. And as a result, I was probably behaving like a fool.

At breakfast I felt conspicuous, as if everyone were watching me. Mr. Waverly, still sober at so early an hour, was especially odd, it seemed. When he spoke, his words surprised me.

"You look so much like your mother in that dress," he said, his words almost kind. "You have her same coloring. Auburn hair and golden skin so well suited for wearing white."

I'm sure it must have been my puzzled stare that caused him to laugh softly. Mrs. Waverly glanced toward Benjamin, but she made no comment.

"You knew my mother?" I asked.

"Everyone knew your mother," Mrs. Waverly said, her look scathing, her words cold and ridiculing.

"What does that mean?" I demanded. I put my fork down and, sitting very still, I looked into her eyes, challenging her.

She was a bit taken aback, I think. She was not used to anyone in the house challenging her authority, or her words. But she hid it well, dabbing delicately at her mouth with her napkin before answering me.

"It simply means that everyone on the island knew Lucinda Demorest," she said, with a lift of her brows. "She was quite talented and quite beautiful and I daresay every man on the island was enchanted with her. Isn't that true, Father?" Her gaze, cold and daunting, moved to her husband.

It was the first time I think I realized that Mr. Waverly was actually a mild-mannered man who was quite intimidated by his haughty, well-bred wife. It was only when he was drinking that he became daring and outspoken.

He cleared his throat and his dark eyes met mine. In them I saw sadness and regret, even apology.

"As my wife said, Lucinda was a beauty," he said, his voice soft and quiet. "And you are a lot like her, I think. Your mannerisms, your kindness . . ." His voice trailed away as if he were too embarrassed to continue.

I can't explain how much his words surprised and touched me. Until that morning I had never regarded Jordan's father as a real person. He was a joke in the household, someone to be pitied and ridiculed, and I had never thought since the time I came that he noticed me one way or another.

"Thank you," I said, hardly knowing what else to say.

The room had grown very quiet and as I glanced toward Ella, I saw her eyes upon me, cautious and wary before she looked away.

"I wish I knew more about her," I said, aiming my remark at Mr. Waverly.

"Oh, Father can tell you all about her. But I'm not sure it's anything you'd want to hear," Mrs. Waverly said with a sneering tone.

I was so exasperated with her and with the entire mystery of the household. Suddenly, her disparaging manner toward my mother, even though I hardly remembered her, was more than I could bear.

"What is it exactly you're trying to say, Mrs. Waverly? I'd prefer you just come out and say it. I for one have had enough of the innuendoes in this household. If you have something to say about me or my mother, why not just say it?"

I'd shocked them. I could see it in their faces, hear it in the stifling silence.

"All right," Mrs. Waverly said, staring at me. Her cheeks were flushed, her eyes sparkling with resentment. "I will say it. I never wanted Jordan to marry you, it's true. He could have done much better. If all he wanted was a brood mare, then I'm certain he could have found someone more suited. You are an arrogant, independent young woman—I suppose education does that to some women. A man needs a woman who is supportive and unpretentious."

"Like you?" I said the words before I thought and as my eyes moved from her to her husband, I saw I'd hit the mark.

She responded only with a lift of her brow. Then she continued, her words slow and measured.

"My marriage to Mr. Waverly is really none of your business," she said. "But since you've so tastelessly brought up the subject, I will tell you about it. Our marriage was arranged, much like your own and, I daresay, by the time you are my age, you will have reached the same conclusion as I. Love between a man and a woman is a ridiculous goal, hardly worthy of such melancholia and longing as young people put themselves through. I'm sure Jordan has already discovered that. Perhaps that's why this time he chose another reason as the basis for marriage, a much more practical one." Her eyes were glittering with triumph.

Mr. Waverly stood up, throwing his napkin on the table and staring at his wife with disgust.

"You've gone too far this time, Mother," he said.

"Your remarks to Shelley are rude and entirely out of order. And I daresay Jordan will not be pleased."

Without another word, he left the room.

I bit my lip, determined that she would not make me cry or flee the room as Mr. Waverly had done. I was beginning to realize that was exactly what she wanted. She wanted to hurt me, bend me to her will. For the first time I began to understand what torture it must have been for someone like Mary Louise to live in this house.

"I love Jordan," I told her quietly. "And I'm sorry that you disapprove of our marriage. But as long as he wants me, and as long as he is happy living with me, then I'm afraid there is nothing you can do about it."

Her eyes were like shattered pieces of glass. Blue and clear and dangerous.

"Oh," she said with a soft grunt. "Don't be too sure, Shelley. Don't ever be too sure about what I can do and cannot do." She took her time rising from the table and walking from the room, as if nothing anyone said or did could shake her confidence in her own power.

"Oh, Shelley," Ella said, after Mrs. Waverly was gone. "You shouldn't have done that."

"Why?" I snapped. "What's she going to do—send me to bed without my supper? Kill me?"

Ella closed her eyes and shook her head. She had the strangest look on her face. Benjamin, who had been very quiet during the whole ordeal, met my gaze. His look too, was disapproving, and he seemed almost as angry as his mother had been.

"Jordan will not be pleased with you," he said, leaning back in his chair.

"Oh? Does Jordan expect me to sit and take his

mother's abuse? Listen quietly to her ugly insinuations about my own mother?"

"Your mother is hardly worthy of such blind devotion," he said, his voice quiet and soft. "She broke my father's heart when she married Joshua Demorest. And later, when she found it impossible to control her behavior . . . after my father was happily married . . . she broke my mother's heart as well."

"What are you saying?" I demanded.

"I'm saying what everyone on the island already knows. Your mother was a loose, selfish woman, concerned only with her own wishes and her own desires. She never loved anyone except herself. The affair she had with my father was not her only indiscretion. There is even speculation about who your father really might be, though, thankfully, the timing of your birth makes it impossible that *my* father could have sired you."

I jumped up from my chair, slamming my hand down on the table so hard that the glasses rattled.

"That is enough! I will not listen to another word about my mother. You're a liar! All of you are liars."

I stormed from the room, so angry that I wanted to smash everything in my path. I found myself inexplicably longing to tear the lovely, cold paintings from the wall, to knock over the marble pedestals that lined the hallways and held priceless Chinese urns and figurines. I suppose it was only my need to be outside as quickly as possible that kept me from actually doing so.

As I hurried from the house and across the vast, sandy yard, I paid little attention to where I was going. But I wasn't surprised when, moments later, I saw the old fishing shack looming before me. It seemed always to be the place I came to of late when something troubled me.

I was gasping for breath and so upset that I gave no notice to anything around me. When I reached the steps to the shack, and Andrew Benson stepped out of the shadows, I cried out in alarm.

"I'm sorry, I didn't mean to frighten you," he said immediately. He reached for me and pulled me beneath the shelter of the sturdy poles that supported the building. "Here, let's get you out of the wind. It's quite ferocious today."

"What . . . what are you doing here?" I asked. I hardly knew what to say to him, standing there so close in the shadows of the building. The ocean roared behind us and the wind whipped my hair wildly about my face.

"Sketching," he said. He nodded toward the beach where a large tablet lay, its pages held down from the wind by a large conch shell. "I might ask you the same question," he said. "You seem upset. Is anything wrong?"

"No," I said quickly. "What could be wrong? Jordan is away on business and I decided to take a walk, that's all."

"Ah, I see."

He did see, I thought . . . more than I intended him to.

"Well, I should go," I said.

He was looking at me so intently, his brilliant blue eyes clear and honest. They saw too much.

"Shelley, if my being here bothers you, I'll go."

"No," I said, shaking my head. I hadn't intended to hurt him or insult him, and I certainly hadn't intended for him to know that his presence made me uncomfortable. I didn't even know why. "You don't have to go. I don't know what's wrong with me. It's just—"

"You don't have to explain," he said. He made no effort to leave, but instead continued to focus all his attention on me, as if he might read my mind.

"But I do," I said. "I feel that I do." I faced him then, looking up into his eyes. He had given me absolutely no reason to feel so awkward around him. It was all the things that lay in the back of my mind—the confusion about Jordan and my marriage, what the Waverlys might say if they saw us together, and most of all, this man's relationship with Mary Louise. "Could we talk for a while?" I asked.

"Of course."

"Perhaps we could walk back to the trees," I said. I couldn't keep my eyes from glancing up to the old fishing shack above us and I suppose I made it very clear that I would not feel comfortable being alone with him inside.

He smiled, putting me immediately at ease. He took my elbow and steadied me in the sand, bending to retrieve his sketch pad as we passed.

The wind was fierce that day, but beneath the palm trees there was a bit of respite. I watched, fascinated as strands of Spanish moss flew through the air and tumbled along the white sandy beach. But it was quieter here and I felt more comfortable being in the open where anyone walking by could see us.

"Did you read the journal?" he asked.

"Part of it."

He nodded. He was not going to give away anything,

but seemed to prefer letting me find out for myself everything that Mary Louise had to say.

"Enough to know she wasn't happy here," I said.

His lips quirked and the glint in his eyes acknowledged what I'd said.

"I never understood Mary Louise," I said. "All she ever wanted was Jordan and Sea Crest, even when we were children. But in a lot of ways she was so naive, so innocent of life and about marriage." I didn't look at him when I spoke. I probably should not have been discussing such a matter, but it was something that ate at me, this relationship between Mary Louise and Jordan. And I had to know. Andrew seemed to know her better than anyone.

"I'm not sure Mary Louise knew what love between a man and a woman really is all about. I certainly don't think she loved Jordan."

I turned quickly to look at him. He stared into my eyes for a moment before his lids lowered, closing off any emotion I might have seen there.

"Why do you say that?"

"She told me."

"Mary Louise actually told you she was not in love with Jordan?"

"Obviously you find that hard to believe," he said. His smile was wry and amused.

"I . . . yes," I admitted. "I do find that hard to believe."

"Ah, Shelley," he said. His voice was a whispered sigh, an ode of regret tinged with exasperated amusement. "Somehow I had hoped to hear you say just the opposite." He stretched out on the ground with his hands behind his head.

I knew he was teasing me, but somehow I had the feeling that there was a hint of truth in his words.

"Were you in love with Mary Louise?" I asked, not caring that I was being presumptuous. I didn't know why, but I felt that I could trust Andrew Benson, that I could ask him anything. "Was she in love with you?"

"Why, Mrs. Waverly," he said, in a teasing manner. He turned to his side and propped up on his elbow to face me. "What a question."

"Were you?"

His face grew serious then and as he gazed out to sea, I thought his eyes darkened a bit. It was long moments before he spoke.

"No."

I was surprised. There had been something between the two of them—I was almost certain of it. I sensed it in the way he spoke about her.

He turned to look at me then and I could see the pain clearly in his eyes.

"She said she was in love with me."

I don't know why, but the ache in my heart was for Jordan and what he would have felt if he had known. Had he?

"Did she know that you didn't return those feelings?"

"Yes," he said, almost anticipating my question. "Yes, I was honest with her from the beginning."

"The beginning? What are you saying? Was there actually a relationship between the two of you? Did you—"

"Shelley," he said, his look stopping my words. "I hope that I was Mary's friend. That's what I tried to be, anyway. I told you before, I'm not sure she knew what love meant. Mary Louise . . ." he seemed to be strug-

133

gling for words. "Mary Louise, for all her beauty and outward sophistication, was an innocent, just as you said. I think she was searching for love, but just because she declared her love for me doesn't mean that it was true."

I nodded. He knew Mary Louise well. It was exactly the way I would have described her myself.

"And the baby . . ."

He met my eyes and his look became impatient. He stood up and brushed the sand from his trousers, staring down at me oddly.

"It was not mine, if that's what you're trying to ask," he said. For the first time, there was anger in his voice.

I stood up too and faced him. I didn't want him to leave, not until I had learned all there was to know about Mary Louise's life before she died.

"Please," I said. "I'm sorry. I don't mean to insult you, but—"

"I already told you that I didn't love Mary Louise. So, I assume by your question that you think me the type of man to make love to a woman just because she's available and willing."

His words shocked me a little and I felt a flush warm my cheeks.

"No, I . . ."

"The child belonged to Jordan, Shelley. Perhaps you just didn't want to hear that. Perhaps you want to hear me say that Mary Louise had several lovers. But for all her doubts and for all their disagreements, as far as I know Jordan was the father of her child . . . the only one who could possibly be the father."

I stood for a moment, my face burning, as I stared

into his eyes. When I nodded I felt an overwhelming relief.

But it was the *reason* for that relief that shocked me. If Mary Louise's child belonged to Jordan, then I knew with certainty that he could not possibly have had anything to do with her death. He wanted a son so desperately that he would never have done anything to jeopardize his child's life.

The fact that such doubts lay hidden somewhere in the back of my mind shocked me more than I could say. I was beginning to wonder if I really knew Jordan at all.

Chapter 16

I had to sit down again. My legs were trembling as I felt relief wash through my body.

"Shelley?" Immediately he knelt on one knee beside me. He reached forward to touch my face. "Are you all right?

"I'm fine," I said. I knew my voice was weak but I could not help it. "Really, I'm fine."

He continued kneeling beside me, his gaze intently scanning my face. "Let me get you back to the house. You look very pale."

"I don't think that would be a good idea . . . your going back to the house with me."

"Then let me take you to the edge of the lawn."

"Not yet, not until I ask you one more question."

"Ask me anything." The light in his eyes should have warned me. But he was such a kind man, so attuned to others' needs, that I did not think his look might be personal.

"How did Mary Louise seem to you . . . about having a child? Was she happy? Sad? Do you know?"

"I think she was afraid at first. But all in all, she was delighted."

His quick reply made me smile.

"Does that relieve your mind somewhat?"

"Yes," I admitted. "Yes, it does."

"She once told me how happy she was because finally there would be someone here at Sea Crest who would love her, no matter what."

I nodded. I knew how desperately one could feel that way here.

"Now," he said, his voice soft with concern. "Let me see you back to the house . . . as far as the trees at least."

I looked up at him then, smiling at his tenderness. I had not intended it to mean anything except that I was grateful for his friendship. But I saw the light change in his eyes and before I realized what was happening he bent his head and kissed me softly on the lips.

I can't explain even now how that kiss affected me. I loved Jordan, there was no doubt about that. But Andrew's concern, his tenderness, his protective manner toward me . . . I can't deny that I was moved. Although his kiss and his touch inspired nothing like the fiery intensity I felt with Jordan, I found myself wanting to throw myself into Andrew's arms and have him hold me.

Instead I pulled away and stood up so quickly that my head began to reel. I felt his arm steadying me and for an instant I allowed myself the luxury of leaning against him, of giving in to those needs I felt.

"Shelley," he whispered.

"No, Andrew. I can't . . . this isn't right."

He stepped away then and his smile was sweet and rather wistful.

"If you ever need me—if there's ever anything I can do for you . . . anything . . ."

"I could use a friend." I suppose my eyes were as pleading as my voice, although I had not intended it. But Andrew's caring touched me and made me realize again just how alone I was at Sea Crest, especially since Jordan had become so distant.

"You do have a friend in me, Shelley," he said. "I hope you never forget that."

"Thank you." I turned to go and when he reached out for me, I took his hand. "I should go back alone," I said.

He nodded and stood watching me until I was out of sight.

As I walked through the trees, I heard a noise, a rustling sound in the undergrowth. I turned just in time to see a flash of color before it disappeared into the dark green surroundings. I stopped dead still, my breath trapped in lungs that refused to function.

I looked down at my feet and saw a large worn spot upon the ground, as if someone had paced back and forth for a long time. Strands of Spanish moss lay shredded upon the sandy earth.

Someone had been here. Someone had stood right on this spot, watching us. And that person undoubtedly had seen Andrew kiss me.

"Oh, God," I whispered as my eyes desperately searched the undergrowth where I'd caught the glimpse of color.

I hurried back toward the house, my gaze moving cautiously through the palmetto and hanging moss. But

I saw no one else again. As I moved up the steps to the large front porch, I turned to scan the treeline once more. But there was no one.

A shiver traveled up my arms and shoulders to my neck. I could not shake the feeling that someone was still there, hidden in the dark tangle of undergrowth, watching me.

By now it was time for lunch, and although I wasn't hungry, I went into the dining room, intending to see if I could detect anything on the faces of those gathered there. For as hard as I tried to tell myself that the person in the woods could have been a servant, or someone from another part of the island, I had a terrible feeling it was someone who knew me.

Benjamin and Ella were there, but I saw nothing in either of their glances to tell me what I wanted to know. And Mrs. Waverly, although she was cool to me, obviously had seen nothing. I didn't think she was the kind of person to remain silent when she was angry. Poor Mr. Waverly was not at the table and I felt a twinge of pity for him. No doubt he was already in his study, consuming his first bottle of the day.

"Well," Mrs. Waverly said, her eyes scanning my features. "There's a definite flush to your cheeks today, Shelley. Not feeling ill, are you?"

"I'm feeling quite well, thank you," I said.

"I hope you're finding enough here to amuse you," she said.

Was there a glint of amusement in her eyes? A touch of irony in her voice? Perhaps I was mistaken. Perhaps it *had* been Mrs. Waverly.

"Shelley and I are doing embroidery work," Ella said. Her eyes met mine, as if pleading for my confirmation.

"Yes," I said. "We usually work on the front veranda where it's cool. If you're interested, we'd be pleased to have you join us, Mrs. Waverly."

"No, thank you," she said, her lips curled into a jeering smile. "Sewing is not to my taste. But I am pleased to see the two of you becoming friends. I always said that was part of Mary Louise's problem. She never accepted our family and, as a result, I'm afraid she might have sought out ... shall we say, other inappropriate pasttimes."

The room grew very quiet and all eyes turned toward Mrs. Waverly.

"I think you've said enough, Mother," Benjamin said.

His mother waved her hand in the air and gave a haughty laugh. "Good gracious," she said. "All of you are much too sensitive. I simply meant that Mary Louise did not fit in here at Sea Crest, but I'm certain that does not mean that Shelley will not. Let's just enjoy our delicious meal, shall we?"

Later when Ella and I took our sewing baskets and moved outside to the shade of the porch, I could hardly wait to ask what was on her mind. We had spent a few afternoons here, but it was hardly an everyday occurrence, as she had made it seem.

"Shelley," she said as soon as we were seated in the large rattan chairs. "You must be more careful. You are falling into exactly the same trap as Mary Louise."

"What do you mean?"

"I mean Andrew Benson."

"Oh." I closed my eyes and relaxed in the chair. "Thank goodness, it was you who saw us."

"Yes, I did." Her gray eyes looked troubled, even hurt. "I realize that Jordan is moody and sometimes hard to talk to. But you can't let Andrew Benson come between you, not if you really love Jordan."

"I do love him," I said. "And I would never let anyone come between us. The kiss that you saw meant nothing. It—"

"Kiss?" Her eyes were bright and she frowned at me. "Andrew Benson kissed you?"

I stared into her eyes, shaking my head in confusion as she began to explain.

"I followed you to the beach, intending to walk with you a while. When I saw you meet Andrew at the fishing shack, I came back to Sea Crest." She reached forward to touch my arm. "Oh, Shelley. What have you done? What happened after—"

"Nothing happened." My mind was in a whirl as I tried to rationalize what she was saying. If she was telling the truth, if she had come back to the house, then it wasn't her in the woods watching us, and all my fears must begin again. I focused again on Ella's worried face. "Nothing, Ella—I swear it. He kissed me out of pity, I think . . . only out of concern and friendship."

She was visibly relieved, although I thought she still seemed troubled about something.

"Be careful, Shelley. You must be careful about appearances here. Jordan would be furious. He hated Andrew for what he did to Mary Louise."

"What do you mean? What did he do?"

"She was in love with the man, surely you must already know that? And even though it must have angered Jordan unbearably, and hurt him, his concern was only for her. He even offered to let her go, to free her to marry this man if she wished. I remember her ecstasy at the prospect. But Andrew would have none of it. He didn't want to marry her. He didn't even love her and although I personally admire his honesty in admitting it, everyone else seemed to think it was the factor that finally destroyed Mary Louise. Who could blame Jordan for resenting that?"

I leaned forward in my chair and every nerve in my body seemed attuned to her words. "What are you saying? Are you saying that Mary Louise killed herself because of Andrew Benson?"

"I'm only saying that's what everyone thinks," she said. She leaned back in her chair and took up her sewing, not meeting my eyes again. "Everyone in the family thinks that, although we've tried to keep it from the other islanders and from Mary's family."

"But the child, Ella . . . what about the child? I can't believe Mary Louise would ever do anything to harm her unborn child."

"You don't know how she was," she said, a frown knitting her smooth brow. Her gaze moved up then, meeting mine and there was such sadness in the troubled depths of her eyes. "You can't know how destroyed she was. I think Andrew Benson was the first thing Mary ever wanted that she couldn't have. She was a madwoman at first, crying and raving at the drop of a hat. And then she went into this terrible, terrible state of melancholy. She wouldn't eat; she couldn't sleep. The servants often found her wandering through the house in the middle of the night. Jordan was beside himself with worry about the baby and what the state of her nerves might be doing to it. I think she even came to resent the child then, thinking that everyone here cared more about the baby than they did about her and her broken heart."

"How bizarre," I murmured. "Did she actually expect Jordan and his family to feel sorry for her when she was in love with another man?" I knew it was like Mary Louise to behave irrationally, but this was odd behavior, even for her.

"She was not herself. That's all I can say—she simply was not herself."

I stood up and walked to the porch railing, staring out toward the trees and the glimmer of blue ocean that shimmered through in places.

"I don't understand any of this."

Ella put down her sewing and came to stand beside me. She put an arm around my waist and I sensed in her then the need for companionship. She leaned her head against my shoulder and we stood for a moment, gazing out toward the murmuring ocean.

"None of us do," she said. "None of us have ever understood what was in her mind to make her do what she did."

"Ella," I said. "Andrew Benson swore to me that the child was not his. Do you think he was lying? Do you think—?"

"I believe him when he says he never encouraged Mary. But sometimes when Ben makes remarks, I get so confused that I hardly know what to believe. And to make things worse, there was no one here I could talk to about it."

"Not even Benjamin?"

"Least of all Benjamin. I'm afraid he's too busy with his other pursuits to be concerned with my trivial worries. He considers them to be feminine weaknesses."

"Jordan isn't like that," I said. I wasn't sure at the

time if I really believed that or if I was simply trying to convince myself it was true.

"No, he isn't," she said. Her voice was firm, her eyes steady as she looked at me. "Jordan is nothing like Benjamin . . . or his mother. Jordan Waverly is his own man, Shelley, and I hope you'll come to believe that yourself before long."

"So do I," I sighed. "So do I."

Chapter 17

We went back to our sewing, and nothing else was said about Mary Louise. Not that I didn't long to ask Ella many more questions. But I could see how troubled she was.

Ella was a sweet, unassuming woman and I was beginning to care about her very much. I could see the misery in her eyes when she spoke about Benjamin, and I suppose all I wanted that day was to make her feel better.

We sat there, working silently at times. And at other times, when a raccoon scurried across the yard, or when certain birds sang, we would laugh and engage in quiet, meaningless chatter. But it was pleasant and soothing and I suppose it allowed both of us to pretend that our lives were filled with as much contentment as that slow, peaceful afternoon.

That evening when I went upstairs to prepare for dinner, Jordan still was not home. Jillian was in my rooms, turning down the bed.

"Do you need my help dressing, ma'am?"

"No," I said languidly. I felt so tired that I could hardly pull the hairbrush through my hair.

Jillian took the brush and began brushing my hair. She smiled at me in the mirror and her look was filled with curiosity.

"I don't know what's wrong with me," I said. "I've felt so tired today."

"Some women feel tired when they're in the—you know—family way."

My eyes flew open and I looked in the mirror, meeting her inquisitive eyes. She seemed amused by my surprise.

"Oh no," I said. "I—I really don't think . . . I mean, it's too soon."

"I've heard women say that they knew they were expecting a child the very next day."

My glance went inexplicably to the bed, where only last night Jordan and I had been. And as flashes of that scene moved in my mind's eye, I felt my face growing warm and flushed.

Jillian laughed again, a soft mischievous sound, I thought, as if she had read my mind.

"No," I said, shaking my head. "I really don't think that's what it is. I'm just tired, that's all."

"Well," she said, handing the hairbrush back to me. "Time will tell. If you'll not be needin' anything else, I'll be going now."

Jillian was such a pretty girl and she had a look of anticipation on her face. I wondered if there was a young man in her life, someone who waited for her now, even as we talked. I turned around to face her.

"Jillian, before you go, could I ask you a question . . . in confidence?"

"Of course," she said.

"You've been here a while and you knew Mary Louise. Did you ever notice her being unhappy?"

"Everybody noticed it," she said, glancing once toward the door. "So I guess I wouldn't be tellin' you something you won't hear from somewhere else. She wasn't happy ma'am, but if you ask me, it wasn't anybody's fault but her own."

"Really?" I said frowning at her.

"She was a spoiled, snooty young lady, always intent on having her own way. She didn't appreciate anything, even though she had everything a woman could ask for. Her beautiful clothes didn't please her; she always wanted more. She whined and dragged around as if she was living in poverty somewhere. As if she didn't have a man who is the nicest, most handsome . . ." She stopped and her hand flew to her mouth. "Beggin' your pardon ma'am," she said. "I didn't mean to be disrespectful."

"No, Jillian," I said. "You're not. I understand." I smiled at her, hoping to put her at ease again. "I quite agree with you—my husband is all that and more."

I suppose for a moment I let myself daydream about Jordan and when I shook myself and refocused my eyes toward her, she had the strangest look on her face.

"You love him," she said, her voice soft and quiet.

"Yes, I do," I said. "Very much. You sound surprised."

"Oh, no ma'am," she said. "Its just . . ."

"What? Go ahead, you can tell me."

"It's not proper, me bein' a servant here, askin' you such personal questions."

"I don't mind, really. If it's something I don't want to answer, I'll tell you."

"It's just that I heard your marriage to Jor . . . I mean, Mr. Waverly was arranged—you know—a marriage of convenience."

"That's true . . . it was," I said. I was a little surprised by her question and by her interest. "But I've known Jordan since we were children. I suppose I've been in love with him all my life."

"Oh, I see," she said.

"Jillian . . . is something wrong?"

"Oh, no ma'am. Nothing at all. It's just strange, that's all . . . the way things turned out. What with him bein' so crazy for the first Mrs. Waverly, then marryin' her best friend."

"Yes . . . I suppose it might seem strange."

She seemed to be asking whether or not Jordan loved me in return. But that was something I didn't intend discussing with her.

"Well, I have to go."

"One more question," I said.

"Yes?"

"Did you ever see Mary Louise with Mr. Benson?"

Her eyes changed then and grew dark and glittering.

"Yes ma'am, I did."

"I've been told he considered her as only a friend."

"Huh," she grunted. "Last time I saw 'em together, they looked like more than friends to me."

"The last time?"

"The day before she died, it was. Seen 'em over toward the marsh, near his house. They were arguin' and she was cryin'. He took her by the arm and shook her."

Her eyes met mine and I could see there was more that she wasn't saying.

"Then what, Jillian?"

"She threw her arms around his neck and I could hear her voice, like she was beggin' him. And the kiss she gave him was a lot more than friendly, ma'am, if you understand my meanin'."

I felt my face stinging. Had Andrew Benson lied to me? Had he blatantly and purposefully misled me? I couldn't understand why he would lie.

Jillian lowered her voice and leaned toward me. "He didn't look like a man tryin' to get away, if you get my meanin'."

"I don't understand this," I said, more to myself. "I just don't understand any of it."

"She was a wicked woman," she said, her voice a hissing sound. "Jordan Waverly didn't warrant what she done to him and if you ask me, she only got what she deserved."

"Jillian."

"Beggin' your pardon ma'am," she said. "I know she was your friend. But I'm afraid you didn't know her as well as you thought you did."

I'd heard that before. Ella had said almost the same thing.

"Well," Jillian said, a bit self-consciously. "If there's nothing else."

"No, Jillian, nothing. And thank you. I hope you won't mention our conversation to anyone else."

"No ma'am, I won't."

When I walked down the stairs and into the hallway that led to the dining room, I saw Jordan and his mother. The sight of him set my heart to pounding strangely. He stood at the end of the hallway, his dark head bent as he listened to something she was saying. I stopped. Neither of them saw me.

I could see Jordan's rigid stance, and hear the rumble of his deep voice. And even though I couldn't make out his words, there was anger and disapproval in the sound.

His mother lifted her chin, like a stubborn child who'd been reprimanded. She turned then, seeing me, her gaze finding mine and holding for a few moments. But in those moments, I felt a chill race from my head to my toes. She was looking at me as if she hated me, almost as if she could kill me. Then she turned with a flounce of her dress and went into the dining room.

Jordan saw me, too, and began to walk toward me. He must have just come home. He was still in a business suit and his eyes had a tired, weary look. He didn't smile, but continued down the hall with a purposeful stride. The look of him, the breadth of his shoulders and the sheen of light on his thick dark hair made me feel light-headed and shy. When he took my hands I could hardly suppress a sigh.

"Your hands are cold," he said, as if he had not been gone all day. "Are you feeling all right?"

Why did I have the feeling that everyone in the house was waiting . . . just waiting for me to announce a pregnancy? I was beginning to understand exactly how Mary Louise felt.

"I'm fine."

He stepped back and held my hands out, his gaze moving over me. For a moment I felt a little of the companionship we'd always shared; I felt a little warmth returning to his eyes when he looked at me.

"You look beautiful," he said, his gaze moving back up to meet mine.

"Do I?" I couldn't help the catch in my voice. His touch made me feel almost mad with pleasure. It was as if his aloofness, his polite facade made me long even more for the intimacy of our room, and the change that always occurred in him there. His eyes would warm, his mouth would seek mine as if he could not contain himself a moment longer. I longed for that now as I looked at him. I longed for him to be that man—the warmly passionate, responsive man who came to me in my room at night.

"I can't believe you don't know it," he said. His voice was warm and husky and there was a whimsical smile on his lips.

"You . . . make me feel beautiful."

His laugh was soft. He stepped nearer and I held my breath.

We could not have stood there more than a few seconds. One of the servants stepped into the hallway and made a noise to alert us of his presence.

"Excuse me, Mr. Waverly," he said. "Your mother asked me to tell you that dinner is being served."

"Tell them to go ahead," Jordan said, not even bothering to turn around. "We'll be right there."

His eyes were so intent upon me that for a moment I frowned and put my hand on his arm. "Jordan? Is something wrong?"

"I hope not," he said. "I heard about your conversation with my mother this morning at breakfast."

"Oh." I hardly knew what to say and I wasn't sure at first if he was displeased with me or not. "I'm sorry if you think I was rude to your mother, Jordan. But I will not sit there quietly while she makes such remarks about my mother. I realize I didn't know her and I have no idea if what everyone says is true, but I just know that—"

"That's not the point," he said, stepping closer. His head was bent as if he might kiss me and his attitude was so confusing to me that I felt myself growing warm.

"That's not the point?"

"Whether or not you knew your mother is not the point. No matter what she might have done or didn't do, she was your mother and you love her. I understand that."

"You do?"

"After meeting my own mother, you have to ask?" He was smiling now and his look was so tender that I actually felt the warmth all the way to my toes. "I've made it clear to her that I was not pleased with her behavior toward you."

"Jordan . . ." I was breathless. Surprised, breathless and completely charmed. I couldn't believe myself how wonderful his response had made me feel.

He smiled down at me, took my hand and placed it in the crook of his arm. "Shall we go in?"

Oh, how I loved him at that moment. Loved him and trusted him. That night I felt hopeful and happier than I'd been in weeks.

Chapter 18

Dinner that evening was very subdued. Even Mr. Waverly was exceptionally quiet and if he had been drinking, I could not tell. And even though it was what I had longed for—a quiet, pleasant family dinner—I found myself growing apprehensive as I gazed at each face and wondered what was going on in their minds. Mrs. Waverly, although she had little to say, was the only one who seemed her usual self. She gave me withering looks all evening and I could see the resentment sparkling clearly in her eyes.

Later, as we were preparing to go upstairs, one of the servants came to Jordan and whispered something in his ear.

"Excuse me," he said, leaning close to me. "You go on up. I'll be along shortly."

He turned and left with the servant, not bothering to explain why he was being called away. I told everyone good night and went upstairs to wait for Jordan. After his warm greeting earlier, I could hardly wait for him to come to me and for us to be alone in our suite.

I was in my room and I had already changed into a

nightgown when I heard the door to the sitting room. I smiled and waited a moment, expecting Jordan to open the door and step into my room.

Instead I heard the sound of his bedroom door closing.

He was changing clothes, I told myself. Perhaps even bathing, I thought as I continued to wait for what seemed like hours.

Finally I could stand it no longer. I opened my door and went across the sitting room to his closed door and knocked. There was no answer. Had I been mistaken? Was it not Jordan who'd come in?

"Jordan?" I called, tapping at the door again.

When the door flew open, I jumped in surprise. He stood there, glowering at me, his shirt opened at the neck, his braces off his shoulders and hanging at his waist. He made a powerful picture . . . strong and masculine, as handsome as any man I'd ever seen.

And as angry.

The look of resentment in his eyes made me catch my breath. Once again he had changed completely. I stared at him and began to wonder if I was losing my mind. Had it not been warmth and affection I'd seen in his look downstairs? Had I really seen that look in his eyes—that look of desire that moved me and made me tremble to my toes?

"I—I thought perhaps . . ." The coldness in his eyes stopped me. How could I ask him, beg him even, to come to me when he was staring at me with such anger?

"What?" he asked, his voice as cold as his eyes. "You thought what, Shelley?"

"What have I done to make you so angry?" I asked. "When I first saw you tonight you were—"

"Happy to see you?" he snapped. "Moved by your

beauty? Filled with desire for my wife whom I've missed all day?"

"Yes," I whispered. I was frowning up at him and trying to understand the change in him.

"That was before I realized how easily you are able to forget me."

I felt the ache in my heart, felt its trembling even before he told me the reason for his anger. I already knew. Whoever was in the woods today watching me with Andrew Benson had already gotten to Jordan.

"Why do you say such a thing? Jordan, I feel as if I don't even know you anymore."

"Why?" he asked. I could see the clenching of his jaw as his hand moved quickly forward, clamping upon my arms and dragging me toward him. "What is it about Andrew Benson, Shelley? What in hell is it about him that made Mary Louise love him . . . and now you?"

"I don't!" I gasped. "Jordan, I—"

"Don't lie to me," he said, his voice a low growl. "God, don't add lying to what's between us, too. Did you really think you could meet him—kiss him—and I would not know it? Or do you even care? Doesn't it matter to you what I think . . . how I would feel? My God, Shelley!"

"Jordan," I said, pleading. "Let me come in. Can't we sit down and talk about this? Let me explain. There are so many things I want to talk to you about."

He closed his eyes for a moment. I could feel him weakening. Then his hands clamped tighter around my arm and he shook his head.

"Do you know how badly I wanted to believe you?" he asked, his voice a hoarse whisper. "To believe that you were different . . . that one day you and I might share something precious?"

"It's what I want too, Jordan," I said, stepping closer to him. "It's what I've wanted with you for most of my life."

He took a deep breath and with a lift of his head, he stepped back away from me, as if I had struck him. I could see a glint in his eye, a wavering frown on his brow.

"I shouldn't believe you."

"But you do," I said, seeing for the first time a vulnerability in him that made him all the more desirable.

"Shelley . . ." he said, his voice a guttural warning. His gaze moved to my mouth and he closed his eyes with a low groan.

"You want me, Jordan," I whispered, moving against him. "You can't deny it, not to me. No matter what's between us, or what your family thinks . . . no matter how many doubts you have, I know you still want me."

"Damn you," he murmured. But his eyes said something else entirely as he took me by the arm and pulled me into the room with him. "Damn you if you're lying to me Shelley. For I swear if you are—"

"I'm not, my darling. I'm not. I love you, Jordan. All I want is the chance to show you just how much."

With a quiet groan of surrender, he closed the door and wrapped me in his arms. His lips were hot and urgent. There was a hunger in both of us that night that would not be denied. His hands, his mouth, the desperately whispered words he murmured against my ear almost drove me out of my mind. And as we tumbled onto his bed, I felt such ecstasy that I thought I would die from the pleasure of it.

I awoke the next morning, still in his bed. I knew it was late, much later than Jordan usually slept. And as I stretched my arms and sighed happily, I turned to find him watching me. I blushed at the look in his eyes.

"Did you sleep well?" he asked.

"Oh, yes," I whispered, moving to snuggle against him. "Wonderfully well."

I felt his lips against my hair, felt his strong arms pulling me close.

"Promise me you won't see Andrew Benson again," he said.

I looked up into his eyes. The anger I thought had dissipated last night with our lovemaking was still there, banked slightly in the depths. But there nonetheless.

"I won't see him intentionally . . . I certainly won't make plans to—" I began.

"Promise me," he said.

"Jordan, I explained to you last night what happened, how I ran into him on the beach. I was as surprised by his kiss as you were displeased. It meant nothing to me—nothing. I made that clear to the man. It's you I love. It's you that I've always loved."

I could feel him pulling away, distancing himself from me again and I could see the resentment in his black eyes. I didn't know what else to say . . . what else he wanted me to say.

"Darling," I said. "How can you doubt me after what we've shared? After last night?"

His laugh was short and humorless as he swung his legs around and over the side of the bed. I watched him walk across the room, fascinated by his male beauty and his lack of self-consciousness.

"I've found that lovemaking is a guarantee of nothing, love. Nothing at all. It's something that even the basest of creatures can accomplish."

His words cut to the quick and I felt my heart lurch, my eyes sting with hot tears. I didn't understand him at all.

157

I had given him my heart, laid my feelings bare for him to see. Where he was concerned I was as vulnerable as a child and I suppose I thought that he could see that, that he could feel it and appreciate it.

"You sound like your mother when you say such things," I said, suddenly angry with him. "What must I do to prove myself to you Jordan? Is there anything? Will I ever be able to convince you or your family that I love you? That I want nothing more than to be your wife and spend the rest of my life with you?"

He pushed his arms into a robe and tied it loosely about his waist. His muscled chest gleamed golden and warm beneath the folds of silk material. He walked barefoot to the bed and leaned over me, placing a soft, provocative kiss on my lips.

"Just keep trying," he whispered, his voice cold and sarcastic. "I love the way you try to convince me."

With that he turned and went into his dressing room and closed the door, shutting off my protests, closing his back on my tears.

I threw the covers back and got out of bed, pulling on my dressing gown with trembling, angry jerks. I did not intend to be there when he came back.

I rang for bathwater and moments later Jillian stepped into my bedroom without knocking. She seemed as surprised as I was.

"For heaven's sake," I said, pulling my robe back around my shoulders. "I wish you'd knock before coming in, Jillian."

"Yes, ma'am," she said, her gaze dropping toward the floor. "I'm sorry ma'am."

"Oh, heavens," I whispered, slumping down in a

chair. "I'm sorry, Jillian. I don't mean to be so short tempered with you this morning. Please—come in."

"It's all right," she said. "I just came to tell you that Mrs. Waverly says breakfast has already been cleared from the dining room." I saw Jillian glance at my bed, still turned down and obviously not rumpled from sleep. "If you'd like, I can bring breakfast up to the sitting room for you and Mr. Waverly."

"That would be nice," I said, feeling unexplainably exhausted and weary, the way I had yesterday. "Just tea and toast for me—I'm not hungry. I'm sure Mr. Waverly will have what he usually has."

"Well, perhaps I'd best ask him," she said, glancing again at my bed. Her manner seemed a bit strained and I could only suppose it was because of the way she'd entered my room and because she felt uncomfortable about encountering the intimacy of my obviously having just arrived from my husband's bed.

I waved my hand toward her, feeling distracted and anxious for her to leave me alone for a few moments. I had intended to take a long, leisurely bath, and when I stepped to the door to go down the hall, I heard voices in the sitting room. I was surprised to see Jillian coming from Jordan's room. Through a crack in the door, I watched as she hurried through the sitting room and back out into the hallway. I can't explain the odd feeling I had—a feeling of being excluded, almost of hearing someone talking about me. And I wondered why she had been in his room before he was even dressed and why it had taken her so long to leave.

Jillian was a very pretty young woman and she had admitted to me how attractive she found my husband. I didn't like the suspicions that came to mind about her and Jordan. I didn't like them at all.

Chapter 19

After bathing and changing into a new day gown, I went back to the sitting room, expecting to find Jordan there having breakfast. Instead the room was empty. His bedroom door stood open. Someone had already been in and straightened his room and made the bed. An untouched breakfast tray sat on the Hepplewhite table near the brocade-covered settee.

Suddenly, standing there in our parlor, with Jordan's door open on one side and mine on the other, I had such a feeling of despondency that I wanted to cry. I don't think I had ever felt so alone in all my life. My husband, so passionate, so attentive at night in the quiet of these rooms, was someone I hardly knew when the morning light came. I had no idea what I was to do about it.

At that moment I missed my friends in Savannah. I even missed my father, whom I actually saw little during my growing up years. Most of all I missed Mary Louise, the one person besides Jordan that I had always turned to.

I took the toast and a cup of tea and went into my

bedroom, closing and locking the door to the sitting room and the one to the hall. Today I would stay in my room. I would read Mary Louise's journal and sleep and try to rid myself of this overwhelming tiredness and depression.

I threw open the curtains, letting in streams of lovely subdued morning sunlight. Then I sat by the window, sipping the hot tea, and opened the journal. Mary Louise wrote:

This child should be everything to me. How I wish Shelley were here, that I could run down the beach and call to her as I always did. That she and I and Jordan were once again children with no worries, no complications except those that dealt with rain or how Shelley and I were to protect our fair skin from the sun.

I felt my heart lurch at her words. After the nostalgia I'd been feeling, it was almost as if she were speaking directly to me. I read on:

I'm confused about the baby and about Mrs. Waverly's behavior. She does not seem pleased that I'm having a child and I can't understand. Even Ella, who has every reason to resent me, seems happy and pleased. But I'm most confused about Jordan. Every move I make, he seems to know about it. I feel I cannot go anywhere without his questioning me about it later.

I almost gasped aloud. It was as if history repeated itself, as if I were somehow reliving Mary Louise's own life, complete with her mistakes. Certainly if Jordan's behavior this morning were any indication, I'd displeased him just as much.

The only person I talk to is Andrew. He is the kindest, most understanding man I've ever known. And so gentle. I have a feeling that he is the kind of man who would never be demanding of his wife.

With that entry, she ended the diary for several days. I sat for a while, looking out my windows, trying to feel what Mary Louise had been feeling. She hated the physical side of marriage, I already knew that. And I was beginning to see that what she felt for Andrew had little to do with an outward attraction. Certainly it seemed just the opposite, because he was not demanding in a physical sense. Then what about the passionate kiss Jillian had seen them share? Had that perhaps come later, as their relationship progressed?

I rubbed my eyes and continued reading.

Mary Louise's entries became erratic, her handwriting difficult to read as if she sometimes hurriedly wrote the words. Sometimes she spoke of normal, everyday things, the passing of ships, the weather, how she was feeling. Other days, she spoke of her discomfort in living at Sea Crest. Slowly, I could see a fear creeping into her words and with that came mysteries and vaguely worded apprehensions.

"He has warned me again," she wrote. I glanced up to the top of the page and saw that it was only days before her death.

My hands began to tremble and I felt perspiration at the back of my neck. For a moment, I felt ill and nauseated. I took a sip of tea, cold now, and continued reading.

> *He says that if I don't do as he asks, I will be sorry. That I will never live to see my child grow up, at Sea Crest or any-where else. God, I'm so afraid. I don't know who to turn to. I've decided to go to Andrew for help. I will beg him if I have to, to take me away from here. I have been so frightened and distracted. Yesterday as I was hurrying to my room, I fell on the stairs and tonight there are rumors that one of the maids has seen the Sea Witch again. I know that even if he does not carry out his threat, it is simply too dangerous for me to stay here any longer. I fear he is a madman.*
>
> *If only I can get away and speak to Andrew. If he will not help, I will take the dinghy if I have to and row myself across St. Catherine's Sound to the mainland. No one would be suspicious of that as I often go crabbing in the dinghy with one of the girls. Andrew could meet me later on shore and together we will be able to forget the threats and forget that Sea Crest ever existed.*
>
> *This must be the last entry until I am safely away from the island.*

I turned the page and saw nothing except blank pages. This must have been when she gave the journal to Andrew for safekeeping—after he'd refused to help her leave her husband. My eyes filled with tears when I realized that this indeed was Mary Louise's last entry before her death. She had not mentioned suicide and I was certain now that that was not how she had died. She had been trying to get away from St. Catherine's Island and away from the man who threatened her.

The man who was now my husband.

There was a loud knock at my door. I closed the journal with a jerk and in doing so, I knocked the teacup off the table and onto the floor where it landed with a thump.

"Shelley?" I heard Jordan say. "Shelley, are you all right? Why do you have the door locked?"

I could hear the alarm ringing in his voice. I tucked the journal beneath the cushion of the chair and stood up, stunned for a moment by all that I was reading. Why was there such fear in his voice? My God, surely he wasn't afraid that I might be thinking of harming myself.

"Shelley," he shouted again his voice filled with angry impatience. "Open the door."

I stood still, dumbfounded. I didn't want to talk to him and in my confusion I hesitated too long.

I heard his shoulder against the door, then the cracking of the wood as the door splintered around the lock and flew open.

I stepped back, my hand clutching my throat. He looked like a madman standing there in the doorway. The words in Mary Louise's journal spun around and around in my head. Jordan had threatened her, perhaps demanded that she not see Andrew again, just as he had me. But Mary Louise, willful as always, had gone to Andrew anyway. Had Jordan found out about that meeting? He could even have seen the passionate kiss they shared that last day of her life. And if he had, had he carried through with his threat?

"No," I whispered. "Don't . . . don't come near me." I felt the room moving, saw lights flashing before my eyes and I touched my forehead, puzzled by what was happening to me. Jordan was coming toward me and I put my hand up as if to ward him off. That was the last thing I remember.

Then I seemed to be coming out of the mists, my feet heavily weighted by wet sand. I could even hear the roar of the ocean loud in my ears.

"The marsh," I heard someone say. "We're in the marsh." Was it in my own voice, or Mary Louise's?

I began to struggle then, trying to free myself from the treacherous pull of the mud and sand.

"Shelley," I heard a voice whisper. "Darling, what's happened? Can you hear me? Love . . . ?"

Who was it? Whose voice was so gentle, so full of love and concern?

I heard footsteps it seemed and I tried so hard to open my eyes. But it was as if tons of water weighed down on me, closing my eyes and making it impossible to open them. I gave in to it then, simply gave in to the pull of the water and the darkness of the mists.

When I awoke, the room was dim and gloomy. I felt confused and couldn't remember where I was or what had happened. I glanced toward the windows and saw that the curtains had been drawn. There were openings between the material where bright streaks of sunlight could be seen. Slowly I remembered the sunlight, sitting in the sunlight reading the journal, and the sound of the door splintering when Jordan had put his shoulder against it.

I gasped and sat up in bed, gazing toward the door. It was only then that I saw Jordan, sitting near the end of the bed. His shadowed face watching me made me catch my breath. But when he leaned forward and pulled himself from the chair, I could see him better and I could see that he was no monster, no shadowy demon come to slay me. That confused me even more and I found myself leaning away from him.

He stopped dead still, staring at me as if he could not believe my reaction.

"Shelley?" His voice was a whisper, a questioning whisper.

"What . . . what happened?" I asked. I had to look away from his eyes, from the black despair in their glittering depths as he sensed my withdrawal from him.

"You fainted," he said, making no move to come closer. "But not until after I'd broken in the door, I'm afraid. I thought something had happened to you. Why didn't you open the door when I called?"

I shrugged and looked from the door back to his face.

"I . . . I don't know. I wasn't feeling well . . ."

Ella came in then. She glanced rather uneasily from me to Jordan, as if she sensed something was going on between us. Then she walked to the bed and smiled.

"Well," she said. "You certainly gave us all a fright. Are you feeling better?"

"I feel fine," I said, moving my legs restlessly beneath the covers. "I've been feeling rather tired lately and I'd decided to spend the day in my room. I . . . I don't know what happened, just that when Jordan knocked on the door I must have stood up too fast." I glanced toward him and caught his steady gaze on my face.

"We've sent for the doctor. He should be here soon."

"I don't need a doctor," I said, feeling the frustration rising in me.

"Of course you do," Ella said. She fussed with the bedcovers and the pillows. "One doesn't faint for no reason."

"I fainted often as a child."

166

"I don't recall your ever fainting," Jordan said, his eyes dark and skeptical.

"Well, I did. I don't need a doctor."

"Indulge me," he said. "And my husbandly concerns." There was such sarcasm in his voice that I wondered for a moment if he thought I had faked the entire episode.

"Well," Ella, glancing between us. "Let me have the cook fix you a nice bowl of soup."

I felt my stomach churn at the mere mention of food. But I smiled at her, anxious for her to go away and stop fussing about me.

"Thank you, Ella," I said. "That's very sweet of you."

She smiled. My words seemed to cheer her and she left the room, turning in the doorway to glance from Jordan to me once more.

Jordan walked slowly to the bed and sat on the edge. I could not look at him. I found I had absolutely no idea what to say to him.

I felt his hand touch my fingers and pull them toward him, forcing me to look up at him. His eyes demanded an explanation.

"Does my touch bother you?" he asked, squeezing my fingers for emphasis.

"No." I cleared my throat and tried to speak louder. "No, of course not. Why would it bother me?"

"Oh, I don't know. Something in your voice . . . something in the way your eyes don't quite meet mine. I've had a lifetime of learning all your little defensive mechanisms, you know."

I bit my lips. Why was it when he was kind and sweet I felt my resolve weakening, felt like throwing myself into his arms? Why was it that no matter how frightened Mary Louise's words had made me, I could not seem to remember the fear when he touched me and spoke to me in his deep, sensual voice?

"Shelley," he said. "Answer me."

"Oh, Jordan," I whispered, shaking my head. "There are so many things. This place . . . your family . . . and Mary Louise . . ."

I felt his fingers tighten, felt his body tense.

"What about Mary Louise?"

"Are you convinced she killed herself, Jordan?"

"Why on earth are you asking me such a question? Has something happened? Did someone say something to you, or—"

"No . . . I've spoken to no one this morning." I still couldn't meet his questioning eyes. "I just have her on my mind today, that's all."

He took a deep breath and stood up, standing beside the bed and staring down at me. I couldn't tell if there was anger in his eyes or if he was simply feeling the same confusion as I.

"You were afraid of me a while ago." His voice was so quiet I could barely make out his words. "And I want to know why."

"No," I said, forcing myself to meet his eyes. "You're mistaken. How could I be afraid of my own husband . . . the man I'm in love with?"

His lips thinned and his eyes grew cold and skeptical. I saw that closed-off look that I'd seen so often since our marriage. It was something unfamiliar to me, something I'd never seen in our youthful years. And I think that frightened me most of all, that Jordan could close me out so easily and that the closeness we'd once shared seemed to be vanishing with each passing day.

"I'll come back after you've seen the doctor," he said, turning on his heel to go.

I sank back into the bed and let the tears come. God, I loved him so much and I wanted more than anything in the world to believe he was not responsible for Mary Louise's death. As I lay there waiting for the doctor, I found myself repeating the very words she'd used in her diary.

"I have to find a way to see Andrew," I whispered. "Somehow I must speak to Andrew."

Chapter 20

I was becoming obsessed with finding out what really happened to Mary Louise. As I lay in bed, I felt an overwhelming restlessness. I needed to find Andrew and to discuss the journal with him. Somehow I had to find out exactly what happened.

I was already dressed and even though I felt a bit lightheaded when I got out of bed, I hurried to get out of my room before someone else came. I didn't want to see a doctor. I couldn't bear the idea of lying patiently while someone poked and prodded, any more than I could bear the thought of Jordan and Ella and everyone else planning out my every move.

I decided to bypass the sitting room, in case someone was there. Instead I stepped to the private doorway that led directly into the hall and opened the door. Quickly I glanced outside, making sure no one was there, then I hurried toward the back of the house. I would go down the back stairs, past the kitchen and out through the gardens.

As I drew nearer the kitchen, I could smell the fragrance of freshly-baked bread. I closed my eyes as a wave of hunger washed over me. My stomach rumbled and for the first time I felt my appetite returning. There was no one in the small pastry kitchen and I stepped into the room where the bread sat cooling. Feeling adventurous and resourceful, I took one of the small loaves of warm bread and hurried out the back toward the gardens. It was such a reminder of our youthful summers and of Mary Louise that I felt a poignant need to hurry, as if what I was doing could help her somehow. I raced through the beautifully landscaped English garden and was soon in the shelter of the trees that separated the lawn from the beach.

Emerging on the ocean side of the trees, I skirted quickly beneath the hanging moss, eating part of the bread as I went and tossing the rest of it to the gulls.

I only hoped that Andrew was at home and not out painting somewhere on the island. I saw him before I ever made it to his house. He was sitting on a small stool at the edge of the marsh, his gaze intent upon the canvas before him. I stopped behind him and watched for a moment, hesitant to disturb him and the quiet changeable beauty of the marshes that he was attempting to capture. The tops of the grasses swayed with the current of the water beneath them. The light from the water seemed to intensify the color of the grass. A large white crane stepped gingerly through the grass and as it stood poised to spear a small fish or salamander, I held my breath, almost as expectant as the feathered creature.

Suddenly a twig snapped beneath my feet. The crane flew up from the marsh with a soft muted flutter of wings and Andrew turned to see me standing behind him.

His smile was brilliant in the dappled sunlight. He put down his brushes and stood, coming forward to greet me. "I'm so happy to see you," he said, the pleasure evident in his blue eyes.

"I need to talk to you." I couldn't manage much more than that and I hardly knew where to start.

"We can go to the house if you'd like; you'll be more comfortable there."

"No," I quickly, glanced around. I couldn't take the chance that someone would see me there and misinterpret my visit.

"All right," he said with a wistful but understanding smile. He walked back toward his painting and took a shirt from a small brown knapsack. Then he spread it on the ground and held out his hand, indicating I should sit on the shirt.

My eyes were focused on the painting as I grew nearer. It was almost finished and lovelier than ever I could have imagined his work to be. With his oils, Andrew had captured the elusive beauty of the marsh better than any I'd ever seen.

"Oh, Andrew," I murmured, coming to stand before the painting. "It's beautiful . . . absolutely wonderful."

"I'm happy you like it," he said, obviously pleased.

"I'm stunned that your work is so real, that you are able to capture the beauty of this place." I smiled at him. "Like a native."

"Ah," he said, nodding modestly. "The best compliment I could ask for."

I settled myself on the ground and he sat nearby. His eyes were expressive and waiting, infinitely patient.

"I can't stay long," I said. "But I wanted to tell you that I finished the journal."

172

"And?"

"And I'm more convinced than ever that Mary Louise didn't kill herself. She was planning to come here, to ask you to go away with her."

"Yes," he said, looking away toward the marsh. "She did."

"She said someone threatened her."

"Jordan," he said and my heart shuddered.

"Did she tell you that? Did she actually say that it was Jordan who had threatened her?"

"No, she told me nothing except that she wanted me to take her away from Sea Crest. I found out about the threats just as you did—by reading the journal. By then it was too late."

"I can't believe she didn't tell you," I said, shaking my head with disbelief.

"She didn't," he murmured. "And perhaps that is the one thing I will always regret. If she had . . ." Once again his eyes sought the quiet serenity of the marshes. But I could see the pain and regret etched across his features.

"If she had . . . your answer to her might have been different?"

"God, yes!" He stood up, restlessly throwing a pebble across the swaying grass where it landed with a quiet plunk in the murky water. "Of course my answer would have been different. I'd have taken her away from here, if for no other reason than that we were friends."

"You broke her heart that day."

He turned to look down at me. His eyes glittered brightly and he took a long deep breath as if to steady himself.

"You don't have to tell me that. I dismissed her fears

just as everyone else did, and I hate myself for not seeing—for not listening to her. I thought for the longest time that I was responsible," he said quietly. "That she drowned herself because I didn't love her, because I wouldn't run away with her as she begged me to do."

"Until you read the journal," I said.

"Yes, until I read her journal."

"I have to confront Jordan with this. I have to make him see that you were not to blame for what happened to Mary Louise and the baby."

"I don't think that's a good idea," he said, his eyes filling with concern.

"Why not?"

"Do I have to say it? Jordan is the one who threatened her. He probably thinks no one else knows that. He probably doesn't even know the journal exists. What do you think will happen when you confront him? Don't you realize how angry he will be, how defensive? You could be in danger then, Shelley. As much danger as Mary Louise was. The difference is that this time we know it."

"Jordan would never have done anything to Mary Louise. I'm as certain of that as I am of anything."

"Are you?" he asked, staring down at me with a look of challenge.

I wanted to believe it. I *had* to believe it.

Suddenly I felt very warm and a wave of sickness swept over me again. I waved my hand in front of my face, hoping to stir a small, comforting breeze.

"Shelley, are you all right?" he asked, coming to kneel beside me. "You look very pale."

"I'm sorry," I said. "I was not feeling well this morning. I'm just a bit warm and—"

"Let me get you something to drink," he said. "It will only take a moment."

"Yes, all right," I said, nodding.

"Don't get up," he said over his shoulder. "I'll be back very soon."

As he disappeared through the trees, I sighed and leaned back on my elbow. My arm brushed against Andrew's knapsack on the ground and I saw his large sketching pad tucked away inside.

I was so anxious to see more of his work that I did not think for a moment that I was intruding, or that Andrew would mind. I pulled the pad free and began to flip through the pages, smiling at his whimsical sketches of birds and animals, at the beauty of his landscapes and flowers. Suddenly as I turned a page, I saw Mary Louise's face, smiling mischievously, the sunlight glinting in her pale hair.

"Oh, Mary," I whispered, feeling an ache in my heart. The image of her was so real and vibrant, as if she had returned for a moment in all her vivacity. My fingers traced the line of her face, to the crinkle at the corner of her eyes.

I turned the page, finding more sketches of her, each one different, each one real and beautiful. I laughed aloud at the one of her skipping along the beach with her shoes in her hand, glancing over her shoulder. Oh, how many times I'd seen her in that exact way.

Tears of joy filled my eyes and I continued flipping through the pages until there were no more. I sighed and started to put the pad back in the knapsack. Then as the breeze ruffled the paper, I saw another sketch, tucked away in the back of the book.

I gasped when I pulled it free. The woman was beautiful with dark, shining hair and huge gray eyes. Her lips were soft and vulnerable and there was just the hint of a wistful smile that tugged at the corner of her mouth. But it was the look in her eyes that captured me, the look of undeniable love, so deep, so real that I knew she loved the man who sketched her. It was the same look I'd seen in the mirror in my own eyes after Jordan and I were together.

But it was the identity of the beautiful woman that made me catch my breath.

It was Ella.

Hurriedly I tucked the sketch pad back into the knapsack, just before I saw Andrew coming back through the trees. He knelt beside me and handed me a glass of water.

"I brought some flatbread too," He said, laying it on the shirt where I sat. His eyes held a shyness as he looked at me, a questioning look of shyness. "Sometimes when Mary Louise wasn't feeling well, dry bread would help."

I bit into a piece of the dry, salty bread, frowning at him and feeling a tug of amazement at his insinuation. Why did everyone keep making such assumptions about me? Was it possible that I really was pregnant? Did I have a certain look that everyone could see except me? I shook my head and sipped the water, thinking that perhaps I should have waited to see the doctor.

Suddenly I felt an urgency to go back to the house. I wanted more than anything to catch the doctor before he left and find the answer to the question everyone except me had been asking.

"I must go," I said, glancing at him apologetically. "There were so many things I wanted to ask, but something has happened and I really should get back to the house."

"Shelley," he said, placing his hand on mine. "Before you go, there is one thing I've wanted to say to you. An apology . . . for what happened yesterday. It was wrong of me to kiss you, to take advantage of you. But I was feeling . . ." he hesitated and sighed heavily. "To be honest, I was feeling alone and missing someone."

I stared at him, knowing now who he meant. It was Ella he missed, Ella that he loved. I could hardly believe it.

"You are so sweet and warm, so easy to talk to, and I—"

"Andrew," I said, touching his arm. "There's no need. I understand." And I did understand. His feelings mirrored my own.

"I will talk to you soon," I said. "I think I'm beginning to understand more about Mary Louise. And I hope with all my heart that what you suspect is wrong."

"Just be careful," he said. "Promise me you will be careful and if you feel in any danger whatsoever, you must come to me immediately. I don't intend to make the same mistake this time."

"I promise," I said.

But oh, how I hoped he was wrong about Jordan's involvement.

I left him then, hurrying along the beach and back toward the house as if my very life depended upon it.

Chapter 21

I came around to the front of the house this time, just in time to see the doctor's carriage going down the drive. And when I drew closer to the house I saw some of the house servants outside. They stopped when they saw me approaching, their glances filled with a mixture of relief and awkwardness.

From a distance I saw Jordan on the front porch. His hands were at his hips and as he paced back and forth, the tail of his morning coat flew out behind him. Suddenly he saw me. He stopped, dropping his hands to his sides and staring at me with a look that almost made me turn and run.

"Jordan . . ." I said as I approached the steps. From the corner of my eye, I saw the servants go around toward the side of the house, their mission obviously completed.

He didn't give me time to say anything else, or to explain. He was quickly down the steps, clasping my wrists and pulling me toward him.

"Where on earth have you been? I was worried sick. Why did you run off without a word to anyone? God,

I swear you're becoming as willful and flighty as—" He stopped, taking a step backward and staring down at me as if he hardly knew me any more.

"As Mary Louise? Say it, Jordan," I whispered. "You see it too, don't you? How our lives have become parallel, almost as if I'm repeating everything she did."

"Don't say that," he growled, pulling me to him again. He held me so tightly that I could hardly breath. "Don't ever say anything like that again."

"But it's true," I said against his shoulder. "Can't you see? I'm haunted by her, by what happened to her. And I feel this compulsion to know everything I can about her. This is something we have to talk about Jordan."

"No," he said, shaking his dark head. "There's nothing to say. She committed suicide. That's all there is to it and I will not discuss it any further." He pulled away from me then, his dark eyes hot and searching. "Don't you see what it's done to this family?" he asked, his voice anguished. "Don't you see what it's done to me?"

"Yes," I whispered. "I see that all too well, and I can't bear it, Jordan. I love you too much to see you blaming yourself, to see you suffering about something that you could not control."

I hesitated before saying what I knew I had to. I took his arm and tugged at his sleeve, pulling him up to the porch and to the shelter of one of the huge columns. "You must tell me why you threatened her, Jordan. Just tell me. I'll understand."

He grew very still and a small frown appeared between his eyebrows. "What?"

"I know that you threatened her. But I also knew Mary Louise and how dramatic she could be, how exaggerating."

"What are you talking about?" he demanded.

"Jordan, don't do this. Can't you trust me, after all the years we've know each other? After all we've become to each other since . . ."

His look of angry disbelief stopped my words and I sighed, wondering if he would ever trust me, or indeed if I would ever again know the Jordan that I once knew.

I glanced up and saw that his mother had come to the front door. She stood in the open doorway, watching us, a look of dark disapproval on her face.

"Let's go upstairs," I said to Jordan, pleaded. "Where we can be alone. There's something I want to show you."

He pulled away from me, staring down into my eyes with cold resentment.

"Please, Jordan," I whispered.

Finally he touched my elbow and moved with me toward the front door.

"Well," Mrs. Waverly said as we stopped before her. "I see you decided to come home on your own. I hope you know that you had this house in a complete uproar—and that Jordan was worried to death about you." The dislike in her eyes stunned me.

"Mother, that's enough," Jordan said, his voice quiet and steady. "Shelley is hardly a prisoner here; she's perfectly free to come and go as she pleases. She didn't want to see the doctor and she made that perfectly clear. I should have listened."

I looked up at him, surprised and pleased that he had defended me again to his mother. But the look in her eyes told me I should not be pleased at all. At best, her eyes could only be described as threatening.

She stepped aside as if my touching her might dirty her somehow. I could feel her resentful gaze on me as

Jordan and I crossed the entryhall and went up the marble staircase.

Ella was in the hallway outside our suite. She clasped her hands together and came down the hall, almost running when she saw me.

"Shelley! Oh, Shelley, we were so worried. Why did you run away like that? Why didn't you wait to see the doctor?" She took my hands in hers and stared up at me with those soulful gray eyes. I looked at her for a moment, seeing, in my mind's eye, Andrew's sensual portrayal of her. I was beginning to realize that I did not really know her at all.

"I'm all right," I assured her. "I just couldn't face seeing a doctor, although now that I've had time to think about it, I probably should have. I'm sorry if I worried you." I glanced up at Jordan who was watching me with an odd look in his eyes. "Both of you."

I sensed that she intended to go back to my room with me and I suppose Jordan did too.

"Will you excuse us, Ella?" he said. "There are some things that Shelley and I need to discuss."

When he spoke his voice was gentle, as he always was with Ella. I liked that about him, that quiet chivalry that he always used with women. But now I found it confused me even more in light of the accusations Mary Louise had made in her journal.

"Of course," she said, stepping aside and smiling warmly at us. "Shelley . . . will you feel like joining me on the porch later . . . as we usually do?"

"Yes," I said. "I will look forward to it." She was anxious to talk, I knew. But no more anxious than I was myself to find out about her relationship with Andrew Benson.

Jordan followed me into the sitting room and closed the door.

"Now, why don't you tell me what this is all about?"

"Here," I said, going toward my room. "There's something I want you to read. I opened the door and gasped at what I saw.

My room was a wild jumble of clothes and bedcovers. One of the curtains hung raggedly as if someone had jerked it savagely in a fit of rage.

Jordan's murmur of disbelief was deep, a growl almost as he pushed past me into the room.

"What the hell . . . ?"

I ran to the chair where I'd hidden the journal this morning and slid my hand beneath the cushion. The book was gone. I should have known as soon as I saw the room that it would be.

"It's gone," I gasped. "The journal—it's gone!"

"What are you talking about?" Jordan asked, coming to stand before me. I could see the disbelief and the anger in his eyes. And he was concerned for me, I could see that too, and I was certain that he was not pretending.

"Mary Louise's journal. I had it. And when you came in this morning, I—I slid it beneath the cushion of this chair. And now it's gone."

He sighed and turned to me, going to the window to stare out toward the sea. "Why would you feel you ever had to hide anything from me?" he asked. When he turned to stare at me over his shoulder, I saw disgust and hurt in his beautiful black eyes. "Why?"

I shrugged, feeling helpless, feeling defenseless against that look that I saw in his eyes.

"I was confused," I said. "Some of the things she

182

said . . ." I lifted my hands and let them fall again to my sides.

"Is that why you thought I threatened her? What things?" he asked, turning all the way round now to stare at me with eyes grown dark and stormy. "About me? I already told you how badly I felt about the way I sometimes treated her. Isn't that enough? That every day I remember the look in her eyes—the look that I put there? The hurt that probably caused her to kill herself? What else do you want me to say?"

"Not that," I said, stepping toward him, wanting to touch him, wanting to comfort him and banish that tortured look from his eyes.

"Oh, Jordan," I whispered. I didn't want to tell him now, didn't want to confront him about her journal or anything else. All I wanted was to love him and to tell him that I trusted and believed in him.

He took a deep breath and stepped toward me, his eyes glittering in the shadowy room. "What, Shelley? What is it that you're finding so difficult to say?"

I took a deep breath and forced myself to say the words. "She said you threatened her and that she was afraid."

"She was afraid? Of me?" He was frowning, looking down at me with a glowering stare as if I'd lost my mind. "No. Mary Louise might have felt many things about me, but believe me," he said with a humorless grunt, "fear was not one of them. Sometimes I wish she had been afraid of me. Maybe then I could have scared some sense into her."

"She was," I insisted. "She even planned to go to Andrew . . ." I hesitated, seeing the look of warning that came to his flashing eyes. "She wanted him to take her away from Sea Crest Hall because she was afraid."

I could see him grinding his teeth together, causing the muscles of his jaw to contract. His gaze bored into my eyes.

"Andrew Benson," he murmured. "Well, well. Why should I be surprised?"

"No, Jordan—"

"And exactly where did you find this journal?" His voice was cold, filled with sarcasm. "It wasn't with any of her things. And it wasn't left in her room."

"I—I . . ."

"Where, Shelley?" he growled, coming to take my arm in a hard, steely grip.

I hadn't planned on this, hadn't planned on his asking me where the journal came from. And now I couldn't lie.

"From Andrew," I whispered. "Andrew gave it to me, to prove that he had nothing to do with whatever happened to Mary Louise."

"I see." His voice was a quiet hiss. He released my arm and stepped away from me as if I might be a striking cobra. "And in this journal, that has suddenly and conveniently reappeared, Mary Louise said that I threatened her."

"Well," I said, remembering. "She didn't actually use your name. She said 'he'."

"Ah." His voice was filled with sarcasm, his nostrils flared. And as he stared down at me through narrowed eyes, I could see the coldness creeping across his features. "But naturally, you assumed it was me."

"Jordan, it wasn't like that. It—"

"Then how was it?" he said, practically shouting as he grabbed my arms again and shook me. "And how is it that you believe Andrew Benson's innocence, while at the same time, you naturally assume my guilt?"

His face was so close, his eyes blazing into mine, accusing and hard. "I thought you knew me better than that, Shelley," he said, his voice a rasping whisper. "I actually thought you knew me enough to trust that I would never do anything to harm Mary Louise or anyone else. Certainly not my own child."

He released me so suddenly that I stumbled and almost fell. He stalked to the door and turned to face me again, his eyes filled with hurt and mistrust.

"Jordan," I pleaded. "I'm trying to understand. I want to believe you. I—"

"Don't bother," he said. "If it's such a struggle to believe me, then don't bother, love." I saw the agitated rise and fall of his chest, the clenching of his jaw as he stared at me, angry and hurt. "Perhaps you *are* haunted by Mary Louise, Shelley. Perhaps what you really want is to repeat her affair with Andrew Benson and throw it in my face. I shouldn't have married you. I should never have let your father persuade me that it would work." He dropped his voice then to a low, growling whisper. "And I should never have kissed you or held you . . . loved you. I should never have come to you at the fishing shack or here in this room. For somewhere deep in my soul, I knew the day would finally come when I'd regret it with all my heart."

He slammed the door and left me there, standing in the jumbled mess of my bedroom. Leaving my heart as tattered and torn as the chaotic scene before me.

I slid to the floor, holding my arms tightly around my trembling body, wishing I'd never confronted him, wishing I could just have believed him.

Chapter 22

I considered staying in my room the rest of the day and not seeing anyone. The last thing I wanted to do was try to put on a face of contentment when all along my heart was breaking. But I had promised Ella and I knew if I did not go, she would come to find me. Besides, I had to find someone to put the bedroom back in order.

I tugged at the bell pull for one of the maids. Jillian came to the door, her eyes large and shocked when she surveyed my room.

"Oh, my Lord," she said. "What's happened? I know Mr. Jordan has a temper, but surely—"

"Jordan had nothing to do with this," I said. For some reason her words irritated me. Did no one in this house believe in him? Or was I the foolish one, trying to convince myself he was incapable of such violence? "And I have no idea who did." I turned around once, taking in the mess, and I waved my hand ineffectually. "I have no idea what's to be done with all this."

"Don't you worry, ma'am," Jillian said. "We'll have it fixed up in no time."

"I'll be on the front porch with the young Mrs. Waverly if you need me, Jillian."

"Yes ma'am, you go ahead."

"Jillian, did you see anyone come in here this morning? Do you have any idea who might have done this?"

"No ma'am," she said. Her pretty face was solemn as she gazed at the torn curtains and disheveled bed. "I can't imagine who would have done such a thing . . . or why."

"Oh, I think I know why," I muttered as I left. Despite the mess and the obvious attempt to frighten me again, the journal was the only thing taken.

Ella was waiting for me on the porch. I sank into one of the rattan chairs and placed my sewing basket on the floor beside me. Ella moved forward in her chair, obviously anxious to hear about all that had happened.

I told her quickly about the vandalized bedroom and when she gave me an odd look and glanced away, I was surprised.

"Ella?" I asked. "What's wrong? Do you know who might have done this?"

"No, of course not," she said, shaking her head. Still she would not look at me. "I wouldn't want to say unless I'm sure."

"But you do suspect someone?"

She nodded, her eyes focused on the sewing in her lap. "Don't ask me to tell you, Shelley," she murmured. "I can't."

She glanced up at me then and I thought I'd never seen such sadness as was in her eyes. "Just let me handle this on my own," she added softly.

"But if someone meant me harm—"

"Oh, no, I'm certain that's not it." she said. "No, they would never harm you."

I was puzzled and hurt that she felt she had to protect someone rather than tell me. But I said nothing else, hoping that sooner or later she would tell either me or Jordan.

"Where did you go this morning?" she asked. There was a slyness to her voice when she spoke, just as when she asked about my seeing Andrew. And now, after seeing his sketch of her, I knew why.

"I went to see Andrew."

When she looked up, I was waiting for her, not even blinking when she stared into my eyes.

"I—I thought you said there was nothing between you and him," she said, her voice soft and melancholy.

"There is nothing between us," I said firmly. "Except that he knew Mary Louise very well and I thought he might help me."

"Help you?" she said. There was relief in her dark eyes as she stared at me.

"Did you know she kept a journal?" I asked.

Again Ella looked away. Her reluctance to tell me anything that could help me learn about Mary Louise irritated me and made me want to shake her.

"Ella," I said. "Why are you so unwilling to tell me anything? And why do I have a feeling that you know much more about what happened to Mary Louise than you want to share?"

"I like you, Shelley," she said, her voice soft and pleading. "I've grown really fond of you, and I want you and Jordan to be happy. But don't ask me to tell you anything else. I can't."

"Who met Andrew first, Ella? You, or Mary Louise?"

There was only the slightest hint of resentment in the thinning of her lips, in the lifting of her chin.

"Mary."

"Did she introduce you?"

"No. Oh, drat," she said, pulling at a tangled thread. Her fingers were trembling.

"How did you happen to meet him, then?" I tried to keep my voice flat and unchallenging.

"I went to him and told him of Mary Louise's infatuation. I was very angry. I asked him to leave her alone, for the sake of Mary Louise's and Jordan's marriage, as well as for the family." She had put down her sewing and as she gazed off into the distance, I could see the softening of her beautiful eyes as she remembered.

"Did Mary know you went to him?"

"No," she said, going back to her sewing.

"Did she ever learn that you were in love with him too?"

Ella gasped, her gaze flew up to meet mine like a startled bird. In her surprise she pricked her finger with the needle and as she sat staring at me, a tiny drop of blood seeped from her skin and onto the pristine white linen that she stitched.

Still staring at me, she stood up. Her face was white and her lips trembled slightly.

"How did you . . . Andrew didn't . . . ?" Tears welled in her eyes and she could not continue.

"Ella, I'm sorry," I said, standing up and taking her arm. I took a piece of scrap material from the basket and wrapped it about her bleeding finger. "Here, please, sit down."

She looked like a small child, sitting there across from

me, holding her finger, staring at me with wide tear-stained eyes.

"Of course Andrew didn't say a word," I said, wanting more than anything to reassure her. I couldn't bear the pain I saw in her eyes. "This morning I saw a sketch he did of you."

I smiled, hoping to put her at ease again. She was obviously very disturbed that anyone knew how she felt and her reaction told me what I suspected—that it had not been a casual thing between the two of them. "It was obvious," I said softly. "The way he captured your smile, your eyes. And the way you looked at the artist."

"That look, as you call it—it could have been something he interpreted," she whispered. "Or imagined."

"Ella," I scolded softly.

Her hands flew to her eyes and she bent her head. And now her small shoulders trembled as she sobbed quietly.

"I have no idea how it happened," she said finally, her voice muffled. "Dear God, if anyone ever knew . . ." She looked up then and tears streamed from her pleading eyes. "Shelley, please, if Benjamin ever knew . . ."

"Oh, Ella," I whispered, realizing her fears. "Of course, I would never mention this to anyone, certainly not Benjamin. And I promise I won't tell Jordan either if you don't want me to."

"No, please don't," she said, frowning. "Oh, Jordan would hate me if he knew."

"He wouldn't," I said. "Jordan thinks the world of you, Ella."

Finally she wiped her eyes and sank back in the chair, seeming exhausted by what had happened. She held a handkerchief in her hands and pressed it to her forehead as she spoke and gazed out toward the yard. She was beautiful and fragile and she filled my heart with such sympathy that I wanted to embrace her and assure her that everything would be all right. But how could I? How could I think that anything would ever be right in this house again?

"I haven't seen him alone since he did the sketch," she said. "That was the day we knew . . . the day both of us knew that we loved one another. Isn't it ironic? I went to him to plead with him about my sister-in-law and ended up in love with him myself."

"And he loves you."

"Yes," she said with a quiet sob. "Oh, yes— unfortunately, I think he does."

"But what about Benjamin? Were you ever in love or was yours a marriage—"

"Of convenience?" she asked, her voice wry and sarcastic. "Like yours and Jordan's? I didn't think so at the time. But I learned quickly that Benjamin is incapable of love—of the kind of love that most women wish for, anyway. We could never talk about it. You see, Benjamin considers me a foolish, silly woman, unable to think for myself or make a rational decision on my own. The same view he has of most women, I'm afraid."

I frowned at her. Somehow I had never thought of Benjamin that way. He had always been polite and charming to me.

"Surprised?" she asked. She was watching me and my reactions and now she arched her brow in an odd, challenging little way.

"Yes," I admitted. "Although heaven knows I shouldn't be surprised about anything that happens in this house anymore."

Ella stood up and walked to the porch railing.

"Perhaps you should know," she said. "As long as Benjamin continues his present . . . habits . . ." her voice was bitter and filled with an odd resentment. "There is no danger of our having a child before you and Jordan. When we're away from the family, we barely speak to one another. It's been months since we shared the same bed."

She turned to face me, her eyes filled with a meaningful determination.

"Oh, Ella," I whispered. "I'm sorry. I'm so sorry that your life is so . . ." I stopped, not wanting to hurt her.

"Miserable?" she asked, her eyes sparkling. "It is, you know—I do know what it's like to be trapped in a loveless marriage. I understood all too well how Mary Louise felt. Not that Jordan was ever anything but the kindest, most considerate husband in the world. But there has to be love on both sides, Shelley, or it simply cannot work."

"I know," I said, thinking of Jordan and wishing for the thousandth time that he could love me the way I loved him.

"I suppose I was vulnerable," she whispered. "So alone, so unhappy . . . and there was Andrew, ready to tell me all the things a woman longs to hear. He was wonderful and kind," she continued. "And he actually listened to me—he actually seemed to want to know how I felt, what I liked. Is it any wonder that I fell in love so quickly, so completely?"

"No," I said, going to stand beside her. I put my arm at her waist to let her know I did not judge her. Who was I to judge anyone? "It's no wonder at all. But what are you going to do?"

"Nothing," she said. "There's nothing I can do. Benjamin has seen to that."

"What do you mean?"

We stopped talking then, both of us looking up as the front door opened and Benjamin stepped toward us. Ella glanced toward me and I smiled, hoping to reassure her that her secret was safe with me.

"Ah," Benjamin said. "There you are, darling. Mother is looking for you. She wondered if you might like to help her with the invitations for the Captain's Ball? You too, Shelley, if you're interested."

I had completely forgotten the ball, one held annually on the island. This year I knew there was great excitement that it was to be held at Sea Crest Hall.

"Perhaps later," I said. "There's something I need to attend to . . . in my room."

"I'll see you at dinner, then," Ella said.

I had hoped that by dinner Jordan would no longer be angry with me. And although I had not seen him the rest of the day, I'd hoped that he would think about our conversation and realize how much I loved him. I was certain he knew that I could never betray him with Andrew Benson, but there was more to it than that. There was a jealousy there that I could not understand, almost as if he resented even the remotest friendship I might have with the mysterious artist.

I had to admit, dinner that evening was more pleasant than usual. For the first time since I came, Mr. Waverly seemed completely sober. His eyes were clear and bright and he held a conversation with his sons that surprised me with its lucidity. Even Mrs. Waverly was pleasant and seemed very excited about the forthcoming Captain's Ball. It was all she talked about.

But if I expected dinner to soften Jordan's attitude toward me, I was mistaken. He was polite and cool, treating me no more cordially than he might a guest.

Later when we went up to our suite, he turned without a word to go into his bedroom, closing the door softly behind him. I felt as if my heart would break. With a quiet sigh I went to my room, gazing about at the new orderliness of it.

As I prepared for bed, my thoughts turned again to the morning, to the journal and to my reaction when Jordan burst through the door to find me. My eyes darted now to the door, seeing the newly-installed lock. I wondered what the servants must think about us. Did they whisper and laugh behind our backs? I was sure they did.

And I thought too of my illness and how Andrew had so kindly brought flatbread for me. I decided then and there that I must see the doctor. Our old family doctor lived on the north end of the island. I would go early tomorrow morning and see him, then visit my father as well.

Strangely, I felt it was a trip and a purpose about which I should tell no one.

Chapter 23

Jordan had already left his room the next morning when I bathed and dressed. I called Jillian and asked her to have a carriage brought around to the front steps.

"Goin' visitin'?" she asked.

"Yes, I'm going to see my father today."

I didn't bother to mention that I would also see a doctor or that I wanted to learn if I might be expecting a child. Jillian was not the person I wanted to hear that news first.

It was a glorious morning and I asked the driver to take the carriage along the wide sandy beach. It seemed years since I'd seen the ocean or breathed in the tangy scent and let the wind whisk away all my worries. That morning I let myself give in to all the joys of those years gone by when Jordan and Mary Louise and I were together. As I rode, I wondered if she could somehow hear my prayers and if she knew how desperately I loved Jordan. Could she see how much I longed to see him smile and hear him tease me the way he had all those years ago?

We reached the doctor's house at the end of the island almost before I knew it. I saw his buggy outside and breathed a sigh of relief. I suppose I had taken quite a chance coming here this way unannounced. He was often out about the island, seeing to patients and the elderly who could not come to him.

I saw my driver's look of speculation. He knew the doctor's house I was sure, and for a moment I felt like telling him that this was confidential. But then I decided I should wait and hear what Doctor Chambers had to say first.

He seemed surprised to see me.

"Well, Shelley Demorest," he said in his big booming voice when his housekeeper took me to his office. He smiled, the weathered skin at the corner of his eyes crinkling as he did. "Excuse me, I should have said 'Shelley Waverly'."

"Yes," I replied. "Jordan and I have been married over two months now."

"And is this a social visit?" he asked, with a lift of his brows. "Or . . . ?"

"I am here as a patient," I said, feeling suddenly shy and uncertain. Quickly I explained by symptoms, realizing that this morning I had not been sick, not even remotely. I told him that as well. "Perhaps it's nothing, perhaps it's just nerves, or my imagination."

"We'll see," he said with a nod.

Later, after I was dressed, I sat in his office, waiting for him to return. When he came in I could not read any expression on his face and I found I was desperate to know his diagnosis.

He sat for a moment, thumbing through some papers until I thought I would scream. Then he looked up at me and smiled.

"Just as I suspected," he said. "You are in the very early stages of pregnancy."

"Oh." I felt numb. A baby . . . I was actually to have a baby . . . perhaps the son that Jordan wanted so desperately.

His bushy eyebrows lifted as he stared at me and what was, I suppose, my incredulous expression.

"Are you pleased to be having a child? Isn't it what you wanted?"

"It's . . . it's what Jordan wants, very much."

His smile was gentle and understanding. "And what about you, Shelley. Is it what you want?"

I took a long, slow breath. I had known Doctor Chambers all my life and I could not lie, not when he sat staring at me with such kind interest.

"I—I suppose I'm just a little afraid."

What was wrong with me? Suddenly I was wracked with such a sense of foreboding that I felt weak and faint. What if I were mirroring Mary Louise's life once more? What if this child that I carried was destined to die along with me?

"Of course you're afraid," he said. "It's only natural for a first mother to be afraid of the unknown." Of course he couldn't know how I felt or why I was so afraid. "But you're young, and you're a strong, healthy woman at just the right age for bearing children. It will be all right, my dear."

"I know," I said, nodding and feeling absolutely foolish to be admitting my fears to him.

Dr. Chambers walked with me to the front door and I turned to thank him.

"How's your father?" he asked. "I've hardly seen him lately."

197

"I'm afraid I haven't seen much of him either since my marriage. I'm going there today."

"Ah," he said. "Then tell him I said hello and give him my heartiest congratulations on his becoming a grandfather."

"Yes . . . I will," I promised.

As we drove to my father's house, my head was in a whirl. My thoughts alternated between incredible joy and wonder, to despair. What was I to do if Jordan no longer wanted me after the child was born? Would I be relegated to the background, like a dowager mother, content to watch my child grow up as a Waverly, knowing I had done only what was considered my duty? Would I be forced to watch as Jordan took other women, no longer needing to pretend that I had any use for him except as a means to something he wanted?

I felt tears of frustration stinging my eyes as I recalled that day at the fishing shack, the day I'd heard the man's laughter inside, the man who sounded so much like Jordan. I'd told myself a hundred times since then that I was mistaken. But now, as the possibility of a lifetime of such pain and hurt and rejection loomed before me, I thought I could not bear it.

"No," I whispered.

"Pardon ma'am?" the driver said, glancing over his shoulder at me.

"Oh . . . nothing," I said, quickly wiping my eyes.

When we arrived at my old home, my father was not inside. I stepped out onto the porch, noticing that several timbers had rotted and needed replacing. I was surprised that he had not yet used any of Jordan's money on the house.

I glanced around the side of the house and I saw him

there, kneeling at my mother's grave, evidently so intent on his grief that he had not heard the carriage. He looked old and sad.

I instructed the driver to go through to the kitchen and find himself some refreshments in the cupboard. Then I walked slowly out to the small plot of ground where my mother was buried.

He seemed surprised to see me and when he stood up, he stared at me for a moment as if he wasn't quite sure who I was.

"Father?" I said, stopping. I hadn't meant to startle him. "It's me . . . Shelley."

"Oh, Shelley. Of course I knew it was you. It's just that for a moment, you looked so much like her."

"Like who?"

"Your mother," he said, turning toward her grave and waving his hand in a sad, weary little way. "I never realized before how much you look like her."

"Father, may I talk to you for a moment?"

"Of course, of course. Did you bring your husband with you?"

"No. There's only me and my driver. I sent him into the kitchen to find something to drink."

"Shall we sit on the porch?"

"Might we walk a ways?" I asked, pointing toward the ocean. "It's been a while since I walked along this beach. I miss it."

He seemed slower, not only in his walk, but in his speech and in his thinking. I glanced at him from time to time as we walked, wondering if he was ill or if it was just the effects of old age.

"I seem to remind Mr. and Mrs. Waverly of my mother too," I said, watching him carefully.

His eyes darted my way, then back again toward the white-flecked ocean and the pale blue horizon.

"Is it true what everyone says about her?" I asked. I knew almost without a doubt that he knew what I was talking about. I could sense it in him.

"They told you about your mother," he said.

"Yes, or at least they told me their version. Why did you never tell me, Papa? Why did you let me believe all these years that she was so good, so loving?"

"She was," he said. He stopped, frowning at me, his lips drawn into a thin line of disapproval. "Don't ever let anyone tell you different. Your mother was good, as sweet and innocent as a saint. She was no match for John Waverly and his wealth. He stole her away from me as surely as a man might steal a precious jewel. He influenced her with his money and position and he took advantage of my being away so much."

"But Papa, why did you let me marry Jordan— knowing this? Why?"

He shook his head and walked on ahead of me. "It was always my plan for you to marry Jordan," he said.

When I caught up with him and he looked at me, there was a disdain and a coldness in his eyes that I'd never seen before.

"Why?"

"So you would be a part of it," he said. "A part of the Waverly family. And even though I'll probably never live to see it, it gives me tremendous pleasure knowing that one day, all that John Waverly owns will belong to my daughter and to her children. It will be my blood, Demorest blood, that runs through the veins of future Waverlys. And I know that will eat at him and at his high and mighty wife who always thought they were so much better than me."

"Father," I whispered. I felt as if I hardly knew him. In all my life I'd never heard him talk this way about anyone or anything.

He hardly noticed my shocked expression.

"He took my beautiful Lucinda and ruined her, made her forever restless and discontent. Then he shunned her, sent her back to me like someone would abandon an unwanted animal." He turned to me, his weary eyes alive now and blazing with fury. "I want him to pay for that," he said, his voice cracking. "I want him to pay dearly."

What had happened to him? His bitterness and the look in his eyes frightened me more than I'd ever have thought possible.

"Papa," I whispered. "What's brought all this on? Is it memories of Mother? How can you speak this way about the family of the man I married? They will be my child's grandparents now. They—"

"Your child?" he said, turning suddenly to me. His eyes glittered and his frail, bony hands bit into my arms. "What are you saying, daughter?"

The look in his eyes made me tremble . . . that look of triumph, a look of evil, almost. I shuddered and pulled away from him.

"It's true," I said. "I just came from Doctor Chambers' office. I'm to have a child, father."

"Oh, my girl," he said, stepping forward to wrap me in his arms.

I was surprised at the frailty of his body, at how slender he had become since my wedding. He seemed to have aged twenty years.

"My girl," he repeated, hugging me tightly. "At last. At last I shall have my vengeance on them. Together you and I are going to make them pay—do you hear me? We will use this child to take from them everything they hold dear, just as they did me all those years ago."

"No," I whispered, stepping back from him.

My ears were ringing and I could feel my heart pounding, in rhythm with the heavy, beating surf. This was why he'd arranged for me to marry Jordan. This terrible need for vengeance. Not money, not greed. Something even worse. Something that frightened me and made me wonder what other horrible things he was willing to do to repay the hurt the Waverlys had caused him.

"Yes," he said, staring down into my eyes. "Oh, yes— this is only the beginning. Nothing is going to stand in my way now. You've given me a reason to live, my dear. A very good reason to continue my struggle to live."

He hugged me and pressed a kiss against my brow. Then he turned and walked down the beach, leaving me there alone. It was as if I didn't exist any more.

I loved Jordan and yet I'd felt used when the doctor told me I was expecting a child. But that feeling of hurt and betrayal was nothing compared to what I was feeling now.

My own father had used me too. And now he intended using my child.

Chapter 24

I felt only numbness as we rode back to Sea Crest Hall. The sparkling ocean held no fascination; not even the crying gulls and warm wind could capture my attention that day, and suddenly, the nausea was back, stronger than ever in the swaying carriage and relentless wind. I could hardly wait to be back in the cool, quiet comfort of my room.

I would not let myself think about the child. I suppose it was too soon to believe it was real. And I was finding that I actually had to fight my resentment, knowing that this was all that Jordan required of me and that now he would focus his attention on the child and not me.

I spent the rest of the afternoon in my room and when Ella came to inquire about me, I told her I was tired and not feeling well. She bit her lips as if she wanted to stay, as if she wanted to continue the conversation we had started yesterday. But I turned my face away, not wanting to talk, not wanting to have to face anyone at the moment.

I was asleep when Jillian woke me for dinner.

"Ma'am," she said, tiptoeing to the bed. I heard her

voice from a distance and felt her hand lightly touch my arm.

"Yes," I said, opening my eyes. "I'm awake."

"Didn't want you to be late for dinner, ma'am," she said. "Mrs. Waverly is in a snit today anyway. Seems the champagne she ordered for the ball wasn't on the ferry this afternoon. She's fit to be tied."

As I lay there, trying to come fully awake, I realized the nausea was gone. In fact I felt wonderfully energetic, even optimistic after the nap. I decided I would wear something new to dinner. The weather had grown very hot. I would sweep my hair up and dress in something light and summery, and tonight, after dinner, I would ask Jordan to walk outside with me. And I would tell him.

I thought of Mary Louise's wedding as I dressed—how angry I'd been that she wanted me to wear pink. The dress I chose tonight was a light shade of pink, although I preferred to call it peach, a more suitable compliment to my auburn hair and fair skin. It was a delicate French muslin, almost like chiffon, and my arms were covered by soft pleated drapes that looked like butterfly wings. The dress smelled new and rich and as I stared at myself in the mirror, I felt alive, even beautiful.

After Jillian finished my hair, she placed a wide comb decorated with silk flowers at the back of my head.

"Well," she said, standing back to survey her handiwork. "You look beautiful," she said, her voice a whisper. "Really beautiful."

"Thank you, Jillian." My cheeks were glowing and I wondered if that were one of the effects of being pregnant. I stared at myself, unable to believe that I was here in this beautiful house, wearing clothes I could once only have dreamed of. And even more incredible than that, I was expecting a child by Jordan Waverly.

I took a silk fan, painted with peach-colored flowers and decorated in green and gold, and I went downstairs to dinner.

Jordan was the first person I saw when I entered the dining room. His lips parted slightly when he saw me and his eyes darkened, then moved slowly from my face down to my toes and back up again. He came forward, offering his arm in what I knew was only a show of politeness. But he could not deny the spark I saw deep in his beautiful eyes.

I smiled up at him, feeling young and beautiful, feeling all the power that a woman feels when the man she loves looks at her that certain way.

"You look exquisite," he murmured.

I would have been pleased, except that the words he muttered were said in an almost resentful tone. As if I'd made him see and feel things he never intended.

"Indeed," Benjamin said as he bowed and pulled my chair away from the table. "Between you and Ella, I'm afraid the other women attending the ball will be put in the shade."

I glanced at Ella and saw her admiring eyes on me. She smiled warmly and as I was to sit next to her, she reached her hand forward and welcomed me to the table in a friendly, companionable gesture. I was beginning to feel, at last, as if I had a sister, and I found that I liked that feeling very much.

During the meal I found my eyes moving of their own will toward Jordan. He was so handsome. I watched his hands, his brown, artistic fingers, as they reached for a wine glass, as they fiddled with the silverware when he talked. He would turn and catch me watching him, then he would frown and look away.

He made my heart catch, made me feel breathless with longing, and I was beginning to feel another emotion that I couldn't quite explain, except perhaps as due to my condition. I felt blessed and grateful that I was the one to have his child, that I was the one who shared his name, if not his heart. And I vowed that night that I would give our relationship a while longer, for I knew without a doubt now that I couldn't leave him, even if I tried.

Mrs. Waverly was obsessed with the ball and I had to admit that her enthusiasm influenced even me. It would be wonderful having the house filled with guests, hearing music and laughter. And I hoped the ball, to be held in a couple of weeks, might even be the beginning of a new era here at Sea Crest Hall.

After dinner, I moved closer to Jordan.

"Could I speak to you alone?" I whispered. "Perhaps we could walk out to the front porch."

He nodded to Benjamin and Ella, then extended his arm to me. Together we walked through the splendid house and out into the velvety darkness. Here on the porch there were only lanterns to cast a dim light against the night and I immediately felt an intimacy envelop both of us.

Jordan didn't ask what I wanted and he didn't refer to his anger about my behavior, or the journal. He simply backed against the balustrade, crossed his arms over his chest, and waited for me to speak. His gaze was cool and uninvolved, nothing like the pretense he'd managed at dinner. It was awkward, and for a moment I had no idea how I was to tell him.

"I . . . I went to see my father this morning."

"I know."

I don't know why his quiet reply surprised me so. I had already suspected that he had someone report to him regularly about my whereabouts. Or was he simply concerned when he didn't know where I was? By his cool gaze, I couldn't be sure of anything.

"While I was there, I also went to see our family doctor . . . Doctor Chambers."

Jordan become instantly alert, pushing himself away from the railing. His arms came down and slightly forward as if for a moment he meant to reach out to me. Then he stood very still and lifted his chin in that defiant way I knew so well. And he waited.

"Are you ill? Is anything wrong?"

"Not wrong," I said, suddenly feeling more shy than I'd ever been in his presence. This was the man I'd known all my life, the man I considered my best friend. And now, because we were husband and wife, because we had shared such breathtaking intimacies, I felt as shy as if I'd just met him.

"I . . . I'm to have a child," I said. I was surprised that my voice could not seem to get above a whisper.

"Shelley," he murmured.

Suddenly he was there in front of me, close. He wrapped me in his arms and rocked me back and forth, murmuring soft little words that I could not quite hear. I felt his lips against my hair, whispering my name and I felt such joy, such confusion. He was the most exasperating and changeable man I'd ever known.

"Are you certain?" he said, pulling away and looking down into my eyes. "Are you all right?"

"The doctor seemed positive," I said, shaking my

head at the new tenderness in him. And at how quickly he had forgotten our earlier disagreement. I should have been thrilled—delighted—but I found his behavior more puzzling than ever. Was he so eager to have a child that he could forgive me this quickly? Or was he simply willing to overlook my shortcomings now that I had fulfilled my duty?

"But are you all right? God, Shelley . . . I was so angry with you before. I'm sorry. I shouldn't have upset you that way."

I laughed then, thinking I'd never seen him in such a state. Jordan could be solemn and stoic, withdrawn even at times, but it had been a long time since I'd seen this old delightful enthusiasm.

"I'm fine," I said.

With a quiet groan, he kissed me, cradling my face in his hands as tenderly as if I might break. "You should have told me sooner," he said "I'd have gone with you today."

"I wanted to be sure," I said. For a moment I thought about telling him about my father's bitter, angry words. I suppose I felt a new bonding with Jordan at that moment, a new optimism about us. And for a second I wanted to tell him about the resentment my father held against his family. But I didn't. I just couldn't bear to spoil the moment, or the look I saw on his face.

"Oh," he said, breathing a whispered sigh as he held my face in his hands. "Do you know how happy this makes me?"

"I know it's what you wanted," I said, still feeling a sting when I said the words. "Why you married me."

"No," he said, touching his lips softly to mine. "It's more than that, now—don't you see? It's much more—

we're more than we were before. This is something we'll always share," he whispered. "That no one else can share with you except me . . . this child, my son."

I was amazed at the way he said the words, at the fierce possessiveness in the tone of his voice. I'd been warned about that possessiveness.

But I was so touched when I heard him say the word 'son'. There was a reverence in his voice, a boyish awe as if he could hardly believe it himself.

"Are you so certain it will be a son?" I asked, smiling up at him.

"Of course it will be," he said, laughing finally. "And if not, then I suppose we'll just have to try again." There was a teasing quality in his voice as he held me there so safe and secure in the shadows of the porch. In the distance came the beloved sound of the ocean and around us the sound of night creatures filled the air. We could even hear the low booming sound of a bull alligator in the marsh.

Suddenly it all seemed so right for us and I felt a sweet sense of relief wash over me as I snuggled against him. Even my reservations about the house and his family faded away into the background when he held me that way, when his words were so soft and tender.

I told myself then that everything would be all right. I even pushed away all the niggling little doubts about Mary Louise and her death. I would not allow myself to think that my father's words today had any significance at all in our lives. I could see happiness ahead for us. For the first time since coming to Sea Crest Hall, I actually thought Jordan might even come to love me as I loved him. I foolishly pushed every other thought far away into the back of my mind.

Chapter 25

I think that those days before the ball were among the happiest I'd ever known in my life. Jordan was more attentive than I ever could have imagined. And if there were still resentments about Andrew, or questions about Mary Louise's journal, we both chose to put them behind us and go on with our lives.

The news that I was expecting a child seemed to put a glow on everyone's face; even the servants when I would meet them in the hallway couldn't resist smiling. And Mrs. Waverly surprised me with her remarks.

"I'm delighted, both for you and for Jordan," she said. Her voice was hesitant and if she did not quite meet my eyes that day I told myself she would come around once the baby was born. There was even a hint of shyness in her voice, a humbleness that was very uncharacteristic. But in my new state of happiness I welcomed it and did not let myself dwell on the whys and wherefores of her behavior, or the way she had treated me in the past. I hoped this was to be the beginning of a new cordiality between the two of us.

Unfortunately, Mr. Waverly began to drink again,

and I wondered if Jordan's announcement about the baby had anything to do with that. I could never be sure, for any new occasion seemed to send him back to his bottle and turn him into a jeering, sarcastic man, completely different from the man he was when sober. All I could do was avoid him.

I had worried about Ella's reaction, but she seemed genuinely happy for me and began immediately to plan a layette for the baby.

I suppose in my happiness and in the plans for the ball, I was completely distracted. One day, about a week before the event was to take place, I was in my room, resting before dinner. Jillian came in, unannounced as usual. It was a habit I could not seem to get her to break.

"Jillian," I began, rousing myself and propping up on my elbow.

"Sorry," she said. "I forgot to take your dress downstairs to be pressed."

"It's all right," I said, frowning at her. She seemed different today, sullen and moody, which was a departure from her usual ebullient ways. "I'm sure the dress is fine."

"Oh, I wouldn't want to disgrace you, ma'am, by having you appear in something unsuitable to your status."

"For heaven's sake, Jillian. What on earth is that supposed to mean? Are you angry with me about something?"

"No," she said, her eyes bright and alert. "What would I be mad about? Everything's fine." She went to the large cypress wardrobe and pulled out the dress I was to wear to dinner, draping it across her arm as she turned to leave the room.

"I'll have this back shortly," she said.

I sat there in bed, staring after her and wondering if I had done something to hurt her feelings. I couldn't think of anything . . . in fact, I had hardly seen her lately. I lay back against the bed and closed my eyes, wishing the nagging doubts that bothered me would go away and that I could sleep. I placed my hand on my stomach, thinking of the baby and what a difference it had already made in the household, and finally I drifted off to sleep.

I dreamed about the dress, a white polished cotton with green and gold ribbon streamers. I could see myself whirling around, allowing the wide skirt to flare about me. There was a man in the distance, obscured by a pale, fast-moving mist. He was coming closer and closer and I could feel my heart pounding in anticipation. I held out my hand to him, not certain if what I felt was fear or pleasure, somehow, the feelings were all tangled up together. As he continued walking toward me, I never seemed able to see his face, no matter how hard I tried. I realized that I could not move . . . something was holding me back. I turned to see what it was and I heard myself moan—a quiet, whispered moan of fear.

Mary Louise's face, pale and deathlike, loomed just behind me. Her hands gripped my dress, holding me away from the man in the mists. There was a look of horror on her face and although her lips mouthed silently, I realized that she was trying to tell me something, to warn me somehow.

"Don't go," she whispered in an eerie, unearthly voice. "You must not go."

"Why?" I asked. "Tell me why."

"Shelley?" I heard somewhere in the mists. "Shelley, wake up."

I came awake suddenly, seeing Jordan's face before me. For a moment I thought he was the man in the dream, the man coming toward me. But it was his eyes, warm and tender and alive, that convinced me otherwise. I moved quickly into his arms and he held me close against him, smoothing my hair and whispering words to soothe and quiet me.

"I was dreaming," I said against his shirt. "Mary Louise was there, her hands clutching my dress." I gazed around the room, wondering if Jillian had come back in with the dress. Perhaps that was why I'd had such an odd dream. But the dress wasn't there.

"Shh," he whispered, still cradling me in his arms. "What's this about?" he asked. "Is it the journal? Are you still worried about her journal and the accusations she made?"

As I looked up into his eyes, I could see his concern and that little hint of pain that seemed always to linger there.

"No," I said, touching his face. "Whatever she said in the journal, she must have been mistaken. I believe you when you say you never threatened her."

"Shelley, listen to me," he said, clutching my arms. "Has anyone here ever threatened you . . . made you feel afraid, uncomfortable even? You would tell me if that happened, wouldn't you?"

"Jordan—what's wrong? Why do you ask—"

"Haven't you thought it could be someone else who threatened her? Have you forgotten about the scene we found in the sitting room on the night of our wedding?

213

And the way your room was destroyed when someone took the journal." He shook his head and stood up, pulling away from me, taking the warmth and light with him.

"Yes, of course I've thought about it," I said. "I've known all along that someone wanted to frighten me away from here. What I didn't understand was why. But now that there's to be a baby—"

"The baby might only make things worse," he said, his eyes sharp and troubled. "Whoever wants to frighten you could feel even more intimidated by the birth of this child."

"Who," I said, shaking my head in denial. "Surely you don't think Ella, or Benjamin—?"

"I don't know," he murmured. "I just don't know."

It was happening again. All those deep, disturbing feelings rushing over me, bringing that dark sense of foreboding. I had tried so hard not to let myself dwell on the way my life seemed to be mirroring Mary Louise's since coming here to Sea Crest. But now, as Jordan stood before me, so real, so genuinely concerned, it all came rushing back with frightening clarity, and I began to wonder how long it was between Mary's discovering she was to have a child and her death.

"Jordan, you're frightening me. What's happened? Something must have happened to make you say these things to me."

He stepped quickly back to the bed and gathered me into his arms, holding me as if he would never let me go, as if he could keep me safe by his own strong will.

"I went to visit her grave today," he said. His voice was quiet, a hoarse whisper in the quiet room. I sat very still, holding onto him and listening.

"There was a black wreath on her grave, Shelley. Someone had fashioned a wreath out of blackened seaweed and dried marsh grass and tied it with a black ribbon. The servants are frightened to death. Some of them are even threatening to leave Sea Crest for good."

"What do they think it means?" I asked.

And why did I immediately associate marsh grass with Andrew Benson? "Exactly what do they think it means, Jordan?" I repeated.

"They say it means another death in the house."

I could feel the shudder running through me, feel it shaking me from head to toe.

"I'm so sorry for frightening you," he murmured, pulling me close. "Mother said I shouldn't tell you, that I should just leave it alone and try to dismiss it as a silly prank. But I want you to know. I want you to be aware of what's happening and to be careful. I don't intend to let you out of this house until I find out who's behind this. Do you hear? You are not to be outside alone for a moment."

I found it odd that he thought the danger lay only outside the house. Did he not feel the same dark sense of wickedness that I sometimes felt in this house . . . or was it only my imagination? Worst of all, I was afraid I might be becoming more and more like Mary Louise—fragile and afraid of everything and everyone.

"All right," I murmured. I felt stunned and lifeless and I hardly knew what to think about all that he had said. There seemed to be so many dangers, so many threats here that I couldn't properly discern them all. "Whatever you say."

"Now," he said, attempting to smile. "I want you to get dressed in one of your most beautiful gowns. After

215

dinner, we'll walk along the beach if you like, the way we used to do. You always said it was quiet and soothing after everyone else went inside, that the beach belonged only to us . . . remember?"

"Yes," I said, brushing my lips against his cheek. "I remember. Will you be here after I'm dressed?" I knew that sometimes Jordan preferred going down early and talking with Benjamin while I dressed.

"I don't intend leaving you for a moment."

I felt tired that evening. Even the nap had not seemed to help. But after Jillian brought the gown and I was dressed, I felt a bit better. I was only troubled that the usually happy and cheerful maid still seemed distant and angry.

That night at dinner, I found Benjamin's eyes on me several times. Did Jordan really suspect his own brother of trying to frighten me? When I smiled, he would look away. Ella saw it too and it seemed to bother her. I could only assume his looks were inquisitive, almost as if he thought he could already see the changes that pregnancy had made.

I realized that evening just how strongly my father's remarks had affected me where the Waverly family were concerned. I saw Mr. Waverly in a different light, although I had to admit it was hard seeing him as a young lover, competing for my mother. And I longed to ask him about her, to ask him if what my father said was true—that he had used her, then tossed her back to her husband when he grew tired of her.

He caught me staring at him and he smiled, a quiet, mysterious smile that made shivers run down my spine.

I felt Ella nudge me and the look in her eyes made

me quickly forget my thoughts about Mr. Waverly and my mother.

"Could I speak to you a moment?" she asked.

I glanced toward Jordan who was deep in conversation with Benjamin. The servants had just brought in dessert and there was a murmur of conversation about the table.

"Of course," I said, smiling at her. "What is it?"

"I don't want to discuss it here," she said, her eyes glancing toward her husband. "Perhaps later. Could you meet me somewhere?"

I thought of Jordan's concern and about his vow that he would not leave me alone for a moment. I frowned.

"Jordan and I are planning a walk along the beach after dinner. Perhaps you and Benjamin—"

"No," she said quickly. "No, I wouldn't wish to intrude on your time alone with Jordan. Might we excuse ourselves for a moment now? Step into the hallway?"

I looked around the table. There was no reason why we couldn't. I nodded.

"Will you excuse us for a moment?" Ella said. "There's something I want to show Shelley."

Jordan turned, catching my eye and frowning. I saw the glint of warning and concern there and I smiled, hoping to reassure him.

"We'll just be in the hallway," I said to him. "Only a moment." He nodded and I could feel his gaze upon me, following me from the room.

As soon as we were in the hallway, Ella pulled me to one side, away from the doorway where the servants moved in and out.

"I have a favor to ask," she said. "A very big favor."

"Of course," I said. I smiled at her, thinking it probably had something to do with our sewing, or my helping her with material or lace. "What is it?"

"I must see Andrew."

She winced when she saw the alarm that her comment had caused.

"Ella . . ." I began.

"Now listen," she begged. "Hear me out. There's no reason why he shouldn't be included in the invitations to the ball, is there?"

"Heavens, I don't know," I said, shrugging. "Mrs. Waverly knows how Jordan feels about him, doesn't she?"

"Yes," she said, frowning. "Unfortunately, everyone knows."

"Then, I don't see how—"

"You must convince Jordan to invite him," she said. "It's very important, Shelley. I must talk to him and this is the only way I can do it without arousing suspicion. I'm afraid to go to him, afraid that someone might tell Benjamin." I understood her fear. It was obvious that someone in the house reported my activities and I could only assume that they did the same with Ella.

"Ella, do you think this is wise?"

"No," she said. "It isn't wise. It doesn't make sense. But it's imperative. And please, Shelley . . . don't ask me anything about it. This is just something that I must do. As soon as I've spoken to Andrew, I'll explain everything. I promise."

Her words troubled me. I didn't like keeping secrets, especially from Jordan, not after our new fragile truce. But I understood her need, perhaps better than anyone. Sea Crest Hall was a breeding ground for secrets and I completely understood how she felt.

"All right," I said finally. "But I can't promise anything. Jordan is very firm about my having nothing to do with Andrew Benson. He practically hates the man for what he thinks he did to Mary Louise. I have no idea how I am to convince him to let bygones be bygones."

"You can do it," she said, her eyes brightening. "Please . . . for me . . . you must convince him. This might be the only chance I have for real happiness."

"Ella . . . ?" I began, feeling a pang of apprehension at her words.

"Please. Just try." she said. Before I could reply, she had turned and walked back toward the dining room, leaving me wondering what I had gotten myself into.

I had no idea how I was to convince Jordan to let Andrew Benson become a part of Sea Crest Hall's social life and the island's once again. No idea at all.

Chapter 26

I could not think of anything the rest of the evening except how I was to go about accomplishing the favor that Ella wanted. I suppose I was always of the opinion that it's best to plunge right in and not to put things off. I decided that our stroll along the beach would be the perfect time to ask Jordan.

I loved the ocean when it was the way it was that night. Calm and still, with the waves lapping gently against the sand. In the moonlight we could see the scurry of small fiddler crabs, racing in their silly patterns down to the water.

But I had to admit that as we walked hand in hand with the full moon beaming down upon us, I felt apprehensive. What would I do if my mentioning Andrew Benson made Jordan angry again, and made him withdraw from me the way he had before. Seeing him this way, with a smile on his lips and the frown of worry gone from his forehead, I thought I could not bear for him to distance himself from me again. He had become too precious for me ever to want to relinquish him again.

I hardly knew how I was to begin.

"Jordan, there's something I wanted to ask you."

"Anything," he said, his voice deep and quiet.

"I wonder if you would consider allowing Andrew Benson to come to the ball."

Jordan stopped dead still and turned to stare at me.

"Why?" His voice was immediately hard and suspicious, his jaw held tightly in place.

"He is a wonderful artist . . . I did see some of his work." Hearing his deep intake of breath, I continued hurriedly. "Now, Jordan," I said. "I'm trying to be completely honest with you—it is what you want, isn't it? That honesty we always shared as children?"

"Yes," he muttered finally. "Dammit, it is, but—"

"I've never seen anyone capture the beauty of the island the way he has, Jordan—never. He loves it here, you can see it in his work. I'd hoped we might even ask him to display some of his paintings in the ballroom. And . . ." I hesitated, finding myself short of breath because of my excitement and anxiety.

"And?" There was nothing on his face to indicate he might say yes. But somehow, now that the subject was between us, I had to continue. It was something we should have put an end to before now.

"And . . ." I tucked my arm into his, hugging him close and walking down the beach. "I'm convinced that Andrew did not encourage Mary Louise. You knew her, Jordan, perhaps even better than I did. And you know how flighty and willful she could be."

I felt his body tense, felt him hesitate beside me. But I continued walking, glancing up at him and seeing his face in shadows against the night sky. I didn't want to make him angry again. But I wanted him to admit it, wanted him to let go of all those memories of the past that he held so tightly. And I have to admit that I also wanted more than anything for him to tell me that it didn't matter now. That I was the one he loved and not Mary Louise.

But he said nothing.

"Jordan?"

"What do you want me to say, Shelley?" he asked, his teeth clenched tightly together.

I stopped, stepping away from him and looking up into his dark eyes.

"I want you to admit that Mary Louise was wrong in what she did. I want you to admit that Andrew was not completely responsible for her actions. And more than anything," I said, fighting the catch in my throat. "I want you to put the past where it belongs and let us start over."

"You're not asking much, are you?" he said, his voice hard and sarcastic.

"Is it too much?"

He sighed heavily and shook his head. His hands reached out for me, hauling me against him with a bit of his old impatience.

"Yes, damnit," he said. "It is too much."

I felt as if I might strangle on the sobs that rose in my throat. But I fought it as I fought the anger that whipped through me. I was so tired of being second to her, so tired of having to put my feelings on hold while Jordan came to grips with his first wife's death. I whirled around, intending to run away, for I simply could not face hearing him tell me that he could never love anyone the way he loved her.

"Shelley," he said, catching my arm. He turned me

around and I thought I heard him chuckle as I jerked my arm away from his hand. "You're as stubborn as ever."

"And you are as overbearing as ever," I snapped. "I won't humble myself because of this, Jordan. If that's what you expect from a wife, then perhaps you did choose badly."

"Shelley," he said with a heavy sigh. He shook me slightly and I heard a humorous grunt. "You have a bad habit of never forgetting anything that's said to you."

"That's right—I don't." I lifted my chin and stared into his glittering eyes.

"And sometimes you're so impatient that you don't listen properly."

"I'm listening now," I said.

His hand reached forward to stroke my cheek. It surprised me. The gentleness, the sweet erotic touch of his fingers made me catch my breath.

"What I intended to say before your temper threatened to make you run away was, yes it probably is too much to ask. I hated Andrew Benson for what he did to me."

I started to protest but he placed his hand over my mouth to stop the words. "Listen . . ." he said, grinning. I couldn't understand why he kept grinning at me as if I were a willful child. "I needed someone to blame— don't you see? I couldn't blame myself. And what kind of man would blame his poor dead wife for such pain . . . such agony? I couldn't. So I blamed Andrew."

"What you're saying—"

"What I'm saying is that even though it is too much to ask . . ." He stepped forward, cupping my face and reaching with one hand for my waist. He pulled me against him and his mouth touched my lips softly, teasingly until I found myself leaning against him, yearning, expecting more. "For you, it's nothing. A mere pittance of what you're worth."

I couldn't believe it. I stood staring at him, wondering if I had heard correctly, wondering if he really meant what I thought he meant.

"Do you mean it?" I whispered.

"Yes," he said, laughing. "I mean it."

I threw my arms around his neck, bouncing on my toes and spraying sand over his trousers and my skirt.

"Oh, Jordan! I love you! I love you so much."

He laughed and held me tightly, kissing me, nipping at my lips with his teeth until I squealed with delight and we stumbled in the sand.

"Careful," he said, laughing softly. "I don't want you to hurt yourself."

"You will ask your mother to invite Andrew then?"

"My mind tells me I should," he said slowly, as if he was still unsure of what he would actually do.

"You were always fair and honest, Jordan," I said, pleading with him. "It would mean a great deal to me knowing you're willing to put all that behind you."

He growled, but I could see the flicker of his smile in the moonlight.

"All right. I'll tell Mother to add his name to the guest list. I suppose the ball is a celebration of the island and its people. If his paintings are as good as you say they are, perhaps they should be a part of that celebration. What better time to put the past behind us than this?"

"They *are* good—you'll see. Oh, thank you, Jordan," I whispered.

"Just don't make me regret this," he warned. His lips were so close, and his eyes held a glittering promise of all I'd longed to see there.

"I won't," I said, reaching up for his mouth. "I promise, you won't regret it. The Captain's Ball will be a night neither of us will ever forget."

How was I to know that those words would return to haunt me?

The next few days were spent in preparation for the ball. The house was filled with the scent of spices which had been added to cleaning solutions. Flowers in the gardens were marked for gathering at just the proper moment the day before the ball. Rooms were opened and aired, rooms that often stood empty for months. The whole house came alive in a way more beautiful than I'd ever expected. I loved the excitement and gaiety, and this new vision of the house was beginning to make me think I might even grow to love it too, in time.

Jordan, true to his word, was never far away from me. I would catch his eyes on me, warm and watchful, as I went about helping with the preparations for the party. Sometimes he would step out onto the long shaded porch in the afternoons. He would see me sewing with Ella and he would smile quietly, then stroll casually back into his study to continue his work.

"You're so lucky," Ella whispered one day.

Was I? I didn't dare agree, not even in a hopeful way for the future. I was so afraid that something would happen to spoil it. That some dark, evil thing would come and whisk it all away. When I had those thoughts, my heart would pound for a few moments, until gradually I could manage to focus my mind elsewhere.

On Monday of the week before the ball, I was feeling especially tired and ill. I suppose it was evident for anyone to see in my pale face and listless movements. That day, as Ella and I sat on the porch sewing, one of the maids came out to ask if either of us would like refreshments.

"Lemonade would be nice," Ella said.

"Nothing for me," I said. "I think I'm going up to my room to rest for a few moments."

"Oh, must you?" Ella said. I knew how much she liked my company and I hated to disappoint her, but I was feeling quite ill.

"I'm sorry," I murmured, standing up to go. I turned to the maid. "Would you have someone bring a pot of herbal tea up to my room? I think that might help." Normally I did not care for the strange tasting brew. But Mrs. Waverly had convinced me that it was the only thing that made her feel better during her own pregnancies.

"Yes ma'am, right away," answered the maid servant.

"And would you please tell my husband that I will be upstairs resting?"

"Yes ma'am."

Ella stood and walked with me across the porch. "I don't mean to be so selfish where you're concerned," she said with her arm around my waist. "But sometimes I feel as if you're the only friend I have on this island."

"You have Andrew," I said. I hesitated to say his name out loud in that house where even the walls seemed to have ears.

"How can I ever thank you for arranging for him to

come here Saturday? You have no idea how much it means to me."

"Yes," I said, "I think I do. And you don't have to thank me. I just hope you won't do anything to get yourself in jeopardy."

There was an odd look in her eyes. A secretive look that troubled me and made me hope I had not made a mistake by intervening. But that day I reminded myself of Ella's sweet nature. All I could do was hope that things turned out for the best—not only for her, but for the rest of the family as well.

In my room, I took off my clothes and slipped into a soft silky wrapper. By the time I had finished, Jillian was there, bringing in a tray containing a silver teapot and a plate of orange scones.

"Anything else, ma'am?" Jillian said. The young woman still was not herself, but I was feeling much too ill to try and appease her that day.

"No, Jillian, thank you. That will be all."

The tea was still very hot and although the taste was slightly bitter, I did find it soothing and comforting. I finished the cup quickly and ate a few bites of the scone, then I lay on the bed, snuggling down into the soft coverlet and closing my eyes.

I don't know how long I slept; it might not have been long. But when I woke, I felt more ill than I'd ever felt in my life. Perspiration beaded on my forehead and above my lip. My stomach felt twisted in knots with pain.

I gasped and slid my legs over the bed.

"Jordan . . ." I whispered. I could hardly force the words out because of the pain that shot through me.

The muscles in my stomach contracted painfully until I could barely stand. I was nauseated and dizzy with pain.

I clasped my hands to my stomach, suddenly afraid. "Oh, no," I murmured. I don't think I have ever felt such fear and anxiety as I felt that day. I knew something was terribly wrong and I knew that somehow I had to find someone to help me.

I dragged myself to the bell pull, feeling the nausea and dizziness clutching at me, pulling me down into a dark, bottomless pit. With each step, the pain was agony.

I remember reaching for the pull before darkness finally descended in a soft, muted roar, pulling me down, down into the spiraling depths.

Chapter 27

I remember hearing muffled voices around me, a quiet murmur of concern as I was lifted and carried to the bed. I remember a deep male voice, softly spoken curses, and hands that caressed and soothed.

"Jordan?" I asked, opening my eyes.

"I'm here," he said. "Shh . . . I'm right here. I won't leave you."

"What is it? What's wrong?" I cried out then, the agony of the cramps causing me to draw my legs up against my chest.

"Shelley . . . sweetheart." Jordan turned from the bed, shouting at those gathered in the room. "Mother, Ella—do something! Can't you do something for her? Has anyone been sent to bring the doctor? Her doctor—Dr. Chambers?"

"Yes," I heard his mother say in a quiet concerned voice. "But it will take a while. You know that, darling."

"Shelley, can you hear me?" I heard him ask. "Hold onto me, sweetheart."

I remember gripping his hand so tightly that I thought my fingers might break. "Don't . . . don't leave me," was all I could manage to whisper through teeth clenched in pain.

"I won't," he promised, brushing my hair from my face. "I won't leave you."

I closed my eyes, gritting my teeth and willing the pain to go away. I could hear them talking in the room, talking about me.

"She's strong, Jordan . . . she's young." Whose voice was it? I couldn't be sure.

"She was drinking this tea," someone else murmured. I heard the clink of a china cup and the opening of a drawer. Still I kept my eyes tightly closed, feeling that if I opened them, I might drift away on the pain and mist that seemed to hover in the room.

"What is this?"

"Cottonwood bark," I heard someone whisper.

Cottonwood? What were they talking about? Something in the tea? I didn't remember ever drinking it before.

"Oh, dear heavens," I heard Mrs. Waverly say.

I opened my eyes then, forced them open, even though the dizziness was overwhelming. I looked toward her and saw that she held a small bag in her hand. She was staring at me as if she had seen a ghost.

"What have you done?" she whispered. "My God, what on earth have you done? Where did you get this concoction and how much of it did you take?" She walked to the bed, dangling a small dirty looking bag before my eyes. "Answer me," she demanded, her eyes glittering with anger. "Tell me how much you took."

I looked at Jordan, saw the puzzlement in his eyes, and the anger.

"What is it?" he asked.

"It's one of those herbal concoctions, something from the swampland," she said, still holding the bag as if it were a poisonous snake. "Something that poor women have taken for centuries, no doubt . . ." She stopped as if hesitant to say any more.

"For what Mother?" he asked, his voice as cold as the winter ocean. "What are you trying to say?"

"For heaven's sake, Jordan—to relieve a woman of the burden of too many children, that's what," she said, her voice a hushed, embarrassed whisper in the quiet room.

"No . . ." My whispered denial was lost in the murmurs, in the look I saw in Jordan's eyes. I felt the pain sweeping over me again, harder and stronger than ever. And I felt his hand slip away from mine, saw his lips part in disbelief, his eyes cloud over with disappointment and pain. He stared into my eyes, as if he sought some kind of truth there. But I was gasping from pain now and as I squeezed my eyes shut, I felt tears trailing down my face.

"It's not true," I whispered. "Jordan, you must believe me . . . it's not true . . ." He didn't answer, but simply turned and left the room.

"Call Aunt Rosa from the kitchen," Mrs. Waverly said sharply. "Tell her to bring extra sheets and hot water. Tell her to hurry."

I knew I was losing the baby. By the time Doctor Chambers arrived, more than an hour later, it had already happened. The beds had been changed, and I had been bathed and dressed in a clean white gown. I lay very still in the bed, alone in the room except for Jillian who sat in a chair and watched me as if I were someone who needed to be guarded. Neither of us spoke.

As soon as the doctor stepped into the room, I began to cry. I didn't see a doctor so much as a familiar face, someone who knew me and trusted me and would believe without a doubt whatever I told him. His look was sympathetic, and filled with kindness and understanding.

He looked at Jillian. "Leave us alone please, miss," he said.

First he pulled a chair to the bed and sat down, taking my hand in his.

"Not a good day for you, my dear," he murmured.

"No," I managed weakly, shaking my head from side to side.

"I'm sorry I couldn't be here when you needed me, although I'm almost positive I could have done nothing to prevent your losing the child. I spoke with Aunt Rosa and Mrs. Waverly."

"What did they tell you?"

"Well . . ." he said, his eyes troubled and speculative. "They seem to think you took one of the swamplady's herbal remedies. That you wanted to be rid of the baby."

"No," I cried. "No, it's not true. I drank some tea . . . just plain herbal tea from the kitchen. Mrs. Waverly seemed to think it was harmless, or I never . . . Oh, Doctor Chambers, I never would have—"

"Shh, child . . . don't upset yourself. There is nothing in herbal tea to harm an expectant mother. No, no, the dosage of whatever you ingested would have to be very large indeed. It could have been added to the tea, though, as it has much the same flavor."

I don't think I ever felt such horror as at that moment. All along I had thought it was my fault, that I shouldn't have had the herbal tea. But if what he was saying were true, then someone else would have had to put the stronger herbs in my tea. Someone who didn't want me to have a child, perhaps even wanted me to die in the process. I began to cry then. I felt so alone, so empty. All I wanted was Jordan and the comfort of his arms.

But I'd seen his eyes before he left the room, the quiet accusation, the disbelief. How could he ever forgive me if he thought I did this to myself and to his child?

Before Doctor Chambers left he gave me something to ease the dull pain and to help me sleep. But I would not take it until I spoke with Jordan.

When he came in I wanted to remain calm. I tried. But I couldn't control the trembling of my fingers when Jordan sat beside the bed and looked at me with such puzzled concern. I reached out and placed my hand in his and I could feel his need to pull away.

"Jordan," I whispered. "I had nothing to do with this. You must believe me. You know me . . . you know I could never—"

"I know that," he said, leaning toward me. His dark eyes were so expressive, so troubled. I felt his hand tighten against my fingers. "I do believe you. Forgive me if sometimes . . ." he sighed heavily as if he too were having a problem controlling his emotions. ". . . if sometimes I seem disapproving and distant. I didn't used to be that way."

"I know," I said, reaching up to touch his face. "I understand. So many things have happened. You've been hurt so badly—"

"I've been hurt?" he blurted out, clutching my hand and bringing it to his lips. "What about you, Shelley? I should have thought about you first. But I let the past and my bitterness send me away when you needed me most. I don't know if I can ever forgive myself for that."

I stared at him, seeing the tears in his eyes and unable to believe his words. I lifted my arms to him and he gathered me close against him, rocking me and crooning soft words as both of us let the emotions we were feeling have free reign over us.

"I've disappointed you . . ."

"No," he said, swearing. "Don't ever say that. You are not to blame, and nothing you could ever do would disappoint me."

"I'm sorry," I murmured against his shirt. "I'm so sorry."

"So am I, love," he replied, placing soft kisses against my brow and my hair. "So am I. It was too soon . . . it was just too soon." He pulled away and smoothed the tears from my face. "I want to have you to myself for a while now. I want us to become reacquainted, the way we should have in the beginning. We'll go away. As soon as you're feeling better, we'll take a long cruise. The ocean breeze, and the sun—it will be a wonderful place to begin again. Would you like that?"

"Oh, yes," I whispered. "I'd love it."

"Then it's settled. Now," he said, kissing my hand again. "I want you to get some rest. Everything is going to be all right."

"Jordan," I said as he stood up to leave. "What about the mixture that was in the bag? Someone did this deliberately. The same person who's been trying to frighten me away has taken our child from us."

"I know," he said. I could see the slow clenching of his jaw, the hard look in his shadowed eyes. "And I swear to you, I'm going to find out who's responsible for this. No one is ever going to hurt you or frighten you again. Not as long as there is a breath left in me. Can you trust me to do that?"

"Yes," I said, feeling safe and secure . . . feeling loved.

He handed me the medicine that Doctor Chambers had left. "Sleep," he said. "I'll be back soon."

When he opened the door to the sitting room I saw Jillian just on the other side. She stepped quietly into my room, her gaze immediately falling on me. The curtains had been drawn and in the dim shadowy room I think she thought I was sleeping. Her look was unguarded and as I saw her eyes, I gasped, and the feeling of well-being was immediately swept away from me.

There was hatred in those eyes—resentment and hatred, even a small glimmer of triumph.

And I knew she was the one.

"Jillian, please go find Ella. I'd like her to stay with me." I couldn't accuse her—not yet. Not while I lay helpless and drugged.

She stood for a moment staring at me, as if she might refuse. I felt my heart skip a beat, felt the laudanum I'd taken beginning to take effect. How could I defend myself if I had to? Finally she turned and left.

I willed myself to stay awake until Ella came. I could not go to sleep now, not suspecting what I did about Jillian. Thoughts whirled and jumbled through my head. I began to doubt my own mind. Why would she do such a thing? Why?

Ella came in moments later. She hurried to the bed, her brow furrowed with worry.

"Darling . . . what is it?" She placed a cool hand on my forehead. "Are you feeling ill again?"

I took her hand, glancing toward the door where Jillian stood watching us. "Stay with me, Ella," I said, fighting the overpowering drowsiness. "Promise . . . you will stay . . . till Jordan returns."

"Of course I will," I heard her say from a great distance.

There was such pleasure in her voice, a strange gratitude that I remember wondering at just before I fell into a deep, dreamless sleep.

Chapter 28

When I woke later that evening, I turned my head and saw Jordan sitting beside the bed. He smiled and leaned forward, touching my face and pushing my hair away.

The house was quiet and here in my room there was only the ticking of a small clock on the mantle to fill the silence. I was so sleepy, so incredibly sleepy. And even though I wanted to tell him about Jillian, I found myself drifting back off to sleep against my will.

I woke several times during the night and always Jordan was there, his hand quick to soothe, his voice soft and comforting in the long, still night. Sometime near morning I woke again and saw his dark head against the bed near my shoulder, his fingers touching mine while he slept.

I touched his hair and he stirred.

"Shelley . . . ?" he murmured, coming awake quickly and looking into my eyes.

"I'm fine," I said. "I feel much better this morning."

"Good." I could actually see him relaxing then and as he shrugged his shoulders, I thought how incredibly tired he must be, after sitting here beside me all night. I couldn't remember anyone ever being so attentive, or doing such a personal thing for me, not even my father.

My father. How would I tell him that I'd lost the baby? He had seemed buoyed by the news and now as I thought of it, I wished that I had not been so hasty in telling him. His health was not good and I was afraid that this might cause him to decline even further.

"What is it?" Jordan asked. "What are you thinking about?"

"Oh . . . about my father. About how disappointed he is going to be."

"He knew?"

"Yes . . . the day I first saw Doctor Chambers, I went to see my father as well."

"Yes, I remember."

"But there's something I need to tell you Jordan," I said, glancing toward the door and wondering where Jillian was. "Something I wanted to tell you last night."

"You can tell me anything," he said, taking my hand. "Don't you know that by now?"

"It's just a feeling . . . a very disturbing feeling I had when I saw Jillian last night."

"Jillian?"

"I think it was her, Jordan. I think she was the one who brought the herbs to my room and who placed them in my tea."

A cold glitter appeared in his black eyes, the coldest I'd ever seen. And for a moment I wondered if I should have told him at all. Perhaps I could have handled it myself, sent Jillian away forever. But I'd agreed that there would be no more secrets between Jordan and me.

Besides, if Jillian was capable of doing such a heinous thing, how was I to know what else she might do?

"I know it sounds ridiculous and I know I have no proof, no reason even . . ."

"There might be more reason than you think," he said thoughtfully. I had no idea what he meant by his comment.

He stood up and walked toward the windows, gazing out as if he were thinking about something.

"I can't believe it . . ." he began.

"You can't believe that she would do such a thing?" I wondered why this seemed to bother him so much. He hardly knew Jillian.

"No . . . nothing," he said, turning back to me. "I'll take care of this no matter what it takes. And no one is going to stop me from resolving it." His smile was reassuring, but still tense and angry and I knew he was only trying to put me at ease. Yet I couldn't explain the terror I felt at what he might be facing—the terror both of us faced.

"Do you feel like eating breakfast?" he asked, trying, I knew, to make everything appear as normal as possible.

"Yes . . . something light perhaps. Doctor Chambers said I could get up today if I felt well enough."

"Do you?" There was such tenderness in his eyes, such a look of protectiveness. It made me feel warm . . . loved even, though I knew I should not assume anything where Jordan was concerned. He bent to place a light kiss on my lips. "I'll have Ella stay with you while I change. We'll have breakfast together in the sitting room if you feel up to it."

"Yes, I do."

239

He rang the bell and waited until one of the maids stepped into the room. I wondered where Jillian was. I even wondered if she had run away and if we would ever know for certain what she'd done and why. Jordan did not leave until Ella came into the room.

I didn't tell Ella about my suspicions of Jillian. She was so sweet and attentive, and she talked mostly about our sewing and about the forthcoming ball. I knew she was trying to cheer me and keep me from thinking about what had happened. Not once did she ask about the herbs that had been found in my room. And I thought if anyone understood how I felt, it would be Ella, although I wondered if her despair at never conceiving a child could compare with mine at losing one. Still, I welcomed her kindness and her sympathy.

"I'm certain the doctor won't allow you to attend the ball," she said, glancing at me with those soft gray eyes.

"Oh," I said. "That's the last possible thing I'm concerned with right now."

"I know," she said. "I'm sorry."

"It's all right," I said, clamping my lips together to keep them from trembling. "Everything will be all right. I even think Jordan and I . . ." I stopped, reluctant even to express such a hope to Ella.

But she seemed to know my thoughts. She only smiled and nodded.

When Jordan came back for breakfast, Ella and I were waiting in the sitting room. When he walked over and took my hand, then sat beside me, Ella murmured a quiet excuse and left the room.

I felt very close to him that day. Closer than I had since before his marriage to Mary Louise. Neither of us spoke about the baby we had lost, except when he spoke about my recovery and the trip we would take together.

"Have you seen Jillian? What's to be done about her, Jordan?"

"No, I haven't seen her, although I understand she's still here. I don't think she has any idea of what you suspect. And that's the way I'd like to keep it for a while. But if you think it will be too difficult, I'll ask that she be assigned somewhere else."

"But why? Why can't you just confront her? Ask her point blank if—"

"Because I think someone else is involved, and in order for me to prove who that someone is, I need Jillian to continue thinking that she's safe."

Someone else? Someone here in this house? Not Ella, I thought, wishing the odd notion had never popped into my head. No, it couldn't possibly be Ella.

"All right," I said, taking a deep breath., "As long as I don't have to see her. I'm afraid I might kill her with my bare hands."

Jordan's eyes were hard and cold and I knew he understood exactly what I was feeling. For a moment, he held me in his arms, then we ate our breakfast, attempting to make the day seem as normal as possible. I was grateful to him for that

As the days passed, I grew much stronger. I felt restless and eager to leave my room. I suppose it was only old-fashioned standards that made everyone think I should remain inactive, but by Friday I had decided I would go outside and walk around the grounds. Jordan had a meeting that day with two gentlemen from the mainland and I could sense that he did not want me to go out alone.

"At least ask Ella to accompany you," he said, his eyes dark and concerned. "And promise me you won't leave sight of the house."

"I promise," I said, standing on tiptoe to kiss his lips. "Your mother says I must regain my strength slowly, so I won't venture far."

"See that you don't," he said, his voice teasing and warm.

Ella and I walked through the gardens at the back of the house. They were beautiful now and in full bloom. Several of the house servants were there with baskets, gathering flowers and greenery for the decorations. One of them handed each of us a rose as we walked by, a sweet gesture that brought smiles to both our faces.

We were talking and our steps seemed naturally to take us around toward the side of the house. Before I realized it we were near the cemetery. I remembered Jordan's words about the black wreath on Mary Louise's grave and now I glanced that way. Large trees blocked the view and I could not see clearly, but I knew that nothing remained now to mar the quiet beauty of her resting place. There beneath the hanging strands of moss, the ground was dark and rich, sprinkled with yellow marsh flowers and sprigs of grass.

As we approached, I suppose it was the flash of color that caught my eye at first. Then we were past the spot where the trees blocked our view and I stood very still, holding my breath as I recognized the person standing there.

"Jillian," I whispered.

She stood, head bent, hands clasped to her breasts as

if she were praying. She was at the foot of Mary Louise's grave and the sight of her there sent shivers of apprehension and anger coursing through me until I felt as if I had the energy of seven people.

"How dare she come here," I murmured. I felt my legs moving, felt the muscles tensing as I started toward her.

"Shelley," Ella said, reaching for my arm. "What on earth is wrong with you?" She clasped my sleeve but I shook her off.

I considered Jillian's presence vile and irreverent, to say the least. And as I saw her there, looking so demure, so innocent, actually having the nerve to come here to Mary Louise's grave, I wanted to kill her. I forgot what Jordan had said about keeping quiet until we found the other person.

"You should be praying," I said, my voice a low growl that I hardly recognized.

Jillian whirled and as she saw me coming at her, her eyes were wide and filled with fright. She made an attempt to appear calm, but I did not miss the trembling of her hands, or the way she took a small step away from me.

"Why . . . Mrs. Waverly, how nice to see you up and about. Hello," she said nodding to Ella. "It's a lovely day for a walk. Are you feeling better? I must say you look well and rested."

"Your concern doesn't fool me," I said. "I should kill you for what you did." I took another step toward her and I felt Ella grab my arm.

"Shelley!" she cried. "What on earth are you talking about? Why are you behaving this way?"

"Why don't you tell her, Jillian?" I said through

clenched teeth. "Why don't you tell her that you are the one responsible for my losing the baby?"

I heard Ella's gasp but I did not turn to look at her. I continued staring into Jillian's eyes, daring her to deny it. My hands were clenched so tightly that I could feel my nails digging into my flesh.

"I—I didn't—I swear it." I saw her glance quickly toward the house.

There was such an undeniable fear in her eyes that I turned, following her gaze just in time to see someone moving from one of the upper story windows. Someone had been watching us, someone who frightened Jillian, and I suspected it was the same person Jordan was looking for.

I took her arms then, shaking her until her hair fell about her lovely vacant face. Until her skin was ashen.

"How could you?" I screamed. "Damn you! How could you do such a thing?" I pushed her then and she stumbled backward, catching her foot on a small square marker. She fell hard on the ground and came up on her elbows, staring up at me as if I were some kind of sea monster, come to take her to the very depths of the dark, fathomless ocean.

I was trembling now and as I stared down at her, I felt my legs growing weak and felt perspiration on my brow. I pulled at the neck of my dress, determined not to give in to this weakness until I'd settled this with her once and for all.

"I didn't," she cried. "I swear. I only brought the herbs to your room to make it look as if they belonged to you, but I didn't put them in the tea. It wasn't my idea . . . I swear it."

"But you know who did," I said, standing over her

with my fists clenched. "Who? Tell me or I swear, I'll—"

Out of the corner of my eye I saw some of the servants moving from the garden. No doubt they had heard our voices and saw Jillian on the ground and now were coming to see what was happening. I even suspected that Jordan had sent one of the men to follow us, for when I turned he was very close.

"Stay back," I shouted. "All of you—go back to the house. This is none of your business." I suppose I was like a madwoman, standing there over the girl, fists raised, my face red and angered. But I didn't care. I don't think I have ever been so angry in all my life. I could feel the blood pounding in my ears and coursing through my body.

I turned just in time to see Jillian's eyes flicker toward Ella, then away.

"Tell me," I repeated.

"I can't say," she murmured, not meeting my eyes.

"Yes, you can, damn you," I said, reaching for her. "And you will."

"Shelley!"

I recognized Jordan's voice behind me and I took a long calming breath of air just as he reached me and put his arms around me.

"Stop this," he murmured against my ear. He pulled me away from Jillian and Ella. "Do you know what you're doing?"

I knew what he meant. I knew he thought I had spoiled our chances of proving who Jillian's companion was. But I didn't care. Once I saw Jillian, all the fury I felt toward her and that I'd pushed away before, came rushing back. I didn't care about anything except revenge and assuaging the pain she had caused.

"Yes," I said, hissing the word. "I know exactly what I'm doing. I want her out of here, Jordan. I want her out of my sight today—for good."

"Will you—" He lowered his voice, pulling me further away from the others. "For God's sake, will you for once do as I say?"

"Edgar," he shouted toward the servant who had followed us. "Please take my wife and Mrs. Waverly back to the house."

When I tried to pull away, Jordan gritted his teeth and whispered fiercely. "Dammit, Shelley. Let me handle this."

I think it was the look of horror on Ella's face that made me finally relent. That and the incredible weakness I felt in my arms and legs. She was looking at me as if I were some wild, demented person whom she didn't know.

But I wasn't, I wanted to shout. Anyone would feel the way I did. Wouldn't they?

As we walked to the house, Ella murmured and soothed, speaking to me in a quiet soft voice as if I were truly insane. I turned once to glance back at Jordan and when I saw him reach his hand down to help Jillian up from the ground, I stumbled and almost fell.

The vision of them there together sent alarm bells jangling in my brain. He should hate her. He should jerk her up from the ground and drag her away screaming for what she had done to us.

Yet his touch seemed gentle and as we went around toward the gardens, I saw them standing very close together, his dark head bent as he spoke to her. Jillian was looking up at him and I realized what caused the odd tingle that raced down my spine.

They looked not like enemies . . . but like lovers.

Chapter 29

Inside the dim coolness of the house, I felt Ella pull away from me. I was so distracted that I had hardly noticed her, and we had not spoken since we left the cemetery. All I could think about was Jordan and the way he and Jillian had stood so close together, so intimately. It brought back disturbing memories of that day at the fishing shack ... the day I thought I heard Jordan's laughter and a woman's voice.

How incredible. Was it possible that Jillian, the woman I'd trusted and befriended, the woman who attended me daily and knew everything about me, was that woman in the fishing shack? And that man my husband?

I glanced up then, realizing that Ella had stepped away from me. Then I saw Benjamin coming down the hall toward us.

"Ella," he murmured. "I need to speak to you for a moment, darling."

I watched them walk down the long hallway toward the front of the house. Ella turned once and glanced at me over her shoulder as if I might stop her from going.

My attention was immediately turned from Jordan and my maid. Ella had told me a good deal about Benjamin. How unreasonable he could be, how flirtatious he was, how inattentive to her. But for the life of me, until that moment I could not imagine why she avoided him so vehemently.

But suddenly I recognized the look in her eyes. She was afraid. Ella was terrified of Benjamin, her own husband.

I started down the hallway but they were already out of sight. I stopped one of the maids coming down the main stairway.

"Did Ella and Benjamin go upstairs?" I asked.

"No ma'am," she replied. "I didn't see 'em if they did."

"Thank you."

I hurried past the entry hall, turning toward the long north wing of the house. It was then I heard the murmur of voices coming from the study. As I approached the partially closed door, I could hear that they were arguing.

"We can't go on living this way," Benjamin was saying. "You're my wife, and by God I won't have it!"

"I'm afraid there's nothing you can do about it," Ella said. But even from the hallway I could hear the tremble in her voice.

"Oh, but you're mistaken," he said, his voice turning suddenly soft and treacherous. "There is something I can do. As a matter of fact, I've already done it."

"What?" she whispered, her voice breaking with anxiety. "What have you done?"

"I've had your clothes moved back into our old suite . . ."

"How could you? You know how I—"

"There will be no more closed doors between us, Ella. I mean it. You are my wife and you are going to start behaving like one."

I heard her muffled cry, heard the shuffle of feet as if they struggled together. Just as I started to fling open the door, ready to confront him, I heard Ella's voice again.

"You are my husband," she whispered, her voice raspy and breathless. "And I'm quite aware that you are strong enough to do as you please where I'm concerned. But I'm telling you, I won't be a part of this, Benjamin. I won't."

"Now is the time," he said. "There is nothing standing in our way now to prevent us from having the first child. By the time Shelley has recuperated, we could have an announcement of our own to make." His voice was as cold and calculated as if he spoke about the time of day or the weather.

My breath caught painfully in my throat and I felt the sting of tears at my eyes. I placed my fingers against my lips and leaned back against the wall, knowing I must not let them hear me.

I could not bear to think that Ella had betrayed me too.

"Dear God," I heard her whisper. "What have you done? If you had anything to do with—"

He laughed, a brittle, mocking sound in the stillness of the house.

"Darling, you always did tend to be a bit melodramatic. Of course I had nothing to do with it. How could I? Everyone knows it was Jillian, and so do you. I saw you and Shelley near the cemetery with her just a little while ago. The girl is obviously quite demented." His voice became muffled as if he'd turned and moved deeper into the room. "But I'd be a fool not to take advantage of the situation. My father's proposal is insane—all of us agree. But it's also legal and binding. There's nothing to change it except possibly his death, and by then, there could be several grandchildren to inherit. Do you realize how much money we're talking about, Ella? Enough to keep you and half the state of Georgia in those gorgeous gowns and expensive jewels you like so well for the next thousand years. Would you prefer poverty?" His voice was mocking and harsh.

"Yes," she cried. "Yes, I would prefer poverty to this. Sometimes, God help me, I even think I would prefer death to this farce of a life that I live."

"No, my darling, you are much too alive, much too vibrant for that. And you can change our life," he whispered. "With the snap of those pretty fingers, you can change it forever."

"Never," I heard her say. "I'll never do this willingly, Benjamin. I loved you once, when we were first married . . . but I don't love you now and I won't—"

He laughed then, a loud, raucous sound that echoed through the room and down the hall.

"Oh, my naive little love. You will do whatever I say."

I heard Ella's soft cry of protest, then her footsteps, moving quickly toward the door. I stepped back into the next room, leaving the door open just a crack. I saw her go past, then I saw Benjamin step out of the study. I could see the glitter in his eyes as he watched her, as he stroked his chin and seemed to be calculating what he would do next. For a moment I felt my knees growing weak, and I was afraid he would see me hiding behind the door.

I held my breath until I began to feel slightly dizzy. Finally he turned and went back into the study, slamming the door behind him.

Slowly I expelled the air from my lungs and leaned back against the wall to catch my breath. What was happening in this house? What had started this insanity and how was I ever to escape it?

I went back to my room, exhausted and troubled. How could I help Ella when I couldn't seem to help myself?

Moments later, Jordan came into my room. I was lying on the bed and I felt my heart skip a beat as he came toward me. His look was tender, apologetic even.

"Shelley," he said, sitting beside the bed and taking my hand. "Let me explain." He was talking about his behavior with Jillian—he knew I'd seen.

"Why do you feel the need to explain?" I asked, turning my head away.

"Listen to me," he whispered. He touched my chin, turning my face toward him again. "I've told Jillian she can stay here until after the ball."

"Why doesn't that surprise me?"

"I know how you feel. I—"

"Do you?" I sat up in bed, shaking away his hands when he reached for me. "Do you really? How can you possibly feel this deep sadness, this emptiness and regret for what I've lost."

"What we've both lost," he said, his eyes solemn and serious. "Do you think I don't feel it too?"

"Do you lie awake at night wondering if life will ever be the same . . . if the pain will ever go away?" I slid from the bed and walked to the window, willing myself not to cry.

I felt his arms around me, felt the warmth of his body as he pulled me back against him.

"I am sorry," he whispered against my hair. "More sorry than you will ever know. And a great deal of that sorrow is for you. I should never have brought you here to this house—"

"Don't," I said pulling away. I thought I couldn't bear for him to tell me one more time that he shouldn't have married me.

He wouldn't let me go, but pulled me back around so that I was facing him, and held tightly in his arms.

"I should have taken you someplace else to live," he said, gazing steadily into my eyes. "I knew the dangers here and I thought that I could protect you. But I was wrong, just as I was wrong about Mary Louise."

"Someplace else . . . ? Then you don't . . . you don't wish . . ." How could I put into words all the things I wanted to know?

"What? Do I wish I'd never married you? No, never," he whispered, his voice deep and husky. "Would I rather give up my home and the island than to see you hurt again? Yes, a million times over. Will I ever love you?"

The question seemed to hang in the air as I waited, breathless with wonder at what I saw in his beautiful eyes.

"I already do," he said, his lips very close to mine. "I already love you, Shelley. I adore you, and I think perhaps I always have. I was just too blind to see it."

"You . . . you . . . ?"

"I love you. All those times I tried to push you away, tried to convince myself that I didn't want love in my life. I was trying like hell to tell myself it wasn't love I was feeling for you. I actually thought I could control

252

everything . . . but I've learned where you're concerned, I can control nothing of what I feel." He smiled at me then. "You knew it," he said. "Didn't you? You were right that night when you came to my room and told me so boldly that you knew I wanted you."

"I . . . I hoped. But I was afraid that was all it was—your wanting a child. The nights were wonderful, but during the day you were so different, so distant and moody."

"I was a fool," he whispered. "But it was much more than that, love. Much more."

"Oh, Jordan."

I threw my arms around his neck, forgetting all the doubts, all the longings that had plagued me since our marriage. I even forgot Jillian and my suspicions about her and Jordan. All I could see were his eyes, tender and loving. All I could hear was his voice, so full of sincerity. This was the moment I'd waited for all my life.

As I clung to him, he scooped me up in his arms and carried me to a chair near the window, then sat down with me on his lap.

"There's something I need to explain to you," he said.

I sat very quietly, nestled against him, unable to look away from his expressive eyes, his sensuous mouth.

"I believe Jillian is only the pawn for someone else in this house."

When I started to protest, he smiled and placed his fingers against my lips. Then he continued, his eyes warning me to be quiet.

"She says she didn't realize how deadly the herbs were or what they were for, and I believe her. I think someone used her . . . After all, what would Jillian alone have to gain?"

"But Jordan . . . you're saying . . ." I stopped, holding my breath at the look in his eyes. The pain was deep and torturing to him, I could see that.

"Someone in this house, in my own family."

"Oh, no . . ." I gasped in horror, but I knew it was true. It had to be, just as he said. They were the ones to benefit if something happened to our child. But it was incredible, unbelievable to think that one of them would do such a heinous thing. I'd told myself, even then, that it must have been an accident, another attempt to frighten me away.

"Jillian has agreed to stay, and although she wouldn't come right out and say who this person is, she did agree to engage that person in conversation—hopefully a *revealing* conversation—at the ball. We've agreed on a time and place, so there will be witnesses."

"Oh, Jordan. I know how much you must hate doing this."

His eyes glittered dangerously.

"Do you think I would put any one of them above the life of my child . . . above your life?" His look was so fierce and determined that for a moment I felt a shudder race through me and I reached out for him, afraid and troubled.

I remembered the conversation I'd overheard in the study, and I hesitated, knowing how hurt Jordan would be. But I could not keep it from him.

While I related the story quickly, I saw the pain in his eyes deepen and turn stormy. But there was no surprise.

"You . . . you knew, didn't you?"

"I suspected Benjamin, yes. He is the obvious choice, isn't he?"

"Yes, or Ella I suppose, but—"

"He and Jillian were lovers at one time," he said.

"I should have known," I said slowly. "I should have realized from all the things Ella said about him." I looked into his eyes, feeling such elation. "Then it wasn't you—it wasn't you and Jillian."

There was a small impatient wrinkle at the corner of his mouth and he shook his head as if he didn't understand. "What are you talking about?"

"At the fishing shack, weeks ago. Oh, Jordan, it wasn't you."

"No," he whispered, pulling my head near for his kiss. "If you're asking if I was ever in the fishing shack with Jillian, the answer is a firm, unqualified no." His kiss was hungry, reflecting an impatience that was so familiar.

And convincing.

"Oh, Jordan—do you know what this means to me? Can you imagine how relieved I feel at this moment?"

"It means, my love, that after the ball, all this will be behind us. And you and I will take that cruise and start our marriage all over again . . . the right way, this time."

Chapter 30

I have always hated the ironies of life. I find sweet expectations that are blended together with an unknown cruel deception to be obscene and frightening.

I insisted on going to the ball, even though Mrs. Waverly was adamantly against it. I could certainly not stay away now, not after what Jordan had told me. I wanted to be there. I wanted to see Benjamin's face when he was found out and when he had to admit his part in what had happened to me.

I dressed carefully that evening, wanting to look my best, not only for Jordan, but to prove a point to his mother. Besides, my father would be there, and I wanted him to see me that way too. Perhaps it would lessen the sting of hearing that there was not to be a grandchild.

Jordan, although he now slept with me in my bed, had gone to his room to dress. When he came out I had just stepped into the sitting area and we stood for a moment, staring at one another across the room.

I heard his quiet murmur of approval, and we both

moved together into the center of the room. He held me away and turned me around slowly.

My ballgown was made of Bandekyn, a fabric of silk and gold thread. It shimmered and changed colors beneath the lights and the full skirt swished with every movement. The skirt was caught up in the back to form a slight bustle, falling in rows and rows of ruffles to a short train that swept the floor. I thought it was the most beautiful creation I'd ever seen.

"You are exquisite ... stunning," he said between kisses.

I laughed and clung to him, noting the cut of his evening jacket, the way the black material emphasized his strong shoulders and narrow waist. He was the most beautiful man I'd ever seen and my heart still caught in my throat when I looked at him. It was almost frightening to think that he was mine, that he actually loved me. As I looked into his black eyes that night, I thought of those ironies of life and how deceiving a happy moment can actually be, and I shuddered.

"What's wrong?" he said. "You're trembling."

"Nothing ... nothing. It's just that I'm so happy and I feel so lucky," I evaded.

"I'm the lucky one," he said.

We went down the hallway and the stairs, arm in arm, laughing and talking the way we had always been able to. We *were* lucky, I decided. I had everything I'd ever wanted. We were going to build a life together and there would be children—the sons Jordan had always wanted. Nothing was going to spoil it for us this time— not the evening, not even the possibility of Benjamin's confession.

"When is Jillian to meet your brother?" I whispered just before we walked into the brightly-lit ballroom.

"At midnight near the cemetery, when the orchestra begins to play the last dance."

I shivered again, pulling slightly away from Jordan so he wouldn't notice. I knew how difficult this night was going to be for him and I didn't want him worrying about me as well.

The room was already crowded when we arrived. I had not seen Ella since yesterday. She had not come down to dinner the night before and I was worried about her. But seeing her now, I was relieved. She looked radiant, more beautiful than I'd ever seen her. She wore a rose-colored silk dress that brought out the natural blush in her cheeks and lips. Her dark hair glimmered beneath the lights and was sprinkled with small pink roses.

"You look beautiful," I said, coming to take her arm. She was standing near Mr. and Mrs. Waverly, greeting guests, but her husband was nowhere in sight.

"Oh, Shelley," she whispered, her voice soft and filled with awe. "No other dress could ever suit you better. The gold . . . the colors . . . don't you think so, Mother Waverly?" she asked, turning to Jordan's mother.

"She is indeed a vision," she said. "As are you, Ella." And for once I think she actually meant it. "I must admit you look quite well, Shelley. But remember your promise—no dancing tonight."

"I'll remember," I said, although I had every intention of dancing one dance with my husband before the evening was over.

I met Mr. Waverly's eyes. They were soft and filled with a look, some long-lost sweet remembrance. I smiled at him and for the first time I thought my father must be wrong. This man couldn't possibly have done such cruel things to my mother.

I took his hand and whispered to him. "I hope you will keep me company while the others dance."

"I would be honored," he said.

His eyes sparkled. When he smiled that way he looked so much like Jordan. I found that I genuinely wanted to get to know him better.

We saw Andrew Benson enter the hallway and move toward the room where we stood. I could feel Jordan stiffen beside me and I tightened my grip on his arm and looked up into his face.

His smile was one-sided, rather wry, and when I looked into his eyes I knew he was trying desperately to get over his resentment of this man. I intended to help him do it if I could.

I glanced toward Ella and saw the deepening flush on her face, the way her eyes darted anxiously around the room, then back again to Andrew. As he approached, his eyes hardly left her face. His look of love and concern moved me and I found myself wondering what on earth the two of them were to do about this powerful emotion that was between them—especially after Benjamin's ultimatum to his wife.

Mrs. Waverly was amazing. In her black lace dress and with her regal bearing, she seemed to will herself to project grace and a quiet dignity as she greeted Andrew. One would think nothing unpleasant had ever transpired between the Waverlys and the mysterious artist.

"Mr. Benson," she murmured. "We're so happy you could come. As you will see, the paintings you sent are displayed at various intervals around the room. We've already had a great deal of comment and I believe after tonight you will find yourself with more commissions than you can possibly fill."

"Thank you," he said with a modest dip of his head. He allowed his eyes to linger only a moment on Ella as he glanced around at all of us. He stepped forward then, gazing directly into Jordan's eyes.

"Jordan . . ." he said, extending his hand.

There was complete silence around us. Even the sound of music seemed muted and far away as we all waited awkwardly for Jordan's reaction.

"My wife was right," Jordan said, taking Andrew's hand. "Your paintings are excellent—a celebration of our island, I believe she said. Glad you could come tonight."

I think we all breathed quiet sighs of relief.

It was a splendid evening, even though I'm sure both Jordan and I dreaded what was to come at midnight. I wondered what he would do if Benjamin actually confessed to having a part in poisoning the herbs in my tea. I didn't even want to think about it.

I don't think anyone had any idea about Ella and Andrew. He asked her to dance and from time to time I would see them standing together, engaged in quiet serious conversation. Ella's hands fluttered as she stood looking up at him and once I saw him lean forward and touch her. I wondered where Benjamin was all this time and why he had not come to claim his own wife for a dance.

He finally appeared near supper time, just as everyone was standing in line at the buffet tables near the end of the long ballroom. He went directly to Ella and took her arm, pulling her to him. She almost cringed away from him and her eyes darted toward Andrew.

I have never seen such a look of quiet desperation as was on Andrew's face. He stood for a moment, his eyes quiet and pained as he watched Ella and her possessive husband. I knew how it must hurt him. I touched Jordan's arm, as he stood talking to some of his old friends from the mainland.

"I'll be right back," I said.

His eyes radiated concern and I knew he did not really want me out of his sight.

"I'll just be over there. I want to speak to Andrew."

He nodded and his gaze followed me before he finally looked away and went back to his conversation.

"Andrew," I said. "Are you enjoying the evening? I'm so glad you came."

He breathed a heavy sigh and there was still that look of pain and desperation in his eyes as he glanced toward Ella.

"She'll be all right," I murmured. "Ella is stronger than I ever would have believed," I added, remembering her conversation with Benjamin and her resolve.

"How . . . how did you—"

"How did I know about the two of you?" I smiled at his frown and the way he glanced around to make sure no one heard me.

"It's all right," I said. "No one knows except me."

"Did Ella tell you?"

"Do you remember that day I came to you about the journal? The day I felt ill and you went to bring me something to drink?"

He nodded.

261

"I looked through your sketch book. As soon as I saw your drawing of Ella, I knew."

"God," he murmured, shaking his head and looking down at the floor. He seemed so lost, so different than he usually was. "I have no idea what I'm to do. As long as I didn't see her, as long as we couldn't speak, couldn't touch . . ." I saw his eyes searching for her. "But this— what I thought would be such joy—this is torture."

"I know," I whispered. "I'm so sorry that it has to be this way. For both of you."

"It doesn't have to be," he said, suddenly snapping to his old confident self. "I wanted to take her away from here. You might as well know—it's why I came tonight."

I couldn't help gasping with surprise. So that was why Ella was so desperate for me to invite Andrew. She was actually thinking of leaving Benjamin and Sea Crest Hall for good.

"Oh, Andrew . . ."

"But something is wrong. She's afraid. She says she has changed her mind."

I frowned and followed his gaze to Ella where she stood quietly beside Benjamin. She glanced our way once, then her eyelids lowered and she looked away.

I knew why she was afraid. I'd heard Benjamin and his ugly threats and I knew exactly what he had in mind for her. And now my heart skittered as I wondered if he had already accomplished his goal. Had Ella slept with him last night? Was that why she did not come to supper, because she was too ashamed to face me? And now, she was too ashamed to face Andrew, the man she truly loved.

"I'll speak to her," I murmured. I touched his arm and turned to walk back to Jordan. "I promise you, Andrew, I'll talk to her later tonight and find out what's wrong."

The meal was light and delicious, complete with Sea Crest's famous she-crab and cold tomato soups. There was also wild duck, succulent ham, and a variety of seafood, along with candied fruits and ices, not to mention Mrs. Waverly's favorite imported champagne.

But I found that my appetite had vanished, probably because I couldn't stop thinking about Ella and how horrible she must be feeling. Andrew was here; the man she loved had come to rescue her, and now something had happened to make her feel that she could not follow through. What was it? Did it have anything to do with our suspicions about Benjamin? Did she suspect him too?

But that was not my only worry. My father had not appeared and as the evening wore on, I began to wonder if something had happened or if he was sick. The thought of him in that small house, alone and sick, was troubling, to say the least.

"What's wrong?" I heard Jordan say beside me. "You've hardly touched your food and your eyes haven't left the doorway since we sat down to supper."

"I'm worried about Papa," I said. I turned to smile at my husband, my handsome, caring husband whom I adored, without whom I simply could not live.

"I'll send someone to look for him," Jordan said immediately.

"Oh, Jordan . . . would you?"

"Of course I would," he said, smiling and shaking his head. There was such tenderness in his eyes. I don't think I shall ever forget his tenderness that night. "Don't you know I would do anything for you?"

He bent to place a quick kiss on my lips and I heard his mother's disapproving noise, a discreet cough. But Jordan only smiled at her.

"Finish your meal," I said. "You don't have to go now. If he hasn't appeared by the time supper is over . . ."

"It's not that late," he said, smiling indulgently. "It won't hurt to give him fifteen more minutes."

We had just finished eating when I felt Jordan's hand at my elbow.

"Sweetheart . . ." he said, nodding toward the open doorway.

I saw my father then, dressed splendidly in his old captain's uniform. He walked slowly into the ballroom, his tall frame gaunt and thin.

"Oh, Jordan," I whispered. "Isn't he magnificent?"

"He is indeed, love," Jordan replied. "Shall we go say hello?"

The orchestra started playing again, a plaintive old folk song, one I'd heard my mother sing when I was very small. Several people came to speak to my father. He was, after all, a legend on our small island and still well respected. Seeing him in his uniform made me so proud. It reminded me of how he was when I was a girl, and I suppose I simply forgot for a moment all his harsh words about the Waverly family and how he would have his revenge.

As we grew nearer he saw me and smiled. I reached out my hand to him.

"Dance with me, Papa," I said as I touched his arm.

His smile was wistful and sweet, filled with pride as he saw his only daughter dressed in the most elegant gown in the room. He took my hand and together we began to dance toward the center of the huge room.

Slowly the dancers parted and stood away from us, smiling and nodding as my father led me around the floor. His steps were slow and sometimes faltering, but I thought that besides Jordan, he was the most handsome, the most elegant man at the Captain's Ball.

When the dance ended, I hugged him. I could hear the applause of the other dancers and the observers around the room. It was the highlight of the evening, and I don't think I have ever been as happy as I was that night.

Chapter 31

We left the dance floor and I walked to where Jordan stood watching us with his mother and father. My father stopped and I could sense his reluctance to be in their company.

"You still cut quite a dashing figure, Captain Demorest," Mrs. Waverly said. "And you, young lady, you promised you would take care."

I frowned at her, not wanting my father to hear about the baby this way. I wanted to tell him in as gentle a way as possible, certainly not standing here in front of the people he despised.

Earlier we had begun to hear thunder rumbling in the distance, far out over the ocean I hoped and away from us. But now as we stood making polite conversation, I noticed the delicate silky curtains at the long open windows blowing in the wind. The smell of salt and a hint of moisture drifted into the room on the night air.

I glanced at Jordan just as the large grandfather clock near the door began to strike midnight. There was a pause in the music before the last dance and now the striking clock and the distant thunder cast an ominous sound into the glittering room.

The orchestra began to play, softly at first, then louder and more forcefully. Jordan took my hand, pulling me out toward the dance floor.

"I believe I have the promise of this dance," he said, smiling down at me. "With the most beautiful woman in the room."

"And I with the most handsome gentleman," I answered, laughing up at him.

To see us, no one would have dreamed what was on our minds and in our hearts. We looked like nothing more than a loving young couple dancing the last waltz of the evening. But as soon as we were away from his parents and my father, I saw Jordan glance around toward the open doorway that led through the garden and beyond it to the cemetery.

In the last few moments, neither of us had seen Benjamin, although Ella and Andrew were dancing near us. Jordan moved me that way and leaned over to them.

"Ella, are you ready?"

I was surprised that Ella was involved in this, that she even knew about Jordan's intention of setting a trap for his brother. But when she replied, I understood.

"I have no idea what this is about, Jordan." She looked at me as if for an answer and I remained silent. "But if you say it is important, then yes . . . I'll go with you to the cemetery."

Without another word, she took Andrew's hand and started through the crowd of dancers toward the open french doors. A few moments later, Jordan began leading me that way as well.

The gardens were well lit by lanterns that swayed

now in the stiffening breeze. But out past the gardens, underneath the huge moss draped live oaks, it was dark and quiet. The flicker of intermittent lightning illuminated the small white tombstones and cast an eerie spell over us all.

No one said a word as we made our way through the gardens, past laughing couples and strolling partners. When we moved past the last string of glowing lanterns and out into the grassy lawn, I shivered and moved closer to Jordan. With a motion of his hand, we began to angle away from the cemetery so that we might enter it from the back, behind the stand of trees.

The impending storm had quieted the tree frogs and night birds. Even the marsh to the west, usually alive with sounds, seemed eerily still and silent.

Jordan took my hand, leaning low and pulling me beneath the moss that dripped from the tree limbs. Even from this distance we could see the glimmer of white in the murky darkness and the dim outline of two people standing near the ghostly tombstones. We stopped, just near enough to hear what was being said. In the darkness we could not see to whom Jillian spoke, only that it was a man.

"Who's there?" The man's voice echoed across the ground toward us.

The four of us beneath the trees froze behind, hoping he had not actually seen us. I felt Ella's hand grab mine and squeeze tightly. She had recognized the voice just as I had.

It *was* Benjamin, just as Jordan suspected and feared.

"It's nothing," Jillian said. "Just some night creature seeking shelter from the storm."

"What do you want, Jillian? And why in God's name did it have to be here in this place?"

"You know what I want, Benjamin." I was surprised at the girl's calmness.

"I've told you—all that was a mistake. Things have changed now. My wife and I are back together. Any expectations you might have had——"

I could feel Ella's hand gripping mine. How horrible for her that Andrew must hear this.

"Expectations?" Jillian cried. "It was a promise. You promised me, Ben. You promised that we'd go away as soon as—as things were taken care of. I've done everything you asked. I even put the wreath on the grave and talked about it to the other servants the way you said."

"My dear girl," he said, his voice a growl. "I have no idea what you're talking about."

"You liar!" she said, her voice rising with the keening sound of the wind. "You lied to me. You said if we frightened her away, we could leave here together, that you and I would have the first child and when we came back your father would have to accept it whether he liked it or not. It wasn't my idea to scare Shelley away, and I sure didn't mean for anything to happen to her baby. You said to do it, Benjamin, and you can't deny it."

We could hear his laughter, soft and menacing through the darkness. Lightning flashed just above us and the thunder rumbled behind it. I could feel my heart pounding and I knew we should not be here beneath the towering trees in the approaching storm.

"A man says a lot of things in the throes of passion, my dear. You should know that by now." He laughed again and I saw Jillian lunge at him.

"Damn you!" she shouted. "You're a devil—a devil!" She was fairly breathless with rage and frustration. "I don't know how poor little Miss Ella stood you this long!"

He caught her hands and we could see them struggling as the wind buffeted Jillian's dress and her hair. In the flickering lightning I glanced at Jordan. He turned and shook his head and I could see the fury in the glitter of his eyes. He turned his gaze back toward the two people beneath the trees and muttered beneath his breath.

"Say it, Jillian. Damn it, just say it," Jordan whispered.

We could hear Jillian's soft cries as Benjamin subdued her and held her arms behind her back.

"It would be best if you leave here, Jillian . . . under the circumstances," Benjamin said. "Or you could end up just like poor Mary Louise."

I was touching Jordan's arm and I felt his muscles tensing as if he would spring up and throw himself at his brother. I held on tightly, knowing this was no confession.

"Wait," I whispered.

"But it was suicide—you told me that yourself. My God, you . . . *you* didn't kill her?" Jillian asked, her voice soft and filled with a horrified disbelief.

"Hell, no," Benjamin said. "The wretched creature killed herself as far as I know. She played right into my hands and I didn't have to do a thing. But this one is different. I knew I'd have to intervene. I do thank you for that, love."

I could feel Jordan leaning forward, straining to hear every word. It was getting harder to hear Benjamin's

270

deep voice with the roaring wind in the trees and the rumble of thunder coming nearer and nearer.

"How can you thank me for something like that? Why didn't you tell me what was going to happen? I'd never want to harm an innocent child—never! You betrayed me, you bastard, just the way you betrayed your poor wife. And I hate you for that. I'll hate you forever," Jillian spat at him.

Benjamin laughed. I was amazed at his heartlessness, at his cold cruelty. Nothing seemed to bother him. Nothing seemed to touch his conscience.

"For God's sake, Jillian, don't be so naive. You knew perfectly well what you were doing, so don't play the innocent with me. I'll admit my part in the deed—I meant to get rid of the little whelp and I did it for the money. And so did you, by God. So did you."

I heard Jordan's growl, felt his muscles rippling beneath his jacket as he sprang forward from a low crouch. Ella was crying softly behind me. But I couldn't be concerned with anyone else now. I was worried only about my husband, the man I loved more than life. I knew the fury that was in him and I couldn't let him kill his only brother.

"No, Jordan," I cried, going after him.

"Let him go," Andrew growled, reaching for me. "Benjamin deserves it."

I jerked away from him and ran. The wind beat at me, whipping my dress about my legs, raking my hair from its pins. I could hardly see and the noise about us had become deafening.

I saw the motion of Benjamin turning, just as Jordan leapt across the ground and the impact of his body threw both of them into the dirt. There was a loud groan as the air left Benjamin's lungs and he hit the ground. Then the two of them were tangled together, fighting desperately. Jordan was like a madman and I could hear his voice rising against the furious wind.

"I'll kill you . . ."

"No, Jordan!" I screamed as I drew near and stood watching helplessly.

Jordan hit him again and again, the sounds of flesh on flesh sickening. In the distance we saw others running from the gardens as they realized something was happening beneath the trees.

It was Andrew who finally pulled Jordan off his brother. I knew Jordan's temper—I'd seen it often as a girl. But this fury in him left me weak and stunned. I'd never seen him like this before and all I could do was stand there watching, knowing I could not calm him. No one could.

He stood over Benjamin, his fists clenched, legs apart, and he taunted him. His anger was like a shield, as if he could not be defeated, as if he didn't care.

"Get up, damn you," he roared.

Benjamin rose a bit and his hand moved upward, waving toward Jordan as if to say he'd had enough, as if to say he had surrendered. Then he fell back exhausted against the ground.

Ella stepped forward then and took Jordan's arm. She was crying.

"That's enough, Jordan," she said, her voice soft and soothing. "Don't waste any more of your grief or your effort on him. He isn't worth having on your conscience for the rest of your life."

"She's right, man," Andrew said.

Lightning flashed above the house, illuminating it like

a giant candle. The thunder that followed was immediate and dangerous, a loud boom that shook the ground.

"Jordan," I said, going to him. "We must get back to the house. The storm——"

"You go," he said, waving me away. "Benjamin and I are not finished."

It had begun to rain, coming in fine, misty sheets that blew first one way and then another.

"Please, Jordan," I shouted above the rain.

It was then that I heard the sound, a loud pop, a sound like that of a Chinese firecracker swept away by the wind.

I saw Jordan clutch his chest and stagger backward and for a moment I couldn't understand what was happening. I just stood there, frozen ... trying to understand, even looking toward the sky to see if lightning had struck near us.

"Jordan!" I ran to him, catching him and steadying him so that he would not fall. He was a strong man, but I could feel the trembling of his body and his legs as he willed himself to remain standing.

I heard his soft surprised grunt of pain and for a moment I felt as if my world was ending.

I felt the warmth of blood on my hands and looked up into his dazed, stunned eyes. Then I turned to see a man coming out of the misty rain, the silhouette of a pistol pointing downward in his hand.

It was like my nightmare ... just like the vision of the man in my dreams, emerging from the mists in a steady, deadly march toward us.

Chapter 32

The storm raged and the rain began to fall harder. There were stunned cries around us as people came from the house. But I could hear nothing, see nothing except Jordan and the blood against his white shirt.

He gave a slight groan and tried to stand straighter, as if he intended to face his attacker or die trying. I stepped in front of him and he pushed me away. I was amazed at his strength, even as the wound continued to take its toll on his body.

"Get away from here, Shelley," he said, gasping for breath.

"I'm not leaving you, Jordan."

I turned to see the man coming toward us. I wanted to run. There was a moment when I had an odd, crazy thought that this was one of our childhood games. That now we would turn and run into the woods. We would hide and be safe and we would win. Jordan always won.

But this time Jordan did not move.

I stared at the man and now I could see the glimmer of gold braid at his shoulders. I shook my head, trying to convince myself that this really was a dream and that I would wake any moment.

"Father," I whispered, feeling an incredible sense of unreality.

"Step away from him, daughter," he said, his voice steady and calm.

"Father—what are you doing? You've shot Jordan! He's bleeding and—"

"It's for you and the baby, can't you see that?" His voice was a keening cry now against the wind that raked and ruffled his thinning hair. It blew the material of his uniform against him, revealing a gaunt skeleton of a man. He didn't look like the father I knew. He looked like a dead man.

For a moment I closed my eyes against the sight coming so steadily toward us. He was mad and he intended to kill Jordan.

"No, father," I said, moving toward him.

"I'll kill him now if you take another step, daughter," he said, lifting the pistol toward Jordan.

"Please! Why are you doing this?"

"For you! Don't you understand anything I've said. Can't you see how this is going to work?"

For a moment he stopped, hesitating, as if he were not sure about what to do next. I heard Ella's gasp when Andrew made a move toward my father, then I heard the click of the pistol's hammer.

"Don't come any closer," he warned.

"Don't do this, Joshua." The voice was that of Jordan's Father. Mr. Waverly stood now slightly to the right of us.

Somehow he had managed to slip unseen to the edge of the cemetery. For a moment I hoped he was armed for I thought that was surely the only thing that would make my father stop this madness. There was nothing rational in him . . . nothing at all.

"Well, Waverly," my father said. "So you've sobered up long enough to face me after all these years, have you?"

I could see the glistening rain on his face and on the shoulders of his splendid uniform. I wanted to cry at the sight he made there in the storm, standing so proudly and yet as mad as anyone I'd ever seen. I could not believe this was happening.

"Put the pistol down, Joshua. Let's sit down and talk about this. My son is not responsible for anything that happened in our past."

"Ah, but that's the joy of it, don't you see? I was never able to hurt you before. But after I got rid of the girl, I knew exactly who your boy would turn to, just like he always did. Like Father like son, eh? Waverly men and Demorest women?"

I felt Jordan move beside me and I reached for him, thinking he might collapse. He grunted and took a step toward my father.

"It was you," I said, feeling dazed. "It was you who threatened Mary Louise. Dear Lord, Father . . . how could you do this? Please tell me you had nothing to do with her death . . . please."

"Threatened her? It was no threat. It was a warning. I told her what would happen if she stayed. And why should she want to stay here? She wasn't happy anyway, so she said. She came to me, girl. She was the one who gave me the idea in the first place."

"What are you talking about?" Jordan asked, his voice soft with pain.

"She wanted me to take her to see you, Shelley, wanted you to talk to Jordan, and make him see reason. She was willing to give up the child for her freedom, but she knew he wouldn't listen to her. She thought he might agree if you asked. That's when I got the idea."

"You didn't kill her," I gasped. "Tell me you couldn't have done such a thing."

"It was easy enough to make it look like suicide." He actually sounded pleased with himself.

Jordan groaned and slumped against me.

"Jordan, darling! Father, please, let me get him to the house."

"I knew you always loved him," he accused. "I did it for you, daughter."

"No," I whispered.

"Don't condemn me for what I did, girl. You're just like your mother, always loving the wrong man. But she paid for her mistake."

"My God," I said. I brushed the rain from my eyes and stared at him. My clothes and shoes were soaked and so were Jordan's. I didn't know how much longer he could stand there in the storm, wounded, perhaps mortally.

"What did you do, Papa? Mother was sick . . . you always told me she died of a fever . . ."

"I had my ways," he said slyly.

"You bastard!" Mr. Waverly moved across the space. "It was you. Lucinda's own husband—"

I saw my father lift his pistol into the air, saw the fire explode from the end of the barrel. The echo of the shot seemed to go on forever until I felt as if I were drowning in the sounds.

Mr. Waverly was on top of my father; the two men

rolled and struggled on the ground. By now Benjamin was alert, sitting up and staring at them with a stunned expression. Jordan stumbled forward, almost falling, then catching himself and coming upright again with a pained grunt.

When the gun exploded again, it was a muffled sound, mingled with Ella's screams and those of the people around us. Then there was only silence except for the receding rain and the thunder that had moved off into the distance.

Jordan and I both moved toward the men on the ground, both of us concerned for our fathers. Bitter enemies, men who had loved the same woman yet neither of whom could claim her.

I saw one of the men get to his knees, then stand, staggering slightly. It was Mr. Waverly who came to Jordan, taking his son in his arms and supporting him.

"Are you all right?" Jordan asked.

"I'm fine, son," he said. "It's you I'm worried about. Here, let me get you to the house. Dr. Greene was at the ball tonight. He'll know what to do."

I knelt beside my father and I could hear his ragged gasps. He lay on the wet sandy ground, his eyes open, staring up at the fine raindrops that fell around us.

"Oh, Papa," I sobbed.

From the corner of my eye I could see Jordan pushing away from his father. He knelt beside me and I realized the cost to him in pain. He put his arm around me and cradled me against him. Then he took the pistol from the ground near my father's hand and tossed it away.

"It's all right, my girl," Father said. "I see the *Sea Witch* coming for me. She's coming through the storm with her sails furled, waiting for my command. Hoist the mainsail, mates," he muttered, lifting his trembling hand slightly. Then he sighed heavily and there was a weak smile on his face. "I'm ready . . . I'm so tired . . . so tired . . ."

He didn't seem to have any idea what he had done, even now, or the damage he had done to this family . . . to us all. He had been living a fantasy for all these years and now he would die in it as well.

"Help him," I begged Jordan.

"It's too late, sweetheart—too late." Slowly he closed my father's eyes as I watched in horror.

I couldn't believe he was gone, that he had slipped away so quietly after the violence of the night. I couldn't believe any of it. My father had not only been responsible for Mary Louise's death, but possibly for my own mother's as well. And all those eccentricities that I'd wondered about and sometimes attributed to his missing the sea were madness all along.

I heard Jordan's soft groan of pain and I realized that for a moment my sorrow and stunned disbelief had caused me almost to forget what had happened to him.

"Oh, Jordan—Mr. Waverly, we have to get him to the house."

"Mr. Benson," he said, motioning Andrew forward. "Help me with my son."

"Gladly, sir."

I stood for a moment, torn between Jordan and my father's still lifeless form on the ground. I felt Ella beside me, felt her arm around my waist, steadying me.

"Go with your husband, darling," she said. "I'll take care of your father. I'll have some of the men carry him to the house."

I went then, not looking back, aware only of Jordan, not taking my eyes from him for a moment lest he slip away from me too.

It seemed like hours that I sat in the sitting room waiting for the doctor to emerge from Jordan's room. Ella had brought a blanket to wrap around my sodden shoulders and she sat with me, waiting. I refused to take the time to change clothes. I was so afraid, more afraid than I'd ever been in my life.

I could not live without Jordan. If I thought I loved him before, it was nothing compared to this. Marriage and the fulfillment of love had brought me closer to him than to any other human being. He was my life, my love, and as I waited I was convinced, with a sinking sense of despair, that I would have to face the torture of a long, dark future without him.

When the bedroom door opened, I jumped to my feet and brushed the blanket aside. My feet, so cold and wet, felt leaden, as if they might not move.

I saw the doctor's smile, but still I could not breath, could not speak.

"He's weak. The bullet lodged in his shoulder, but I managed to get it out with a minimal amount of damage, I think. If there's no infection he should recover fully."

"May I see him?" I asked.

"Of course you may, my dear. But he should be asleep soon from the medicine I've given him, and I'm—"

"I don't care," I said, moving toward the door. "I just want to be with him."

"Shelley, I'm going to bring you some dry clothes. We

can't have you getting sick too . . . not now." Ella's soft voice cut through my urgent fear.

I turned to see Ella and her face was like a sweet familiar harbor in the storm. Suddenly I was so glad she was there, and so happy that she was not only my sister-in-law, but my friend. I turned and walked across to her and hugged her.

"You're right," I said. "Not when I finally have everything I've ever wanted. Thank you, Ella. Thank you for everything. As soon as Jordan is well, we'll talk and we'll sort this thing through."

I opened the door to the bedroom and stopped. Jordan's father was there. He had insisted on going in with the doctor in case help was needed. Now, he sat beside the bed, his head bent toward his son.

"I'm so sorry," he murmured. "I blame myself for all of this—for the things Benjamin did, for the hatred that Joshua Demorest felt toward me and toward this family."

Jordan's hand moved to touch his father's hand.

"Don't . . . don't blame yourself. I don't want that."

"I was such a fool," Mr. Waverly continued, his voice a bit stronger. "Such a weak, spineless fool. I tried to dull the pain of my life with drink and now it's destroyed everything I ever held dear. Benjamin has left the island. I can't blame you for hating him for what he's done. But he's still my son. I don't know if any of us will ever see him again."

"Your life isn't destroyed," I said, moving into the room. "You still have Jordan . . . and me and Ella . . . and a wife who I think really loves you if you'd only give her a chance."

Mr. Waverly stood up and I could see the tears in his

dark eyes. He brushed his fingers across his face and turned away as if he were ashamed for me to see.

I went to Jordan then, kneeling beside the bed and taking his hand. His eyes were languid from the potion Dr. Greene had given him, but there was love there and I thought for the first time I saw a hint of peace as well.

"Everything is going to be all right, Jordan," I said, leaning over to kiss him. "You're going to be well and we're going to be together."

"I'm sorry," he whispered. "I'm so sorry about your father and that I didn't see this . . ."

"Shh," I whispered, brushing my fingers across his mouth. "It wasn't your fault. It wasn't anyone's fault. We all have to stop blaming each other and go on." I turned to glance at Mr. Waverly. "Can we do that? Can we try?" He stood a bit straighter and nodded to me. Slowly he cleared his throat to speak.

"Shall we start by my saying how lucky we are to have you here, Shelley? How lucky I think my son is to have a woman like you in his life?"

He was thinking of my mother and the love they'd lost, and I knew then as surely as I've ever known anything that he had truly loved her. I didn't know what had transpired between them or why they had not married, but I knew he loved her. I could see it in his eyes and hear it in the bittersweet sadness of his voice.

"Thank you, Mr. Waverly."

"Well," he said, looking away. "If you will excuse me, I'm going to go down and tell your mother that you're all right, son."

I could see that Jordan was growing weary and that the medicine was taking effect.

"You always believed in me," he whispered.

"I told you I always would."

"I love you," he murmured. "Always."

He closed his eyes and I could barely hear his voice when he spoke.

"Stay with me." His dark lashes fluttered and opened again and for a moment his look was so clear and intense. "I want to see your face when I wake tomorrow . . ."

"Yes, I will," I whispered, taking his hand and bringing it to my lips. "I'll never leave you, my darling . . . never."

"Tomorrow, love," he whispered. He was smiling as his eyes closed. "I'll see you tomorrow . . . and all our tomorrows."

Epilogue

As soon as Jordan was well, we left on a cruise from our little island of St. Catherine's. It was a time of healing, a time of renewing our love for one another and of coming to terms with all that had happened at Sea Crest Hall.

It was the most glorious adventure of my life.

We pieced together some of the facts about what happened at Sea Crest that night of the Captain's Ball, although I'm sure much of what my father did and his reasons for it will be lost to us forever. We learned later that he burned our house before he came to Sea Crest Hall. I think he meant to put an end to everything that night, even his own tortured life. But I can't really be sure if he intended it to happen the way it did.

We buried him on the north end of the island beside my mother, where the oleander blooms. It was painful for me to do it. I suppose I was still confused then, still disturbed and uncertain about both my parents and whether or not they had ever loved one another, or me.

It helped when Mrs. Waverly told me that she thought my mother married my father for security, that she felt herself too unrefined and unsuited for a marriage with someone of Mr. Waverly's status. And from what I remember of my mother, I think she was probably right. For the first time I began to see how Mr. Waverly's love for another woman had changed Jordan's mother, and often made her seem callous and cold. But she was so different with Jordan when he was recuperating, so loving and tender that I began to see how hard she had to try to cover up her natural feelings. She was a survivor, much like myself, and I think that one day we might come to terms with one another. We both adore Jordan, after all.

We have not heard from Benjamin since he left the island that night. Some say he is in Europe, living the kind of life he always wanted, that of a carefree Lothario, free from the bonds of marriage and responsibility. I know how worried his parents were; even knowing what he had done, they were torn, for they still loved him and still grieved for the loss of him from their lives. But I don't think they will ever forget or forgive what he did.

But it was not to be helped, we all knew that, and after a while I hope we will come to accept that as well.

Ella received a quiet, very discreet divorce with the help of Jordan and his family. She and Andrew are together now and even though Mrs. Waverly thought it was too soon, I encouraged the marriage.

"You've waited so long for this, Ella," I told her. "So long for love to come. This is right. You know it and so does Andrew. Don't let another moment go by without him in your life."

"It's what I want," she said. "But I love Mrs. Waverly

and I respect her, and after all, we will be living here on the island half of the year at least."

"She'll be all right," I said. "When you come back after Christmas, she will be ready to accept you into her life again . . . I'm sure of it."

It was the same thing Jordan told her when we both kissed her goodbye. Both of us were there to see her onto the ferry to meet Andrew on the mainland where he had gone to secure tickets to New York.

"Write to me," she said, waving goodbye.

"I will," I said, throwing her a kiss. "And I will see you just as soon as you can get here in the new year. Spring on the island is glorious, you know."

"I know," she said, waving and smiling. "Andrew will be in heaven."

I'd never have expected at first that Mr. Waverly would become like a father to me, but he has. He's sweet and gentle—nothing like the man I once thought him to be. He will be, I think, the perfect grandfather one day for all the children Jordan and I plan to have.

The vision of the ghost ship *Sea Witch* has never appeared again on the south end of St. Catherine's Island. I don't believe it ever will.

We haven't seen Jillian since that night and no charges were placed against her. I, like Jordan, believe that she was unknowingly used by Benjamin. As for him, I'm not sure either of us will ever forgive what he did. But he is Jordan's brother and there are days when I see the lost look in my husband's eyes and I know he thinks of him and their boyhood together.

That's when I go to him and hold him, tease him the way I did so long ago. We race on the beach, or seek shelter on warm, wonderful afternoons in the old fishing shack. Sometimes we fish in the wide, glorious ocean and cook our catch over a fire in the sand. In these good, happy days as we both grow tanned from the sun, as both of us grow strong and well, I can see a bright ray of hope for our future. Even for the future of Sea Crest Hall.

And when the doubts come back to assail me, I remember those days . . . the laughter and the love that we shared.

I know our life together will always be the way it is now. Filled with so much love.

About the Author

CLARA WIMBERLY is a native of Cleveland, Tennessee, where she has lived all her life. She has always been fascinated by the history and traditions of the Old South and has taught creative writing and worked for many years for the U. S. government. She is married and has three children—two sons and a daughter. Clara is the author of six other Zebra Gothics, *Natchez Moon*, a novel in the Pinnacle Magnolia Road series, and *Tomorrow's Promise*, her first mainstream novel for the To Love Again line.